The Troubled Texan

The Troubled Texan

PHYLISS MIRANDA

KENSINGTON
Kensington Publishing Corp.
www.kensingtonbooks.com

KENSINGTON BOOKS are published by

Kensington Publishing Corp.
119 West 40th Street
New York, NY 10018

All Kensington titles, imprints, and distributed lines are available at special quantity discounts for bulk purchases for sales promotions, premiums, fund-raising, educational, or institutional use. Special book excerpts or customized printings can also be created to fit specific needs. For details, write or phone the office of the Kensington special sales manager: Kensington Publishing Corp., 119 West 40th Street, New York, NY 10018, attn: Special Sales Department; phone 1-800-221-2647.

KENSINGTON and the k logo are Reg. U.S. Pat. & TM Off.

First electronic edition: March 2014

ISBN-13: 978-1-60183-120-0
ISBN-10: 1-60183-120-X

First print edition: March 2014

ISBN-13: 978-1-60183-224-5
ISBN-10: 1-60183-224-9

Printed in the United States of America

Dedicated to Chris and Natalie Bright, who taught me a lot about ranching out on the Sanford Ranch, one of the oldest original ranches established in the Texas Panhandle in 1895.

And in memory of my Uncle Chalmers Michael Goodwin who passed from this life without having to experience the full agony of Alzheimer's disease.

Special dedication to all the caretakers who devote their lives daily to their loved ones who suffer from Alzheimer's disease.

IN MEMORY
of
THE REVEREND BILLY HOBBS

1946–2004

Two-time All American from Texas A&M University
Southwest Conference player of the year
Cotton Bowl MVP
National Defense Player of the Year
Texas A&M and Panhandle Sports Halls of Fame
Linebacker for the Philadelphia Eagles
and the New Orleans Saints

Chapter One

LIFE WITHOUT PAROLE! the April 12th *Los Angeles Tribune* headline shrieked up at Maressa Clarkson.

The word "failure" might as well have been scrolled in neon. Not being able to get the death penalty for a murderer who made Charles Manson look like a schoolyard bully was totally unacceptable, nothing but a sign of weakness, unworthiness. At least that was the way her father would see the verdict.

District Attorney, Judith Mason, had stood alone with her, the only one to understand the emotional hell Maressa had been going through as lead prosecutor in such a high-profile, gut-wrenching case. Maressa suspected the DA figured that, since she was up for reelection and her conviction record had been challenged by her opponent, she didn't want to get her hands dirty with such a horrific case. She certainly didn't need the stigma of Alonzo Hunter receiving life in prison hanging over her head when he deserved the death penalty.

Besides her own father and her boss, there were probably thousands of citizens of the state of California disappointed in the verdict, but none more than Maressa herself.

Scoping out her desk, she touched a nutmeg-colored folder labeled "People vs. Alonzo F. Hunter" lying open beside volumes of Cal Stats—*Statutes of California* and *West's California Reporter*. An opaque water ring from an empty Diet Dr Pepper can on her otherwise organized desk reminded her that she hadn't eaten a real meal in weeks.

A bonsai plant she had pampered for five years caught her attention. She checked the soil. Still moist. Plucking off a leaf that clung for survival like an umbilical cord, she tossed the dead twig in the wastebasket beside the credenza.

She turned back for a final look and ran her fingers across the brass nameplate: R. Maressa Clarkson, Deputy District Attorney.

The pathetic looking bonsai seemed to plead with her not to be left behind.

Don't look so sad, little guy. With rare spontaneity, she snatched up the front page of the newspaper and wrapped it around the delicate plant, before securing the pot in a corner of her gym bag.

Sliding on her sunglasses, she headed for the door. Cautiously surveying the outer offices, she checked to make sure nobody was around.

Easing the door closed, she exited through the back and headed for a bank of elevators. Luck was on her side; the doors opened immediately and she stepped into the waiting car.

Adjusting her heavy tote bag slung on her arm, she steadied herself, leaning against the mirrored tiles covering three sides of the elevator walls. The coolness of the glass seeped through her olive-drab blouse hanging off her noodle thin shoulders. She had lost more weight. Barely five-foot-two and a slight one hundred and three pounds, she couldn't afford to lose another ounce.

A gaunt, tired image teetering on this side of anorexia screamed back at her. She touched the dark circles under her eyes. Lack of sleep and stress, compounded by the trauma of prosecuting such a horrendously complicated case and her concern for her safety, as well as that of her staff, had taken their toll. Her normally emerald-green eyes now looked more like mucky moss against her pasty complexion. Pinching her cheeks to add a tad of color didn't work. She needed some sun. And rest, lots of it.

The elevator jerked to a stop on the ground floor where she located her new Lexus. She unlocked the doors, and then tossed her car keys on the concrete beneath the automobile. Exiting the parking garage on foot, she walked seven blocks south.

Although the back streets she took were virtually deserted at this time of the morning, she stopped several times to make sure she wasn't being followed.

Halting near a trash bin, she took a deep breath, opened her gym bag and removed the Prada purse that cost more than a month's payment on her condo. Tossing the turquoise-and-gray paisley printed handbag in a shallow growth of weeds behind the receptacle, she walked away. She had a small, cheap purse she had purchased inside her gym bag.

Someone would find her billfold, complete with identification, and figure she was another mugging victim. They'd take the piddling amount of cash she had deliberately left inside and discard the handbag. Nothing unusual in a city the size of LA.

Once she crossed back to the main avenue, crowds bustled to work around her like screensavers on speed. Meshing with the smell of designer perfume, tobacco, and leftover lust, she made her way another six blocks west before she flagged down a taxi. She told the driver that she wanted to go to the Los Angeles International Airport, where she paid him and mingled amongst the people before she caught a green-line bus and changed terminals. Weighted down with apprehension, she hailed a second cab.

Maressa removed a note Judith had given her from her pocket, and directed the cabbie to a used car lot in East LA, where she picked up her new identity and an ordinary Chevy Malibu. Not exactly a car she would have chosen, but one serviceable enough for her needs.

"Mrs. Michaels, uh, lady . . . Rainey—"

Jerking her head up, she responded, "What? Yes?"

She needed to get accustomed to her new alias since the last time anyone in her family used her first name was when she was baptized as an infant thirty-two years before. Her father hated the name Maressa, but had agreed to allow it to be put on her birth certificate only to appease her mother. The LA County DA insisted that "Rainey" didn't sound professional and that using Maressa, along with her first initial, would set her apart from the other thousand-plus deputy DAs.

Rainey Michaels did have a secure ring to it.

"Don't act scared. It's a dead giveaway that you're on the run. You paid a lot of money to get lost, so get used to it," chided the slick-talking son-of-slime. "The registration and insurance docu-ments are in here." He handed her an envelope. "Keep 'em with the car 'cause you can't afford to get stopped. Gotcha a New York driver's license . . . everything you wanted, including a burner phone. You okay, Mrs. Michaels?"

"What? Yes, I'm fine. Thanks." She handed over a manila enve-lope. "All the money is here."

Deal closed, the man slithered back to the hole he called his office.

Slipping behind the wheel, she exited the parking lot . . . off the emotional roller coaster that had taken her for a nasty ride. She needed separation to heal, and plenty of it. Hopefully, given enough time, she could put the daily, sometimes hourly, images of the hideous crimes of Alonzo F. Hunter behind her and begin to live again.

Merging into traffic, she headed toward small-town USA where she could blend in like a single boll of cotton in pale moonlight.

A frightened deputy district attorney didn't resign . . . she vanished.

And in R. Maressa Clarkson's, rather Rainey Michaels's case, she carried way too much baggage with her in the form of horrific memories.

Chapter Two

Alternating blue and red lights flashed from behind, jolting Rainey Michaels's gypsy mind back to the dusky Texas highway not far off Interstate 40.

Damn it!

A single blast of a siren from a county marked club-cab pickup sliced the air.

"Son of a . . ." She slammed her hands on the steering wheel, tapped the brakes, and pulled to the soft shoulder of the road. *Speeding! I had to be speeding.* And her proof of insurance had blown away when she'd opened the glove box way back in Tennessee.

Trouble had found her and she hadn't been in the Texas Panhandle more than an hour. In this Godforsaken county, she'd be lucky if she didn't get the book thrown at her.

She had carefully selected Kasota Springs to relocate to because it was far enough away from her hometown of Denton, Texas, for her not to be recognized, while small enough to feel at home. Using her new name, Rainey Michaels, she had already prepaid a six-month lease on a building sight unseen in the Podunk city. She had planned to slip quietly into town and go inconspicuously about her business. But now . . . that might be impossible.

In the rearview mirror, she saw the silhouette of the officer unfold from the patrol car. He carried himself with a confident presence, an air of authority. Most likely there would be no talking her way out of a ticket.

There wasn't the slightest hesitation in his stride as the tall man approached. No doubt, she had found trouble and he came with a Stetson, a Glock .45 on his hip, and the means to unravel the elaborate ruse she'd constructed.

From the way the deputy pulled the black felt hat low over his eyes and lifted back his jacket to touch his service pistol, he expected instant obedience. A no-nonsense type of person who would enjoy making an example of a commonplace automobile with New York plates speeding through his sleepy Texas county.

Biting on her lower lip, she jerked open the gym bag and retrieved her new driver's license and auto registration. Maybe he wouldn't ask for her insurance card. Not likely, but maybe.

Looks tough and cocky, but great body! she thought. Her tongue danced along her upper lip.

Rainey spoke to her only company, the bonsai plant riding in the passenger seat. "I might even enjoy being handcuffed to that rascal."

Reality snarled at her. *Handcuffed! Arrested! Goodness sakes alive, what are you thinking, girl?* she scolded. The last thing Rainey needed was someone delving into her past. Besides, she expected plenty of questions just being the newest addition to the quaint ranching community.

Shadowed by the remnants of a lazy West Texas sunset, the big man trooping her way reminded her of Donovan Cowan, Sr., the tough-as-nails longtime sheriff of Denton County. To teach the teenagers a valuable lesson, if he caught them speeding, they were an automatic overnight guest of the county. Swallowing hard, she tried to dislodge the knot in her throat. The death of the gruff old hound dog, killed in the line of duty, had been plastered all over the Internet for weeks.

As though she stepped on a grave, thoughts of his son, Deuce, chilled her. After nearly three decades of trying to ignore his existence, why would she think about the baddest good boy she had ever known?

Get back to reality, woman!

Frantic, she searched for a scarf. *I look like a vagrant with my swollen eyes and ratty hair*, she thought to herself.

With a whisk of her hand, she pulled a layer of bangs over her forehead and fluffed her short auburn tresses around her face. Rather,

Chestnut Sunshine the box had read. She thought her hair had turned out looking similar to the color of a Christmas ornament. But then dyeing it in a motel room somewhere in Arizona wasn't exactly an applied science.

Pulling on the headscarf, she slipped on blue-tinted shades, lowered the window, and trained her gaze upward.

Thick forceful thighs, slim hips, and a polished silver-and-gold Texas A&M belt buckle below an obviously taut, planed abdomen were a welcome sight for a traffic stop.

"Good evening, ma'am . . ." His deep-timbred voice kicked her heart into overdrive. "Kinda in a hurry, aren't you?"

Sheer black fright swept through her. *That voice!* She'd know it anywhere. It had to belong to the studly Denton High quarterback and her old study partner, Deuce Cowan. But why would he be in Kasota Springs?

Taking a deep breath before lowering her voice, Rainey nervously stuck out the documents, crunching them into his washboard hard stomach. "Sorry, deputy."

"Thank you, ma'am. This won't take but a minute." He took the cards, pushed her hand away, brushing her fingertips as he did. "And, it's Sheriff Cowan." He tipped his Stetson, turned, and walked back to the pickup.

Sheriff! Not a deputy?

Mother of Joseph! It was worse than she thought. She pulled more bangs over her forehead, and exhaled deeply. Rainey had carefully checked out the town and had been assured that E. L. Kirkwood was the sheriff. And now the position seemed to belong to her old high school classmate Deuce Cowan.

Mercy . . . mercy sakes alive, did she ever have a problem.

Rainey rested her head against the headrest and willed away the tightness between her shoulders. Queasiness flared in her stomach.

Her mind wandered through an array of worse scenarios while she waited for the sheriff to take care of business. The business of checking her out with the Department of Motor Vehicles and Vital Statistics. And realizing she didn't have any proof of insurance.

It seemed like eons before the officer reappeared. His voice clipped the air, sending a ripple of awareness through her. "Mrs. Michaels, open your trunk, please."

Lowering her voice to a whisper, she answered, "Certainly."

Dern, if she knew where to find the trunk release and couldn't afford to open the door . . . she didn't need any more light shed on her. Lowering her head, she looked beneath the console and found a trunk icon. Breathing a sigh of relief, she pressed the lever.

Clink! Slam!

In less than a minute, Deuce had closed the trunk lid, and rounded the car. "I need your proof of insurance."

Her worst fear had just come to fruition. "I lost it, sir." She kept her head lowered and her voice lower.

"It's required in Texas. You'll need to get a replacement and appear before the court." He handed her his ticket book. "Since this is Saturday, the earliest you can see the judge will be nine on Monday morning. Sign here," he ordered in an unsympathetic tone. "I clocked you doing sixty-eight in a fifty-five, plus I'm citing you for not providing proof of insurance. This isn't an admission of guilt, only a promise to contact . . ."

Rainey accepted the pad and scribbled her new name across the signature line, not listening to the spiel that she knew only too well. Never looking up, she handed the form back.

He tore off the top copy and squatted down next to the car. "Passing through?"

Clutching the lapel of her blouse in an attempt to cover her flushed chest, she nodded. She didn't dare look into his face, not even if the heavens threatened to open and scoop her up. And that might be a relief.

Rainey stared straight ahead, afraid of what she might find if she took a glimpse in his direction.

No doubt he wore that lopsided, quirky grin that oozed raw sexuality. A smile that got him whatever he wanted, when he wanted it, without any questions asked . . . from everybody except her. She could bet that a renegade curl had escaped from beneath his hat and hung low over his forehead.

Was that little half-moon shaped scar above his lips still noticeable? She recalled the night a cocky defensive tackle gave the popular quarterback's face true character by taking advantage of a dislodged helmet to plant a cleat in his nose.

She cut her eyes and caught his image in the side mirror. Dang it, whether she appreciated everything about the man or not, Deuce had charisma and a breathtaking ruggedness that could not be ignored. Of course, being a two-time collegian all-American turned professional football player didn't hurt either. So, let him mesmerize other women. She had her personal Achilles heel in the form of one Deuce Cowan. *Excuse me!* Sheriff Deuce Cowan.

Sheriff Cowan returned her documents, leaned within inches of the side of her face, and spoke with an authoritative voice that sent her already racing heart into somersaults. "If you want to stay out of trouble—best stay out of my way."

Chapter Three

"Well, I'll be damned!" Deuce Cowan watched the white Chevy pull onto the blacktop. "Double-dog damned. Rainey musta gotten married."

But what in the hell was she doing passing through his county with a New York driver's license? He leaned against the black-and-white's fender, smiled, and thought back to how sweet she used to look when he'd get her all riled up by calling her Brainy Rainey. How those cute dimples deepened and her eyes flashed with annoyance.

If she was headed for Denton, she was off track. And her only company, some type of deformed, puny bush. More importantly, why was she so intent on disguising herself? Even those ridiculous bangs and that metallic red hair did nothing for her flawless complexion. She looked tired and pale. Nothing like the feisty blonde he had shared a lab station with in high school. The girl that made it her mission to see that he kept up his grades, assuring his eligibility to play football, and ultimately get a college scholarship.

She was always there to help him. He was always ready with a barb or something to tease her about. Like the day he tried to get her goat by asking her about her favorite position on a football team. She simply responded: "The tight ends, regardless of the position they play."

That was Brainy Rainey. He coined the nickname, but he wasn't the only person to call her that. Sporting enough steel in her mouth to make an ironworker proud, thick tortoise-shell glasses, and braids, the library-card toting, pint-size gal was the persona of brainy. A nerd, except softer.

He cringed, thinking back to the day he got an in-school suspension because he decked another member of the football team for making fun of her. Deuce chuckled. The ISS wasn't all that bad except he'd missed ball practice and the coach had made him run the next day as punishment until he threw up. As far as he knew, Rainey never knew he'd stood up for her.

And the thanks Deuce had gotten—although he'd hinted that he needed a date to homecoming their senior year, when he called, he was told by her father never to call again because she didn't want to talk to him. He didn't even get the chance to talk to her. Her father spoke for her, but then that's about what he had expected from the pompous ass of a district judge. And the worst part, she'd never mentioned his call to him.

Yeah, Brainy Rainey had grown up and made lots of changes.

But one thing that she hadn't changed: those adorable little dimples at the corner of her mouth that deepened when she smiled or was nervous. They were still there, and he hadn't even seen a promise of a smile.

And that smell . . . just as he remembered. Sensual and heady, like a blooming field of wildflowers.

When he got back to the sheriff's office, he planned to check up on Miss Maressa Clarkson. Rather, Mrs. Rainey Michaels.

Deuce finished his paperwork before he scouted out The Silver Dollar, one of just two local watering holes, to make sure there weren't any underaged drinkers. He returned to his patrol car in time to catch a call about an alarm at the old, vacant Rock Island Depot. Probably a dog call, maybe a rambunctious teenager who thought he had found a safe haven for his drinking.

"I'm on my way," Deuce responded to his deputy. "Hey, Jessup, got a job for you. When Danny comes on duty, ask him to see what he can find on a Mrs. Rainey Michaels. . . ." He flipped open his book for her New York address. "At . . ."

After giving the deputy all the pertinent information, Deuce slipped back the brim of his hat with a thumb and shook his head.

Hell, I thought tonight was going to be quiet, but from the minute I laid eyes on that brainiac, I should have known better.

Deuce slid into the county pickup. Hopefully, trouble wasn't waiting for him at the abandoned railroad station.

Pulling into the lot in front of the Rock Island Depot, Rainey cut the engine and stared into the darkness at the gigantic beige stucco building sprawled out ahead. Luckily, she had received a letter from her landlord confirming the address. She took the note from her pocket and reread it. There was no mistaking she was at the correct place. One hundred Main Street. The classified ad had read "Historic Landmark" and the lessor assured her that the building had adequate living quarters and was perfect for her new business venture.

Oh, yeah, an antiquated railway station was every woman's dream house! Maybe she should have asked more questions, but she had been too thankful to have found a building so quickly. Next time, she'd make sure of what she would be getting instead of leasing sight unseen.

Rainey sighed, suddenly feeling as though she had been traveling over a long, lonesome highway without a soft shoulder to depend on . . . abandoned and lonely like the deserted building.

Wishing she could go home, realization hit her—that was not an option. Her parents were vacationing in Europe, and when she contacted them, her father seemed more angry that she refused his help than concerned for her safety. She feared her father had brushed off her cryptic message about her parents not talking to the news media. After all, he'd spent most of his life in the public eye. How long had it actually been since she had seen her parents? Three, four years ago? Months before the murder trial began.

She needed to talk with her mother, and figured she could tolerate the man who provided half her DNA. The man with all the answers, plenty of criticism, and an overabundance of ridicule. The man who insisted she call him "Father."

Her mind wandered back to the bitter frustration and regret of LA. Back to the reason she was forced to return to Texas. Back to the sordid images of the bodies of five women and four children, all products of incest, stacked on top of one another against one wall of the filthy, insect infested house occupied by a madman. Impressions that were so imbedded in her soul that she rarely slept without the invasion of night tremors.

Rubbing her arms, she forced away goose bumps, and instead thought back to Deuce Cowan and their friendship. Friendship? So not true. And their relationship? Like cashmere tangling with steel wool. A pit bull snarling at a bookworm.

It all started in the kindergarten lunch line, where she hunkered close to the girl in front of her to keep Deuce from pulling her charleys, as she called her dog-ears in those days. Then came middle school, and their rapport worsened. By high school, the aggression had reached epidemic proportions along with heightened raging hormones, as they were continually paired as study partners.

From play school to high school, the mismatched duo always seemed to be in one another's face about something. Be it her accusations that he hadn't taken a class project seriously or his obvious frustration with her not understanding the difference between a field goal and a touchback. Just let him continue to believe that she thought the football play was when the offense ran backwards for a touchdown.

After all, she had little desire to know much about jocks butting heads, any more than she'd expect Deuce to understand the real meaning behind Shakespeare's sonnets.

Then there were the teachers who seemed intent on making both their lives miserable. Regardless of whether they made alphabetical assignments for projects or selected students at random, the brain and the brawn seemed to always wind up together.

And they hated every moment of it. Well, she hated it, and Deuce left no doubt that was the only thing they agreed upon.

Years later, after mentoring troubled teens, Rainey realized Deuce's and her relationship had nothing to do with them disliking one another, but rather both of their needs to challenge and be challenged. The truth be known, she had a crush on him and after a lot of maturity settled in, she believed he probably liked her, but just didn't want his jock friends to know he cared about a girl . . . particularly a plain Jane girl like her.

A knot formed in her stomach thinking back to the night she had cried herself to sleep after waiting for Deuce's call inviting her to be his date to the homecoming dance their senior year. A call that never came, although he'd all but asked her when they stood side by side at their lockers.

Rainey knew one thing for certain—until he proved he could be trusted, she'd trust nobody, not even the handsome sheriff clothed in charm.

Making no move to get out of the car, she tucked the past in the back of the recesses of her mind and focused on the future.

Visions of the captivating sheriff resurfaced: the fully-grown, mature version of the man who obviously needed a dose of reality. He was no longer the captain of the football team or a lineman for the Steelers, but a small-town sheriff. Jeeze, if he wasn't even better looking in person than on *Monday Night Football*. Not exactly a pretty boy, but handsome to just the right degree. . . . But it was the charisma dripping from him that scared the hell out of her.

A warm feeling shot directly to her most vulnerable spot, remembering Deuce's capricious smile and dazzling white teeth against a sun-bronzed face. The shadow of his beard profiling dark against the setting sun. No man deserved to have such a monopoly on virility and good looks. Particularly one so smug and with such bravado.

But, how in the blue blazes did he end up as the sheriff of Bonita County, Texas? And the badge-toting hunk hadn't even recognized her. At least her disguise worked.

The last she heard, Deuce had returned to their hometown to serve as a deputy under his father. Until now, she had presumed that he had been named sheriff in Denton after his dad's death, not here.

Her stomach knotted. Why did she have to run into him of all people? She had followed her plan to a tee. After leaving LA, she zigzagged across the country paying with cash until she reached New York City, where she rented a Cobble Hill brownstone in the northeastern part of Brooklyn for six months, although she only stayed less than eight weeks.

All of the time, she had watched as many national television newscasts she possibly could to make sure there was no word of her disappearance. So far, her plan had worked perfectly . . . until now.

While in NYC, she had even melded amongst the close-knit families living in the area, making sure that the ever-watching elders of the many extended families in the neighborhood were able to verify her existence. Certainly, they would remember her bonsai. She hadn't stayed there long enough to need to fabricate a story about Rainey Michaels's life before New York.

Was she divorced? Separated? A widow? Damn, now that she had run into Deuce she had to be careful not to raise more questions than she had answers for.

Annoyance thinned her lips. Settling in a new locale should have been as smooth as shooting marbles on a sheet of ice. But now, she had to deal with the brown-eyed handsome sheriff that turned her legs to mush and made her heart flutter as if it were filled with butterflies and ladybugs, while infuriating her beyond belief.

Just because he ticketed her didn't mean she'd have any dealings with him.

Stay out of his way! rang in her ears.

"Well, Mr. High and Mighty Sheriffman, I can promise you that you don't have to worry about me getting in your way, but you might want to steer clear of *me*."

Grabbing the gym bag and the bonsai, Rai made her way to the monstrous double doors of the railroad station and inserted her key.

She took a deep breath and pushed the doors open. Hopefully, hobbits and gnomes weren't waiting inside.

Flipping on the switch, muted lighting flooded the lobby. She glanced at the ceiling. The majority of the fluorescent tubes were unlit, casting a dusky haze on the aged linoleum floors. A musty smell of ghosts of bygone years attacked her nostrils. The room looked big enough to hold all nine hundred plus LA deputy DAs for Thanksgiving dinner.

What had she gotten herself into? A need to cry engulfed her, but she had never been allowed to cry. It showed weakness, lack of control. Or that was what her father had always drilled into her. Crying was a luxury she couldn't afford.

She set the bonsai and her purse on a counter. Looking around, she shivered. Few options were available to her. This way station must serve as her safe haven. She'd make it work, no matter what.

Maybe this was exactly what she needed. It was the last place a mentally deranged criminal would look for her.

Only one good thing came from running into her old classmate. If she needed the most contemptible, baddest bruiser around for protection, she had his number.

Any peace of mind was only momentary, suddenly interrupted by a shrill earsplitting wail.

She jumped half of her height and clutched her chest. The noise came from a burglar alarm high above her head.

Rainey's heart raced.

Mr. Wilson, her new landlord, had mentioned an alarm, but said he would clear it with the security company.

The noise scrambled her thought process. Where was the most logical place for a control pad? She darted toward the ticket agent's cage, searched the walls, and ran her hands beneath the desk. Briskly turning toward the squealing, she located the command center and punched in the code Mr. Wilson had sent her. She tried a second time with no results. After she located the emergency contact sticker on the wall, Rainey punched the toll-free number into her cellular telephone.

Surely, the owner had given her name to the security company and authorized her access to the property. Surely?

She leaned against the rough counter, shifted her weight for the umpteenth time, while she provided information to a faceless service rep that seemed to be having difficulty recognizing the urgency in her call.

"I leased this building from a Mr. Wilson." Rainey tapped her sandaled toe against the baseboard. "I have a money order right here for the payment and a lease agreement."

The high-pitched scream of the alarm going off seemed to kick up a notch as the sound bounced off the hallowed walls like a pinball machine.

"Yes, Rainey Michaels . . . M-I-C-H-A-E-L-S." She leaned forward and cupped her hand over her ear. "If I had the correct code, we wouldn't be having this conversation, now would we?" She pressed her phone closer and plugged her other ear with her index finger. "Oh, jeez, please don't put me on hold. . . ."

Suddenly she felt a presence in the room, an eerie feeling of being watched. Biting a trembling lip, Rainey tucked the phone deep into her shoulder, which was no easy task, and searched for something to use as a weapon. Spying a weathered switchman's lantern, naked without the glass globe, she swallowed hard and choked back panic. Her heart sped up like a runaway train.

A large shadow crossed the floor, drawing her attention away from the canned music coming out of the phone. *God, this is supposed to be a security company!* If only the idiot had stayed on the line, she could signal for help.

The silhouette neared.

Her heart soared out of control, and the knot in her stomach tightened as fright assaulted every inch of her body. She fought back bile, and her mouth felt grainy, like a sandpaper breath mint.

The deranged mass murderer had kept his promise. . . . Alonzo Hunter had found her!

She dropped the phone. Hitting the floor, it skidded across the mucky-yellow linoleum.

Whirling, she grasped the lantern and hurled the antique through the air before driving every ounce of her petite body into the intruder.

The man ducked in time to miss the flying object, let out a four-letter word, and grabbed for Rainey with his long reach. He quickly subdued her. Reeling her around in one brisk movement, he locked her hands behind her back and pulled her tight against his chest.

She jerked and kicked at his shins with her heel, not giving a flying frog if she rearranged his cojones in the process, but missed as he leaned back out of her reach.

"You spitfire!" Deuce Cowan's harsh words sounded a bit playful, but the meaning was crystal clear.

The familiarity of the voice and the security of his arms unnerved her. She allowed relief to sweep over her momentarily, but only long enough to catch a breath.

"Let go of me, you . . . you animal!"

"What are you going to do if I let go?"

"I'm gonna kick you in your—"

"Well, in that case, hang on." He picked her up, tucked her under his arm like an unruly child, and hauled her kicking and cursing toward the security keypad. "Close your eyes."

"Close my eyes?" She made an unsuccessful lunge at freedom, all four limbs slicing the air.

"Shut them or I'll let this alarm bellow all night."

"You dumb buffoon!" Her voice echoed in the empty tomb. She squeezed her eyes shut. "I can't see a thing. Are you happy?"

"As happy as I can be trying to corral a wildcat." He punched in the disarm code with the wiggly woman still under his arm. "And I might be a buffoon, but I'm not dumb!"

Silence.

"Now, Miss Michaels—" his voice rang with command.

"*Mrs.* Michaels," she shot over her shoulder. "And how do you know my security code?"

"I'm the sheriff, remember? Right—now, Mrs. Michaels, you can either settle down and explain why you are trespassing, or I'll charge you with assault and haul your sassy butt to jail."

"Officer Smart-Ass. Oh, excuse me, *Sheriff* Smart-Ass . . ." She squirmed until she loosened her right arm. "I'll have your hide for manhandling me—"

"I'd love for you to have my hide any time, any place—"

"Get your mind out of the gutter. I promise, I'll . . ." Giving little thought to the fact she was assaulting a peace officer, she rammed her forearm against a wall of muscle.

Her offensive launch didn't faze him.

"You'll what? Kick and scream your way out of here? I don't think so." He took a step forward, dangling the woman at his side. "Sweetheart, if you can't stand the heat, get out of the kitchen."

"It isn't the heat that's bothering me—"

"Couldn't tell by the way you're acting." He stalked toward the ticket counter. "But it's bothering me."

With a wild unexpected shot of adrenaline and fury, she jabbed her elbow in his solar plexus, causing him to momentarily gasp for air, lessening his hold.

"You hellion! If that's your answer . . ." With both hands, he plopped her on her feet, grabbed her around the waist and hoisted her, not too gently, onto the ticket counter.

In a flash, he removed his handcuffs from his hip, and clicked one cuff on her wrist and the other to the wrought-iron grill. "Well, this ought to give you some time to reconsider your answer."

"Let me down." She spaced the words evenly, before rushing on. "I'm going to file abuse charges. I'll send you to the penitentiary, t-to . . ."

Rainey cast a scorching gaze from Deuce to the floor and back up to the fiery-eyed man and considered her options.

No doubt kicking was out of the question. With legs not much longer than a good-sized man's arm, she could never touch him. Jumping off the ledge wouldn't be advisable. She'd end up dangling like a watch fob on the end of a chain.

She blazed a stare at her captor. Simba faced Mufasa.

Madder than a hornet with the hives, Rainey tried unsuccessfully to keep her eyes above his waist, but with him standing so near, her attention was drawn to his bulging crotch. For a moment, she allowed the images of what lay behind his tight-fitting jeans to ramble through her mind.

Heat crept up from somewhere deep in her stomach. Christ on crutches! Now wasn't a good time to blush like a schoolgirl getting her first glimpse of a *Playboy* magazine.

Sheriff Deuce Cowan dusted his palms off, reached for a nearby ladder-back chair, and turned it around. Straddling the seat, he tilted back his Stetson with a thumb and shot her one of his killer smiles.

"Well, ma'am, I warned you to stay out of my way unless you wanted trouble." His words were as cool and clear as a mountain stream. "So, the way I see it, you can either settle down or I'll leave you there until you learn to behave."

Chapter Four

Deuce draped his arms over the chair back and watched the green-eyed vixen attempt to stare him down. Although still appearing too fragile to cause such a ruckus, Rainey's coloring had improved. A rosy shade of strawberry blotched her cheeks and neck.

Suddenly, a rush of heat ramrodded his body, settling way down south in the damnedest sensation he had experienced in a while. Or at least since he swore off females and booze after he woke coyote-drunk and realized he'd rather gnaw off his arm than wake the woman next to him.

Considering Rainey's proclamation of being a married lady, his thoughts were anything but gentlemanly. He struggled to swallow and forced his attention away from his uncomfortable state and back to the problem at hand.

"Okay, *Mrs.* Michaels, if that's what you prefer to be called, what do you plan to do now? And don't even think about going after my cojones again."

"Let me down this minute." She jerked at the restraints. "And, *that* is *not* what interests me in a man—"

"Oh, yeah, it was my brains you were aiming for—"

"One and the same," she said dryly.

"You can make this hard on yourself if you want—"

She cast her gaze downward. "It doesn't appear I'm the only one that I'm making it hard on." She turned her face upward, returning the spitting-nails stare he knew was plastered on his face, with a sassy, disdainful, and purely sensual smile.

Shrugging her shoulders, she said, "You scared the bejeezus out of me and you know it. I didn't assault you. Not exactly." Her grin rapidly disappeared into creases between her brows and tiny dimples at the corner of her mouth. "It was your fault," her silky voice challenged. "But, I'll try to behave. Okay?"

Not much of a promise. Hoping to loosen the tightness in his jeans, Deuce shifted his weight to one hip, cautiously eyed her, and considered his choices.

As much as he dreaded to stand, he pushed up from the chair, stuck his hand in his pocket, and fingered the key to the handcuffs. "All right. If you're sure I'm not going to have any more trouble out of you, *Mrs*. Michaels."

Deuce closed the distance between them, bringing them face to face.

Eye to eye.

Lips to lips.

He halted when sensual, emerald eyes brought him up short, sending his heart head over teakettle. It had been fourteen years since he'd seen Rainey . . . rather, Maressa. When in the hell had she gotten so sexy? Lookin' so good? Why hadn't he seen her that way before? He'd had more than his share of youthful raging hormones, yet he'd never thought of her as anything but a gal friend. A pal, yeah! But never a woman.

She may have changed a lot about herself, and certainly her razor-sharp tongue hadn't dulled a millimeter, but she was as keen and witty as always. Still not taking any crap off anyone, particularly Deuce.

Damn! How in the hell did he get so turned on seeing her shackled and fuming? He fought off the desire to take her in his arms and apologize. Apologize? *You idiot. For what?* Doing his job? No! He had defused the situation. Deuce was the professional with the criminal justice degree. And after all it wasn't personal. Was it?

Jerking the key from his pocket, he uncuffed her. His large hands encompassed her slender waist and he lifted her down, setting her on her feet.

"Thanks, Ace."

As though being blinded by a cornerback blitz, her comment staggered him temporarily. He'd almost forgotten about the nickname.

Few people, hell, nobody except Rainey called him that. Anyone else would have been met with a fist in his gut.

"You meant Deuce. It's Deuce Cowan."

"Sorry." She stiffened. "I won't make that mistake again." She rubbed her wrist. "And I have every right to be here. I leased this place from Harold Wilson, but I think you already knew that." Each word dripped with vinegar. "And call me Rainey."

Reaching for the gym bag, she produced the lease agreement, jabbing the paper at him.

"And I have the responsibility to protect this county." He skimmed the first page, although Harold had informed him of the arrangement. "Seems to be in order, but I think you already knew that," he mimicked her, folding the document and handing it back to her. "How would I know you aren't a drug dealer? You cruise into town, or rather speed through, with almost no luggage, with out-of-state plates, no proof of insurance, and offer no explanation for being here. What was I supposed to think?"

"So, you're an equestrian?"

"Don't answer my question with a question. Of course, I know how to ride. What does that have to do with anything?"

"I was just wondering, because you are so skilled at jumping to conclusions." She tilted her head back, and raised an eyebrow. "You know me better than to think I'd be involved with something illicit. Anyway, how many drug runners drive a four-year-old Malibu?"

"That isn't the point. And no, I don't know Rainey Michaels, but I used to know Maressa Clarkson."

Gnawing at her lower lip, she glowered. "I knew you knew who I was all along, so why didn't you say so?" Eyes flashed as sarcastically as her voice.

"Of course, I recognized you." He curtailed an impulse to roll his eyes at her. "That's my job, as a badge-toting, whatcha call it? Oh, yeah, I remember: buffoon. And I can assure you that I don't wear this .45 for the hell of it." His hand patted the butt of his holstered Glock. "When are we going to stop this game of cop and robber and get down to business?"

And the business he wanted to get down to had nothing to do with law enforcement. He had questions, and she held the answers. He charged on. "Why did you leave an exciting job to move to this one-horse town? And I'll know if you're lying."

"It's a long story and I *am not* lying. All I have to say is that life dealt me a wicked hand, like the dead man's hand in poker. . . ." Irritation deepened her dimples. She stood deathly still and bit her lip. "Uh, I-I fell in love, relocated to New York, and well, things got complicated."

"So, he dumped you?"

"No!" Her gaze bore into his and she prickled up like a cactus. "He certainly did not."

"So you left a promising career, and I heard before I left Denton that you were on the fast track to becoming the next LA County DA, to follow some man across the country? Come on, Maressa . . . Rainey, or what in the hell you want to be called, you graduated with top honors from the University of Texas." He shook his head. "I can't imagine a focused, keep-your-head-stuck-in-a-lab project bookworm like you letting a man separate you from your goals."

Deuce chided himself for adding such a seedy barb, but it was too late. He looked away, avoiding the hurt in her eyes. Wishing the darkness would swallow him, he took a deep breath and knew he had twisted the dagger he had already driven in her heart. "So, what was his name?"

"His name? Uh, Edward. Edward Michaels."

"A man with two first names. And his middle name?"

Her eyes darted around the room. "Burlington. Edward Burling-ton Michaels."

"Convenient." Deuce followed her gaze to an array of vintage metal locomotive signs. Rock Island. Santa Fe. Burlington. "Want to start over on your story?"

"I *am* telling the truth!"

"The lady doth protest too much."

"*Hamlet.*"

"Gertrude. His mother."

Not yielding the floor, she filibustered on. "It's not that simple. You, of all people, know how it is when you fall in love." She pulled a Kleenex from her pocket and wadded it in her hand. "On second thought, a guy like you with a turnstile in his bedroom wouldn't know.

My husband was a, uh, a lawyer and a great man. I didn't mind giving up my career for him. We hadn't been in New York City long when it happened. . . ."

She touched her nose as if checking to make sure she hadn't developed the Pinocchio syndrome. Apparently satisfied, she crossed her arms.

Something stunk to high heaven, and it wasn't the moldy old railway station either.

"What happened?" He added a degree of warmth to his voice.

"He got killed. Y-yes," she stammered, as though the idea was foreign to her. "He was doing charity work in the projects and was killed. Such a good man." She dabbled at nonexistent tears.

"Killed," Deuce repeated.

"Y-yes. He fell off a ladder, hit his head and died before the paramedics got there."

"I'm sorry," Deuce offered, but knew his voice didn't reflect true sympathy.

Such a good man and nary a real tear? Oh, yeah, Widow Michaels, tell me another one.

"Deuce, please believe me." As though she read his mind, her eyes seemed to plead for understanding. "I was frightened and scared, and just couldn't live in such a big city without knowing anyone. At least in LA, I had friends. Trust me, I didn't leave my life behind. . . ." She leveled a piercing stare straight at him. "Or anything else for that matter, just for the hell of it. It was for the best." Her nervous dimples faded and sheer terror shrouded her features.

This wasn't his first time at this rodeo, and he recognized the signs of fear as quickly as lying. Most definitely Rainey wasn't telling all of the truth. But, one of the many things he hadn't forgotten, she was honest. So honest, in fact, that she wouldn't swipe a grape off the school lunch line, unless she paid for it first. The feisty person he grew up with wouldn't run without a very good reason.

The woman he knew, *news flash, Cowan—thought I knew*, was stable, self-assured, and had goals. So what had caused her to change her physical appearance, take on a new identity, and relocate to a quaint Texas town?

Nothing seemed right about the circumstances surrounding her sudden appearance in Kasota Springs. Hopefully, once Danny completed his investigation, some of the missing pieces would fall into place.

"Now, it's my turn." Rainey threw back her shoulders, straightened her collar, exuding a renewed confidence. "How did you end up as the sheriff here?"

"After my pro career ended because of my shoulder injury, which if you watch television any you know as much about it as I do—"

"Oh, yeah, I couldn't turn on any station without seeing your picture splattered everywhere for weeks."

"Have to admit, I was pretty disappointed, but I accepted a position with the Steelers as a specialty coach. Never really had my heart in it. I wanted to play ball, so when I couldn't do that anymore . . ." He took a deep breath, hoping his voice didn't betray his emotions. "Anyway, when Dad got killed I came back to take care of Mama—"

"She's in Kasota Springs, too? Do you live together?"

"No. She's . . ." He hesitated before completing his sentence. "I have a little house near headquarters out on a little spread I bought. The Slippery Elm." He studied her for a few seconds. "Been around for over a hundred years. Shares a fence line with the Jacks Bluff."

"I've heard of the Jacks Bluff since they were rodeo stock contractors, but not the Slippery Elm since I didn't grow up in the Panhandle. I never figured you for a rancher."

"It's just an old cow-calf operation, but I had a unique opportunity to buy it and couldn't pass it up. I've got a foreman running the ranch, so I mainly sleep and bark orders out there, if I don't stay in town."

"Sounds like a perfect place to me." She laid her hand on his arm. "Deuce, I'm truly sorry about your dad."

Her touch, soothing like silk against a wound, chased away some of his uneasiness and old fears.

"A basket of roses and a donation to the American Cancer Society couldn't begin to tell you how I ached for your family." She tore her hand away as though suddenly aware that it rested on a hot stove.

"Thanks. Time heals, a little. Dad lived each day knowing that's the way it might end and went out a hero, just like he wanted. And Mama—"

"Your mom is the reason I decided to open an antique shop here in Kasota Springs."

"I'm not surprised. I remember what great friends you were when you worked for her after school." He pulled off his hat and pushed back that renegade lock of hair that hung over his forehead, glad that she had interrupted him before he told her more about his mom than he wanted to. That conversation would have to wait until he saw whether Rainey was serious with her plans to stick around.

"I can remember you lugging in the"—she quoted with her fingers—"'good stuff' your mom got at garage sales and thrift stores, so she could open a bigger shop someday. Did she?"

"No. The old house in Denton is like Noah's Ark. She has two of everything." Deuce replaced his Stetson and chuckled, thinking about the crowded rooms filled with antique furniture and shelves of glassware, not to mention boxes upon boxes of her treasures stacked in the garage.

He shook off the memories, which were just that . . . memories.

Deuce resisted adding, *Like you, life dealt Mama a sorry hand.* Instead, he quickly changed the subject. "Yesterday, Wilson called and said he had leased the building for an antique shop, but he didn't give me your name."

"That was my original plan, but after seeing its disrepair." She looked around and a wistful expression etched her face. "I might have bitten off more than I can chew. It's rather, uh, big." She dropped her lashes, but not before he saw her disappointment. "Are you going to charge me with assault?"

"Haven't made up my mind. Where do you plan to spend the night? There's no running water and it's drafty as a wind tunnel in here. And I bet Wilson told you it had a great living area, too?"

"Something like that, and from what I see, it's like the accommodations a weary traveler who missed his train might expect."

"Yeah. Where this place is concerned, someone put a stop payment on Wilson's reality check." He tried to lighten the mood, not wanting her to head for the hills when he had plenty of questions only she could answer.

"I'll get a rent by the week hotel room." She shrugged, as though answering a pointless question.

"Let's see." He rubbed his thumb along his jawline. "There's four rooms above the Silver Dollar, which is one of our watering holes, and you don't need to spend the night with the creepy crawlers that hang out up there. The two motels are filled with road crews working on the bypass, so there's little choice. You could—"

"I'll sleep in my car," she said a little too quickly.

"Come on." Possessively, he grasped her arm. "I'm taking you out to the ranch. You'll be safe there."

"I can't do that." She hastily pulled out of his grip.

"Sure, you can. I have plenty of room and if you're worried about what people will think, I'll just tell the old hens that you're my long-lost cousin."

A smile fought its way through her mask of uncertainty. "Thanks, but it's best that I make other arrangements."

"Other arrangements? That's nothing but pure ol' stubbornness. Either come along willingly or I'll reconsider the assaulting a peace officer charge and snap those wrist cuffs back on you so fast it'll make your head swim. You can see just how comfortable those cots are in the hoosegow."

"That's being a bully, but under the circumstances I have little choice. I know the law and would rather take the deal than plea bargain for hours."

"Smart girl. You might be the lawyer, but I've got the handcuffs. So, let's get out of here so the things that go bump in the night can come out and play."

"If you promise to be a gentleman—"

"Now, Brainy Rainey, when have I not—"

"You don't want to go there, Ace."

Chapter Five

Rainey halted just inside Deuce's living room and wondered how in the blue blazes she had ended up at his place. After all, a Rhodes Scholar surely knew how to say "no" to the macho quarterback-turned-sheriff.

Although, Deuce wasn't the typical jock, either. Attending Texas A&M on an academic, as well as a football scholarship rather than hinging his whole future on being an athlete, he was capable of understanding the word "No."

Only a ribbon of soft light from the porch flanked the floor. She smelled the room more than saw it. The atmosphere hung heavy with the manly scent of leather, cedar, and Deuce.

He switched on a lamp and light illuminated the gargantuan room. Unbuckling his holster, Deuce removed his weapon. He went into what appeared to be his study and locked it in the gun cabinet.

A massive Bev Doolittle lithograph depicting an American Indian surrounded by an interesting array of wildlife hung above the stone fireplace. Stone and cedar-lined walls on either side of a bookcase brimming with hardbacks, all without dust covers, added to the rustic allure of the room.

The appointments were masculine, all male, all consuming . . . all Deuce. Nothing soft or feminine but bold like its owner. Nowhere did she see football memorabilia. Not a single item to indicate that a talented player lived there.

"Make yourself at home." He hunkered before the fireplace, and soon an infant blaze took hold shooting gilded tangerine and crimson flames upward. "There's drinks in the fridge, but no Diet DP. Still drink it?"

She nodded.

"How about a glass of wine?"

"No, thanks. It'd probably knock me on my keister."

"When did you eat last?" He rested his elbow on the mantel, exposing wisps of curly black hair beneath his gaping white shirt.

"I'm not hungry." She set her purse on the mammoth oaken roll-top desk in one corner of the living room. Above, a deer head with a handsome ten-point rack and stony stare guarded the room.

She glanced up at Deuce and saw skepticism etched in his frown. "I have eaten," she retorted.

"What? Crackers and water?"

"No. Cheez-Its and AriZona tea."

"Real solid food, huh? How about I fix you something?"

"Honestly, Deuce, I'm just not hungry." She halted and gazed at him with a half smile. "But thanks, that's very sweet of you."

It had been a long time since anyone had asked if she had eaten or cared enough to even bother to ask.

Growing up, her mother had been too busy protecting her position as a trophy wife to do little more than make certain her only child had the best of everything. Best clothing. Best education. Best country club. Not to mention hiring a "Rent a Mommy," as Rainey called her au pair. And she wasn't sure her mother would have done that if it hadn't been for Rainey's unbendable father. Regardless, she still loved her mother.

Rainey willed away thoughts of her childhood. Right now she didn't have the luxury to wallow in her dysfunctional family's atrocities. She had to worry about today—not yesterday. Survival depended on staying alert, and mulligrubbing about her past could only get in the way and could get her killed.

The long hours driving from New York, coupled with the challenges of dealing with Deuce and constantly watching her backside, had stressed Rainey beyond her limits. Every muscle ached from exhaustion. She needed a hot shower and some sleep. Food could wait.

She turned to Deuce, who watched her from across the room. His cognac-colored eyes scrutinized her every move, searching her face as though delving into her thoughts.

"I'd like to take a shower and then I want to know about your mom." She picked up her purse and clutched it to her chest.

"I'll show you the way." He strolled down the hall, stopped to grab an oversized bath towel and washcloth, before entering the stark, immaculate bathroom. "Everything you need should be here."

Deuce turned on the bathtub faucet and adjusted the temperature.

Rainey looked down at her wrinkled slacks and remembered the gym bag at the depot. "I don't have a change of clothes."

"There are T-shirts in the top drawer. They'll swallow you, but at least they'll be comfy." He pulled the door shut, only to reopen it. "You'll find a brand-spanking new toothbrush and a small bottle of liquid soap in the medicine cabinet. Have to watch my delicate skin, you know." He offered her a sensual, arresting smile before pulling the door closed.

Rainey sat on the side of the tub and watched the steam billow up from the rushing liquid; she felt too drained to care whether the water was hot or cold.

She jumped at the sound of a knock. "Deuce?"

"No, it's the maid. Here." The door eased open only far enough for his hand to appear and set a goblet of wine on the sink counter. "Drink this. It'll get rid of some of your weariness," he called from the hallway.

"Thanks," she answered, in spite of her racing heart.

Rainey shot to the door, clicked the lock, and plastered her body against the wood.

Nausea attacked.

Inhaling deeply, she fought the foul tasting bile. She closed her eyes and allowed a final wave of nausea to pass, unable to believe she had been so careless as to not have locked the door.

Anyone could have come in . . . anyone!

Somewhat composed, she dragged herself to the cabinet, where she found a nice supply of "girlie stuff." Essence of vanilla shampoo, powder fresh Secret, English lavender gel, and bubble bath. Apparently, her knight-in-shining-armor wanted to be prepared for a sleepover, but she doubted he expected his guest to be a flash from his past.

A bubble bath sounded inviting.

Between brushing her hair and washing her face, she downed the wine. After stripping off her clothes, she eased into the lavender scented tub.

Wine mingled with the steamy water and flushed her skin to a rich burgundy. She closed her eyes and let tranquility engulf her.

Her mind wandered back to the rugged, infernally handsome sheriff with a restless energy that showed in his every move. Glossy like volcanic rock, his eyes were full of life and exuded unquenchable warmth. Yet, amongst the twinkle there was a flicker of pain. She'd seen him in emotional turmoil before, but nothing like what she had seen earlier. She noticed sadness, like he searched for something. The problems she shouldered could only add to what troubled him.

As sheriff, Deuce had a duty to protect her once he knew she was in danger. But, she wouldn't bring him into her problems without a new threat. Maybe she should have identified herself right away and told him why she was on the run. But in the middle of a traffic stop, parked on the shoulder of the highway just didn't seem the right place and she was too angry at him at the depot to do anything but exchange barbs with him.

How could something so simple have turned so complicated so quickly? She had planned to unceremoniously ease into town, blend in like a chameleon in the rain forest, and quietly go about her business setting up shop. Although the building wasn't exactly what she expected, with more work required than she had anticipated, it could provide a comfy place to call home. A much-needed safe harbor. Now she had to get a replacement insurance card and appear before the justice of the peace to pay her fine, which would definitely draw attention to her.

Taking a deep breath, she exhaled to clear her mind. Her plans had gone awry, to say the least, when she ran into Deuce. Now she relaxed in his bathtub soaking up bubbles not intended for her. Probably intended for the person he expected to share his bed with.

Perplexity knotted deep in her stomach at the thought of another woman in Deuce's arms.

Absentmindedly, she lathered up the washcloth. What the hunkster did was none of her business. She had bigger problems than tracking how many women Deuce Cowan had bedded. The sheriff would have plenty of questions of his own, and she needed to come up with answers. Dern, if she hadn't complicated things by allowing the sweet-talking rascal to back her into a corner where she had to improvise a story about her past. And a pretty damn stupid story to boot. Not to mention she was an experienced lawyer accustomed to countering any challenge with quick thinking and self-assurance in the courtroom.

Now she had to deal with questions about a dead husband that never existed in the first place.

Damn it! Deuce had the tools available to unravel the truth, as though the facts were loosely woven into an afghan. Rainey needed to prepare her defense much in the same manner as she would if she faced him in the courtroom.

Flashes of the faces of her last jury surfaced. One by one, each juror turned his or her eyes from the gruesome photos of the nine murdered victims stacked on top of one another like skin pelts.

Why couldn't the memories of the defendant's taunting face go away, instead of appearing every time Rainey closed her eyes?

After hearing the jury foreperson slowly and deliberately state, "On Count One, the jury finds the defendant, Alonzo F. Hunter, guilty of first degree murder," Hunter became enraged like the animal she had proven him to be. As each verdict was read, he became more incensed. After hearing *guilty* for the ninth time and knowing he'd spend the rest of his life in prison without parole or be executed . . . he mouthed a flood of obscenities before bolting from his chair.

Rushing the prosecutor's table, he captured her wrist in a steel-trap grip and spat in her face, before hissing, "Bitch, you're a dead woman." Three deputies subdued and dragged the deranged mass murderer away. Being pulled from the courtroom he continued to yell, "I've got people out there waiting to kill you. Hear me, you're a dead woman!"

The heavy doors to the courtroom slammed shut masking the rest of his threats.

The terror had never let up. Never went away. Always, his smirk. The beady, black snake eyes.

Rainey fought back the need to dash from the bathroom and escape the horrid visions.

Run and never stop.

Run until she could no longer breathe.

Run until she was free from fear.

The gurgle of the last ounce of water swirling down the drain drew her back to her bath. Pain throbbed in her hand. She stared at the stopper chain that was twisted around her finger so tightly that it had cut off her circulation.

Gripping the plug, Rainey sat with a thin layer of bubbles covering her and they were dissipating at rapid intervals.

After rinsing and toweling off, she snatched up the first shirt she found in the drawer and pulled the soft black-and-gold jersey over her head. She eased out the door.

A knot formed in Deuce's throat and his heart did a somersault when Rainey entered the room. Damn, he'd never seen his old football jersey look so tantalizing, although the shirt hung on her like it would on a stick figure. The numeral on the front hid in the folds as the neck dipped low, giving him a nice view of ivory breasts. The hem draped well below her knees.

Her freshly shampooed tresses had lightened several shades. Reflections from the fireplace gleamed shadows of deep gold and rich red against her auburn hair. Eyes the color of green ice behind heavy black lashes peered up.

Barefoot, she padded across the room, tugging at the neck of his shirt. "Thanks. It's a little big but works." She collapsed onto the russet leather sofa facing the fireplace and pulled a corduroy pillow to her chest. "And for the wine, too. It helped."

Oh, yeah, it helped okay! His day had been interesting to say the least, and the two Lone Star beers he consumed while he waited had mellowed him. Now, he couldn't pry his gaze off the feisty wildcat if he tried. But he had to.

"You're welcome," he choked out. "I fixed a snack. Don't want anyone to accuse me of sending a prisoner to bed without supper."

He slid a tray of sliced cheddar cheese, salami, saltines, and a glass of wine on the coffee table. "Eat."

Rainey tentatively selected a cracker and washed it down with wine. "That tastes good."

Although flames crackled in the hearth, a late spring chill filled the air. She shivered.

"Cold?" Deuce pulled one of his mother's Texas Star quilts from a wingback chair. "Here." Testing the waters, not wanting to frighten her, he eased down on the couch and wrapped the coverlet around her shoulders. Adjusting the fabric, he allowed his fingers to linger on her arms longer than was necessary.

Rainey's skin felt smooth, silky and delectable, making him more aroused than ever. He chided himself for responding to her nearness. God only knew what a bad idea it was to get too attached to her, both emotionally and physically. His problems could only add heartache to her fragility and the porcelain-thin emotions she was unsuccessfully trying to hide.

He'd never seen Rainey weak or scared. The girl he knew was high spirited, never boring, and certainly not easily intimidated. What had happened to change the woman?

"Thanks." She set the glass on the end table.

Embers turned to ashes as they sat immersed in their own musings.

Deuce broke the silence. "Hey, I've been thinking. With a good paint job, some serious elbow grease, and a bit of caulking, the old depot can be habitable in no time."

She stirred uneasily next to him, causing the edge of the quilt to fall from her shoulder. "You think I'm the caulkable type?"

"No, but I am." As though his nearness caused her harm, he moved away and leaned forward, watching her intensely. "If you want my help—"

"I need help, Deuce." She touched his shoulder. "I don't want to be alone tonight."

For one dreadful moment, fear in her eyes bridged the differences between them. Deuce saw traces of alarm . . . paralyzing terror. Settling back into the leather cushion, he slipped his arms around her shoulders. Protectively, he skimmed his fingertips over her arm. "I'm not going anywhere."

"Thanks. I feel safe here and it's been a long time." Her eyes closed as her voice trailed off. Within only moments, she slipped off into slumber.

Deuce pushed away a strand of stray hair from her temple and rested his chin on her head.

Closing his eyes, he inhaled deeply. She smelled of yesterday; like a woman he loved more than life and had lost. Of lavender and vanilla. His own eyes drifted shut.

Twelve strikes of the mantel clock woke Deuce. He didn't remember nodding off.

Rainey slumbered soundly in the crook of his arm.

How in the hell did the bookworm and the lawman end up in one another's arms? The last thing Deuce needed was another vulnerable female to look after, and he'd never get any rest with her in his arms. His traitorous body had already told him as much.

With limited choices he scooped up the sleeping angel. Taking two stairs at a time, he reached his bedroom. He laid her on the bed and tucked her in.

A sliver of moonlight shimmered across her face, making it impossible for him to resist placing a light kiss to her cheek.

Pulling the door closed, he leaned against the wall. Frustrated, he ran his hands through his hair.

Rainey Michaels sure as hell hadn't come back to Texas by accident. It didn't take an experienced lawman to see that she was on the run and scared to death.

Deuce swore into the darkness, "Lady, I'll uncover the truth . . . with or without your help."

Chapter Six

White cottage curtains flapped lazily in the open window where Rainey slept. Cloaked in country freshness almost forgotten, she half opened her eyes and enjoyed incredible serenity.

Inhaling, she took in the aroma of fresh coffee and the forceful smell of a masculine bedroom. Rolling over, she nuzzled deep into the pillow. Lingering lavender fused with an outdoorsy scent clung to the linens, making it impossible for her to force herself out of bed.

Dawn peeked through the windowpane and sent cattywampus patterns across the room.

Sunrise!

Bolting upright, she turned the clock on the bedside table so she could read the time. Six-ten and all's well—no nightmares! Just wonderfully satisfying dreams of . . . of what? Deuce?

"Holy bejeezus!" She threw back the covers, realizing that the silver-tongued ruffian had made things way too easy for her to get comfortable with her surroundings. It would not happen again. But allowing the unassuming man to reach into her heart and massage her soul had given her the best night of sleep she had had in months, maybe years, with not even one horrific nightmare. No waves of nausea which normally kept her rushing to the bathroom for relief. No pounding temples. No headache.

Deuce Cowan succeeded in doing what she had not. The mesmerizing man had changed everything—even the air around her, breathing life into her ailing spirit.

Quickly, she shucked his jersey and slipped on wrinkled khaki slacks. After rubbing at a tiny soiled spot on her apricot sweater, she took a whiff. Her first project must be to launder her meager belongings, followed by a much-needed shopping trip to the town's only ladies' shop. She pulled the sweater over her head.

Finger brushing her short auburn locks, she stared in the mirror above the massive oaken dresser. Even without makeup and only a light coat of lipstick, she already looked much better. As a matter of fact, after a fleeting glance, she realized she wasn't even the same person who fled from Los Angeles a short three months earlier.

She touched her cranberry-tinged cheek, moving her fingertips to her lips. Had she dreamed being kissed? Yep, she definitely remembered a kiss. His nearness. So close that she had smelled his breath, a sweet mixture of salty beer and sensuality laden with the realization that she'd always be safe with him.

Sliding on her watch, she added gold hoop earrings before looking around.

The room was so Deuce. Rustic and bigger than life, just like the rest of the house. He had called it a little house. Certainly not her idea of a "little place on the ranch." But then there was nothing half-pint in that man's life.

Atop a chest of drawers, family pictures caught her eye. A smile escaped, as she picked up a photograph of Deuce in his cap and gown, surrounded by his parents. Her stare lingered on the take-control, stately woman with long curly hair standing so proudly next to her son.

What a happy family.

Suddenly, Rainey felt anxious. But for months anxiety had become her middle name, enduring uneasiness about everything from the man in brown delivering a package to a friendly service station attendant in Oklahoma who smiled at her. However, this time she felt eagerness, not dread. She wanted to see Deuce's mother.

A warning voice whispered, reminding her that regardless of how secure she felt at the moment she remained in danger, and thus putting anyone near her in harm's way. She must be careful not to jeopardize the elderly Mrs. Cowan's welfare.

Rainey wiped away a thin film of dust from the glass with the hem of her sweater and studied the picture. "Uh, honor cords." She returned the frame to its resting place. "Funny, I never noticed how easy on the eyes you were in those days. But then you ain't all that bad today. Dern, if I'm not babbling to a picture," she mumbled. "I've got to get out of this house."

She didn't know why the thought suddenly struck her after all of these years, but she couldn't help but wonder why Deuce changed his mind about asking her to the senior homecoming dance so many years ago. But it didn't matter now. Between her father and Deuce she had learned to trust only herself . . . never a man.

The smell of java guided her down the stairs. Except for a steady hum of the refrigerator, the spic-and-span kitchen was quiet.

Mugs, but no sugar bowl or creamer, sat next to the Mr. Coffee. She poured herself a cup and read the note propped up against the canister. "R, Be back later, D."

After checking the cabinets for sugar and finding none, she blew on her coffee before taking a tentative sip. She shuddered at the bitterness. What kind of a man doesn't keep sugar around? A healthy one, probably.

After taking a second sip, she poured the remainder in the kitchen sink and meandered to the back door, then stepped out onto the redwood sundeck. A rowdy blue jay squawked his warning before bombarding a fat, muddily-dun tabby scrunched down on his haunches.

Spiky clumps of bluish-green yucca and spiraea veiled in tiny white blossoms edged the fence line. Outdoor furniture encircled a mammoth hot tub. Rainey ran her hand through the water. Still warm.

Breaking daylight blazed orange beyond a good-sized tack room adjacent to a corral and some stalls.

Crossing the manicured scrunch-grass walkway leading to the barn, she halted at the open door.

Her eyes froze on Deuce's long, lean, perfectly proportioned body, as he lay on his sweat-glistened back with arms stretched high, bench-pressing weights.

Holy cripes, was he ever healthy and in all the right places.

Rainey whirled and blindly rushed back to the cabin.

Had she forgotten that she didn't even like the man, much less his body? Oh, yeah, but she had to admit that, although she didn't necessarily like the package, she certainly enjoyed how it was wrapped. After all, she was a living, breathing woman who could look but not touch.

Just as she hit the safety of the kitchen, Deuce called from behind, "What's the hurry?"

Startled that he had caught up with her so quickly, she halted in mid-stride. Methodically, she turned toward the voice. "I'm on my way to town to buy the things I need to set up housekeeping at the depot."

Deuce tugged a tattered Gold's Gym muscle shirt over his head. "Not this early in the morning, you aren't. There's no Green-Mart in this town, but heard they're planning to put one in, so you might as well stay here for a while—"

"I'd be in your way. Besides, I've imposed on your hospitality enough."

"You haven't. I have plans and won't be home tonight anyway." He grabbed a bottle of water from the refrigerator and loosened the cap. "So, you might as well stay another day or so."

"I'm living down at the depot beginning today." Rainey turned briskly, fleeing toward the staircase.

Strong, calloused hands grabbed her by the arm and she found herself spun around facing him.

"What's the matter?" He loosened his grip.

"Nothing. I'm just going to get my purse and get to town to check on a couple of things before I have the water turned on. And don't forget, I need to obtain a new insurance card."

What was wrong with her? She didn't have to give him an excuse to leave. Besides, she had seen men exercising before. Back in LA, a town filled with leading men and men to lead, she'd seen plenty of them. However, she must admit, none quite as exquisite as the one she'd just witnessed.

"Hey, if I could cancel my plans, I'd help you out, but I can't—"

"Deuce, I need to do the work myself. To stay busy. I'll call you if I get into trouble."

"A promise is a promise. I said I'd help, and come hell or high water, I'm going to keep my commitment." His dark eyes never left hers for even an instant.

"Like *I* said, *I* don't need any help. I've already taken advantage of your good nature too much."

His gaze caught and held hers.

Deuce seemed to study her face unhurriedly before saying, "Like *I* said, I'm going to help you, but not tonight."

Without warning, he leaned into her and kissed her lightly on the forehead. "End of discussion, okay?"

After touching the tip of her nose with his index finger, he bounded up the stairs three at a time, leaving Rainey breathless.

Jiminy Christmas! Had he gone bonkers? Tee-totally off his rocker? Maybe he exerted too much pumping iron and had a blood shortage to his think tank? Or, possibly his shoulder injury story was a cover-up. That was it! Had the quarterback gotten sacked too many times and had a bruised brain?

Gently, she ran her fingertips over her forehead. She should go straight to the bathroom and wash away the kiss. No. Brain injury or not, she enjoyed the attention way too much to let the show of affection go so easily.

Grabbing up her purse, Rainey headed out the door intent on taking care of the business necessary to get the depot at least inhabitable.

Once hitting the city limits, her first stop ended up being the tiny town hall where the utility department was housed She came away frustrated when a wiry clerk, sporting a double whammy of dumbass, informed her they couldn't turn on the water for seventy-two hours per their city code.

Grumbling under her breath, Rainey left city hall. Oh, yeah, in a town so small that everyone knew everyone else's business, yet big enough that they had to read the newspaper to see who got caught, it took three days for water service.

After calling the insurance company and ordering a new proof of insurance document, her next visit was to Gideon's Hardware and Surplus where she bought a hot plate and a dorm-sized refrigerator. She chose a cheap set of dishes. Ones guaranteed to have wobbly bottoms and sport irregular patterns or drips of paint trailing from the design. A set of nondescript white sheets and towels completed her household purchases.

After ordering a futon, she learned it wouldn't come in until the store's next shipment arrived from their supplier. If she wanted it sooner, there'd be an express shipping charge, but even at that, the bed would take about a week to get to her.

She couldn't afford the time it'd take to drive the sixty miles over to Amarillo and back, so she'd have to settle for what she could find in the hardware store. Since she couldn't get the futon any time soon, the fluorescent orange sleeping bag on the shelf seemed her only option. She hated the color orange because it reminded her of a jail jumpsuit. Oh, well, what was another forty dollars this late in the game?

After stuffing a wad of her money into the cash register, the middle-aged, balding store owner quickly requested to be called by his first name. Gideon loaded the merchandise into the Malibu for her short trip to the depot, spouting his pleasure at having a new customer. No doubt the price gouging increased her value to the economy of Kasota Springs.

All of this came with a running dissertation about his first-day issue stamp collection. At least, the shop owner did something useful while he rattled on, by throwing away the moisture-stained newspaper that the bonsai had rested on ever since leaving Los Angeles. Not satisfied, he grabbed an empty Diet Dr Pepper can, a cracker wrapper, and what was left of an old page torn from a legal pad, and crammed them in a sack. What did he think? She'd toss the trash out in his parking lot the moment he turned his back?

Her cell phone rang.

"Excuse me, Mr. Duncan—"

"Call me Gideon," he insisted.

"This is the water department," she said. Thinking her business with Gideon was concluded, she quickly said, "Thank you for your help."

He never made a move to return to his store, seemingly more intent on listening to her conversation.

Once finished receiving bad news, Rainey disconnected from the call and put the phone in her purse.

"At least I know why they can't turn the water on immediately."

She had no idea why she was discussing her business with a total stranger, but felt the need to have someone to commiserate with. "The depot has outmoded clay pipes and by the building code, they can't turn on my water until they're replaced." She hoped her frustration didn't show in her words.

She wanted so badly to add, "Inspected by probably a Turn-On Tech Level One." No wonder they needed lead time. It must have taken them that long to dust the cobwebs from the codebook. She nearly had to bite her tongue to keep from spitting out the words.

"I've got a temporary solution for you, Miss, uh—"

"Michaels, Mrs. Michaels."

"I own the building next to the depot and have running water, although it's vacant. Wanna keep the grass watered, you know."

Pleasantries certainly were not on her agenda, but she said, "I noticed how nice the grass looked."

"You could get your husband to hook up to my water supply until ol' man Wilson gets around to making your repairs."

"I'm a widow," she said softly, then lowered her eyes.

The storekeeper offered his condolences and she accepted, grateful he didn't ask any more questions.

Momentarily, Rainey wrangled with herself over the offer, but with no better solution in sight and a huge desire to get out on her own as quickly as possible, she agreed.

By the time she left Gideon's store, he'd loaded seven of his longest garden hoses in the Chevy and lightened her pocketbook even more. He'd probably bill her for the water by the ounce, but at the moment, she had more important things to worry about.

Minutes later, frustrated beyond sensibility, Rainey pulled into the depot's parking lot and sat staring at the monstrous building. In the daylight, it looked even worse than at night.

From the appearance of the parking lot, someone had poured asphalt over a sheet of dynamite and detonated it. Potholes and trenches layered with gravel. But at least she had everything she needed to start a new life: running water siphoned from a neighbor, a place to keep her food cool, as long as she didn't buy anything bigger than a four-pack of yogurt and a Happy Meal, and a sleeping bag on a concrete mattress.

When she left Deuce's house earlier in the day, she had planned to cut all ties with him, but now, dang if she could. With the prospect of sleeping on a cold floor and taking an even colder shower, maybe she shouldn't have been so hasty in cutting the jockaramus loose.

She sat in her car and made several calls to her property owner's office. Of course, Mr. Wilson had chosen today to take a trip to Odessa. Three calls later, Rainey was reassured by his primordial secretary that the repair would be no problem and she'd have Mr. Wilson contact Rainey. But when? Tomorrow? Friday? Next week?

Not bothering to even unload the merchandise she had purchased, Rainey headed toward a little café she had spotted earlier in the morning. Although she wasn't all that hungry, a cup of coffee sounded good.

Rainey entered Pumpkin's Café and was greeted as though she were a hobo who just hopped off a slow-moving coal train.

Six rough-as-whang-leather workmen sat at the counter, stares glued to a television wedged up high in the corner. Ignoring a vacant stool, she looked for another free seat. The first table near the entrance meant she would have to sit with her back to the door. She refused to willingly be caught off guard.

She eyed a willowy waitress with a short, broomstick haircut clearing off a booth directly across from the lunch counter.

When the woman gestured that she had the table ready, Rainey took a seat.

Shaking off uneasiness, she glanced at the "specials" scrawled on a white board and then picked up a menu strategically placed between the wall and the napkin holder. She opened it and read nearly every item on the menu, but still nothing sounded good.

After ordering coffee, Rainey sat there playing with her spoon and looking out the window, wondering about her decision to stay in Kasota Springs.

Every time the door opened, she shrank down in the booth, afraid of who might enter. She had to stop being leery of everyone she came in contact with. She was a thousand miles away from Los Angeles, but regardless of how hard she tried, she hadn't succeeded at leaving the past behind . . . to being scared of what the future held for her.

The bell at the top of the café's door rang, and the screen door slammed behind a flurry of crinoline petticoats and gingham that whirled in. American Bandstand, circa 1950, sidled between the rows of booths and headed her direction.

"Mrs. Michaels!" the woman buried in the regalia squealed.

Rainey stiffened, debating whether to respond or act like she hadn't heard her, while fighting off the urge to look over her shoulder to make sure another Mrs. Michaels wasn't hiding behind her sipping tea.

The petite woman, probably in her mid-thirties, with a thick crop of chemically induced blond hair teased into an outrageously big bouffant style swished her way, coming to a halt beside the table. "I finally found you," she said, as though Rainey had been lost.

"I'm sorry. I don't believe we've been introduced." Rainey's mind reeled with confusion.

"Oh, golly. I guess you wouldn't know me, but I feel like I know you, since I've heard so much about you." Net and lace crackled as the woman flounced into the seat opposite Rainey. "I'm Sylvie. Sylvie Dewey."

"Uh, please join me, Miss Dewey."

"Sylvie." She deposited her purse on the bench.

The waitress reappeared and without looking at the menu, Sylvie ordered a vegetable plate and iced tea. "I didn't know you were the person who rented a PO box until I put two and two together. Then Deuce fessed up that you were the friend. . . ." She punctuated the word "friend" with her fingers. "Who spent the night out at his place." She batted her frosted sky-blue coated eyelids.

Oh, Jiminy! Why didn't Deuce hire a town crier to go up and down the street and announce her sleeping arrangements? Any minute she expected a full description of her underwear. Dang that Deuce Cowan's hide. He'd ended up shipping her reputation down south in a rickety cotton wagon.

"It wasn't like that," Rainey muttered.

"That?" A dumb-as-a-stump expression curtained Miss Rock 'n' Roll's face.

Dah! Hello! Anybody home?

"You know, uh, anything personal." Feeling uncomfortable,

Rainey raised a questioning eyebrow. "I only stayed at his place because I couldn't find a motel room."

"Oh, yeah, I know. When I came in, Gideon was over in the post office space picking up one of our famous government publications off the rack. He told me that you rented the old depot. I'm the postmistress, you know."

Saved by the sound of the front screen opening, Rainey darted a wary eye in that direction. She could deal with Deuce knowing her true identity, but being absconded by the queen bee of the quilting guild shook her like the aftermath of a Texas twister.

In clipped words, Sylvie continued her query. "And you're a widow. I'm so sorry."

"Huh, yes." Rainey twisted the coffee cup between her palms.

Oh, God, her nose surely grew another inch. Things were getting out of hand. At first, a little white lie didn't seem to hurt anything and served as protection. Besides, doesn't the end justify the means? As though fed Miracle-Gro, in less than twenty-four hours, the whole featherbrained scenario had blossomed out of control.

"If you don't mind, I'd prefer to talk about something more pleasant."

Sylvie nodded. "Sure, but I'll be here if you ever need someone to confide in. You know, girl talk. Things you might not be able to tell Deuce."

"Thanks, but Deuce and I aren't all that close. We just know each other from school."

"Oh, that's not what I heard. I thought you were best friends and all."

Being friendly was one thing, but this conversation had gone from a warm, fuzzy introduction into an interrogation.

"Being the postmistress must be interesting." Rainey took a drink of water, feeding her nausea. She glanced at the food sitting in front of her lunch companion, unaware that the waitress had even brought the vegetarian plate. "Are you married?"

Sylvie poised her fork over parsley new potatoes. "No. Never been." She laid down the utensil and leveled a stare at Rainey. "But I don't plan to be an old maid forever."

"You're much too young to be considered a spinster," Rainey said. "So, you have someone special?"

"Someone *very* special and he treats me really good, too." She turned her attention to her plate. "I grew up here and have worked in the post office since high school. I know just about everything that goes on around here." Sylvie speared green beans. "And I do mean everything—"

Deuce's rich-timbred voice interrupted her. "And you keep it all to yourself, huh, darlin'?"

"Have a seat, sheriff." The bundle of lace scooted across the bench to make room and patted the empty seat beside her.

"If I'm not interrupting a chick moment." He eased into the booth. "See you found her." He cast Sylvie a sideways glance and flashed Rainey one heck of a devilish smile.

"Well, you knew as soon as you told me that we have a new resident, I'd want to introduce myself." Sylvie dabbed her mouth with a napkin.

"I told you?" Deuce quirked a questioning eyebrow at her before turning his gaze back to Rainey. "As I recall the way it came about—"

"Shush!" Sylvie interrupted him. "The most important thing is that we're getting to know one another." She locked a smile on her face. "Real well, like we've known each other forever."

Interrupting, the spindly waitress returned and set down an empty glass and a pitcher of iced tea in front of Deuce. "Well, whatcha gonna have today, sheriff?"

"Whatever she's having." Deuce nodded toward Sylvie's plate. "But make mine with some meat."

"Gotcha covered, handsome." From her apron pocket, the waitress produced Tabasco and slid the bottle on the table. "Here ya go."

Sylvie seized Deuce's glass and poured tea before refilling her own. "You might as well add two slices of Granny's Special Chocolate Cake." She beamed a sweet, wary smile and batted her eyes across the table. "Deuce does love his chocolate."

Deuce shifted his attention away from her, and tilted his face up to the waitress. "Want you to meet a friend of mine, Rainey, uh, Rainey Michaels. She's the lady Wilson leased the ol' Rock Island to."

"Glad to meetcha." Long, I-Can't-Believe-I'm-A-Waitress red, enameled nails reached toward Rainey's hand. "Any friend of his has a hot cup waitin' for 'em here."

Rainey wiped her unmanicured, practical length fingertips on a paper napkin before accepting her shake. "Thanks, Miss—"

"Old man named me Clara, but everybody calls me Pumpkin. Been hitched up more times than a skinny cowpoke's pants, so cain't even remember my ex's last name. Be back in a jiffy." The spunk-fire sashayed away leaving Rainey wondering how much money Pumpkin would save if she fired the janitor and attached brooms to each of her wig-wagging hips.

"I need to powder my nose before I get back to work." Sylvie huddled close to Deuce, touching his bare arm. "If you'll excuse me."

He stood and stepped aside to allow her to scoot from the booth.

"I've got to hurry back to the post office. Today is the release date for the new Forever stamp. Every time there's an increase in postage, they seem to issue another Forever stamp. The new ones should have already been here, but haven't arrived, so I know Gideon will be waiting for me to get back from lunch to see if those new stamps came in on today's truck. He always buys up every first-day issue, so unless I hide them, there won't be any for anyone else. The perils of the government leasing space in Gideon's store for the post office." Giving Deuce a shy, schoolgirl smile, she flounced to the restroom.

Rainey shook her head. "She seems nice, kinda quaint." Taking a chance on Deuce thinking her catty, she looked down. "But doesn't she realize we're in the twenty-first century?"

"Sylvie's a great gal and is honest to the core."

"She has an interesting wardrobe," Rainey said.

"I heard that her father made Sylvie wear her mother's clothes after she died. No telling what other abuse he laid on her. I've always suspected she'll swoon over any man who gives her any attention. Never dates, so now I think wearing her mother's clothes is more about Sylvie missing her mama than any embarrassment from people's comments."

"And what about her father?"

"He died a lonely ol' soul a couple of years ago, before I became sheriff."

"I admire her for being her own self, regardless of what people say."

"Right now, I'm more concerned with you. What's wrong?" Deuce leaned into the table and crossed his arms. "And don't say nothing—those pretty dimples betray you every time. It was that damn kiss, wasn't it? Rainey, it didn't mean a thing."

"Of course not. It didn't mean anything to me either."

"I know you're in some kind of trouble. What?"

"No," she responded a shade too quickly. "I am not in any trouble. It is, well, that I don't want to look like some kind of desperate woman that shimmied out of her widow weeds before the hearse got out of the cemetery."

"Nobody will think that. They don't even know you're a widow, and unless you believe it's important they do, just leave it alone. Let them think what they may."

"But she knows." Rainey motioned toward the bathroom.

"Damnation!" He flattened his hand on the table.

"It's okay. I knew I'd have to tell sooner or later."

"Damn again over!"

Rainey stared at him, trying to piece together the reason he acted so surprised. After all, he had to have been the one who told Sylvie. It seemed that she wasn't kidding about knowing everything that went on in the town.

"She's not a Rhodes scholar, but she's a hard worker and a good friend." He reached out and touched Rainey's hand, as though apologizing for his bluntness. "She'll be your friend, too. If you ask her to keep quiet, she'll do it. So don't get all upset, okay?"

Fat chance of Miss Party Line keeping quiet.

"And if she doesn't?" Rainey asked.

"She'll do it if I ask her to. Trust me, okay?"

Trusting Deuce wasn't the problem, but putting trust in Sylvie might be a doozie, even a double-doozie.

The postmistress appeared from the back, and stopped near the lunch counter, head cocked toward the television.

Over the hustle and bustle of the diner, the voice of one of the men at the lunch counter split the air. "Pumpkin!" he growled. "Change that damn channel. Nobody gives a bunghole about a missing scum-suckin' lawyer all the way out in California."

"Shut up, you buttnocker. I'm trying to get some smarts off that news station," the missing link to the Beavis and Butt-Head combo challenged.

Deuce became instantly alert, zeroing in on the dim-witted duo.

Rainey clasped her fingers over Deuce's hand, encouraging him not to insert himself in the escalating argument between Stupid and Ignorant. She cast her gaze over the counter toward the television and watched as a reporter began a newscast.

Sylvie stood, glued to the news report.

In well-formed words the reporter began: "We are waiting the arrival of the Los Angeles County DA, Judith Mason, to begin her news conference to update our viewers on the case of the reported missing deputy DA. Reliable sources have told CNN that Miss Mason will announce . . . And here's the district attorney now."

A close-up shot of Rainey's former boss and close friend in front of a chorus of microphones filled the screen.

Stark white fear rushed over Rainey. She had seen nothing on the news or in the newspaper about her disappearance, but that wouldn't be uncommon with nearly a thousand deputy DAs employed there. She had presumed that Judith had figured out that Rainey had disappeared on her own, since she was the one who had told Rainey about the son-of-slime car lot salesman who in turn got her the car and a new identity. The only thing she had seen about the LA County District Attorney's office was that Judith has lost the election and would no longer be the district attorney in another couple of months.

But Rainey had to hold it together, although she'd rather be dead than to watch the television report at the moment.

In a confident voice Judith articulated: "Thank you for coming. I have a short statement concerning the reported disappearance of Deputy District Attorney—"

"Pumpkin!" Beavis of the lunch counter sect bellowed, drowning out the reporter. "Get this crap off this TV or you won't be seeing my ugly mug around this place again."

"Dreams do come true," the waitress quipped and then meandered up to the kitchen window and picked up some plates of food. She wandered over to Sylvie and shot over her shoulder, "If you don't like the TV here, go down to Winnie's 'cause that husband of hers won't allow no TV down there."

Rainey stared squarely at the television, as a random selection of library clips of the reported missing DDA appeared in rapid succession.

Rainey quickly pulled some hair around her face and grabbed her purse. She pulled out some reading glasses and put them on. "I'm so hungry," she said as she snatched up the menu. She tried to keep her face hidden as much as possible under the pretense of reading the menu, while peeping over the top at the news report.

Holding a platter high above her head, Pumpkin peered up at the television. "Hey, Deuce, she looks like your friend there." She twisted around and nodded toward Rainey.

"No, she doesn't. That woman's a blonde and that one back there—" Butt-Head tossed his head toward Deuce and Rainey's table.

"Yeah, it does, except that woman up there . . ." the third man joined in and pointed at the screen. "That woman is fatter. A whole bunch fatter. And she ain't as pretty."

"Except for the hair and the glasses, she does look like her." Pumpkin turned and ambled toward Rainey and Deuce. "But, kids, she isn't all that fat. I hear tell that television puts twenty pounds on you."

Panic, stark and vivid, rioted in Rainey's stomach, sending shockwave after shockwave through her body. Paralyzed with fear and scared to breathe, she clenched the menu.

The waitress placed a T-bone steak the size of Rhode Island in front of Deuce. "Whatcha think, cowboy? Think that missin' woman looks like your lady friend?" She planted the tray under her arm and a fist on her hip.

Time halted while she waited for his reply.

"No. The woman in the picture was taller." He grabbed the Tabasco and loosened the cap.

"That could be." Pumpkin glanced back at the television. "Hush up, you jackleg shovel jockeys. None of you got sense enough to spit downwind." She barked at the quarrelsome construction workers, "I wanna hear this."

"Don't getcha drawers in a wad, Pumpkin, or we ain't ever gonna get that bypass built for you."

"What part of hush up don't you understand?" Pumpkin sighed.

Silence. All eyes turned to the interview.

"I will answer three questions only," the district attorney announced, before acknowledging a female reporter in a red suit.

"Ms. Mason, then it's true that Miss Clarkson disappeared willingly?"

"Our investigation concluded that there was no foul play involved. She simply resigned. Next." The DA pointed to a gray-haired man. "Mr. Samuels, you have a question?"

"Yes, ma'am. It's been reported that you know the whereabouts of Ms. Clarkson."

"Sam, you know that it's my policy to neither acknowledge nor deny rumors. I reiterate . . . that Ms. Clarkson willingly resigned. Thank you for coming." Not waiting for the third question, the DA disappeared behind closed doors.

"Well, I still think that girl is fat," Butt-Head snapped.

Deuce spoke up. "Pumpkin, change the damn channel so the Three Stooges over there will can it." A muscle quivered in his jaw, and a shallow frown creased his forehead. "I don't think she looked all that fat."

"How about a refill?" He pushed Rainey's coffee cup toward the waitress, who nodded and sauntered to the corner and picked up the remote control.

Before Rainey could thank Deuce for running interference, he rose to allow Sylvie back into the booth. Apparently, she had changed her mind about the urgency of returning to work. Her eyelids and lips sported a fresh coat of war paint, and the sweet scent of counterfeit White Shoulders hovered heavily overhead.

"That was your pictures on the TV." Sylvie's eyes narrowed and a knowing tone emphasized her words.

"Knock it off, Sylvie. . . ." Deuce lowered his voice. "I've known Rainey for years. She isn't the woman on TV." His in-no-uncertain-terms tone left little room for debate.

Deuce saturated his steak with Tabasco and cut off a bite, exposing a red gushy middle. Setting down his knife with purpose, he stabbed the meat.

"Oh! Okay, whatever you say, sheriff." Catching Rainey's eyes, Sylvie zipped her lips shut with her fingers, twisted an imaginary key, and tossed it over her shoulder.

Rainey fought off a wretched stomach to mutter, "He's right. I just moved back to Texas from New York."

"I didn't know where you moved from, but should have known by the license plates," Sylvie said.

Deuce's brows knitted together in a deep frown as he glared at his potatoes and went to work pulverizing them with a fork.

Sylvie turned to small talk. "I heard you've already butted heads with the security company."

"Yes. Mr. Wilson notified them that I had leased the building, but didn't give me the access code. It was a maddening experience." She cut her eyes back to Deuce, who now peppered his potato with vengeance.

"I can only imagine late at night being at that old spooky depot and new in town." Sylvie picked up the tea pitcher. "I don't know why store owners around here even bother to have security systems since they all use the same code." She filled the glasses. "It only serves to keep out teenagers. Doesn't it, Deuce?" She batted her overly-mascaraed lashes.

The sheriff lifted his head and shot Sylvie a look of disapproval.

Rainey eyed first the hunkasarus, then the shrinking violet who acted like a pair of mismatched bookends, and then replaced the menu and took off her reading glasses. So the code she'd been given by Wilson was the same one everyone else used. Unbelievable! Storing her glasses in her purse, she said, "Not as hungry as I thought I was." She issued a weak smile.

Shifting her focus back to more serious problems that were multiplying quicker than a rabbit on fertility drugs, Rainey took stock of her options. And the most logical choice: Consider the money paid Wilson a bad investment, move on, and try to forget she had ever set foot in Kasota Springs, Texas. Her trying to break the lease would only lead to lengthy litigation and more attention drawn to her. The last thing she needed was to be deposed and be forced to answer questions under oath about her background, particularly a dead husband she never had in the first place. A good lawyer would scour the bowels of the earth to find dirt to be used in a piece of litigation.

Rainey watched the scowl on Deuce's face deepen, realizing she couldn't get out of town quick enough to suit the obviously peeved lawman.

Seemingly snatching words out of thin air, Sylvie piped up, "I'd never do anything to hurt our friendship." She spoke to Deuce, but eyed Rainey, before placing her hand over Rainey's. "I know we just met, but I'll be there for you, too."

"Thanks." Rainey tried to smile, but was abruptly distracted by a man peering through the café window.

Hooded, black, beady eyes bore into hers.

Fear spewed through her like an erupting volcano.

Frightened.

Electrified.

The bell over the front door jingled.

Rainey looked up to see a shadow of someone coming into the café.

Choking back a cry, she barely got out the words, "I've got to go to the ladies' room," before bolting from the booth and slamming her knee against the table leg in the process.

Dishes toppled and crashed, shattering glass in their wake. The tea pitcher hit the tiled floor, bouncing to a stop against the lunch counter baseboard.

Rainey rushed to the restroom, but instead of going inside, she turned towards the back door, fleeing danger. Or she thought she had.

Chapter Seven

"Noooooo!" Rainey screamed.

Butting the backdoor screen with her palms, she ran from the café, zigzagging through empty bread trays and milk crates stacked outside the rear exit. Rounding the building, she tripped on a grease bucket. Mucky, tar-colored liquid splashed her pants leg and ran down onto her foot.

Her heart sped out of control.

Hammering . . . pounding . . . beating uncontrollably against her ribs.

Behind her she heard the screen door slam and boots hitting the hard soil mixed with patches of concrete and asphalt.

Alonzo Hunter had escaped and found her as he had threatened.

Those hooded, beady eyes were undeniable.

Mocking . . . menacing . . . promising.

All the memories of the trial came rushing back. Every grisly image. Every morbid photograph. Every bloody detail.

Brands seared on nine bodies like cattle!

To no avail, Rainey's trembling fingers attempted to unlock the Malibu. Steadying her shaking wrist with her free hand, she tried again.

Click!

Clambering inside, she threw the car in gear and raced from the parking lot, leaving an opaque ribbon of gravelly whirlwinds behind.

The Malibu flew down Main Street. Tiny rocks and hardened earth crackled, propelled from beneath the tires, as she braked to a stop in front of the Rock Island Depot. Whether she had bothered to yield, much less halted at the stop signs, didn't matter. She had to hurry. Time was running out. She had to get her measly belongings and get out of town.

Scrambling through the front door, she locked it behind her before disarming and resetting the alarm. Raw emotions battled fright for control and won out.

Sliding to the floor, Rainey drew her knees tight against her chest, and buried her face. Hot tears escaped, falling into her lap.

Like a scolded child needing comfort, she rocked . . . back and forth . . . back and forth.

Heaving, the tears continued until there were no more.

How could Alonzo Hunter have found her? He couldn't be free. She had watched three deputies subdue him and escort him from the courtroom to be restrained before removing him from the court-house.

Three months later, she had watched a vehicle pull away, heading for San Quentin State Prison, where he had been sentenced to stay for the rest of his life.

Oh, God, would she ever be free from the nightmare?

Seizing composure, weak-kneed, she stumbled to the dinky, filthy restroom, filled her hands with tepid bottled water and washed her tearstained cheeks.

Grasping each side of the sink, she stared into the mirror. Where could she turn? What should she do?

The decision had been made for her.

Piling her dirty clothes and cosmetic bag into her satchel, she headed towards the door.

If she didn't stop any more than was necessary, she could make it back to New York City in two days. Three days tops. Rainey Michaels could melt into the crowd and get lost forever.

She set the alarm and tossed the keys to the depot on the counter, then headed out the door. After wedging the gym bag between the Malibu's front and back seats, she slammed the passenger door shut.

Rounding the car, she skidded to a stop . . . coming face-to-face with one very big and immensely angry sheriff.

His legs were spread shoulder-width apart and his arms were folded across his chest. "You planning on running away? Guess it's easier the second time—"

"I'm not running away!"

"You always take your refrigerator with you when you go out?"

"Deuce, this doesn't involve you. And for your information I just bought the refrigerator and haven't had time to take it into the depot yet." She took a deep breath. "There isn't anything you can do."

"I tried to follow you, but couldn't keep up. There's one thing for sure, I have an issue or two with you, lady; and by damn you aren't going anywhere until I have answers." His look was stony, unbendable. "Do you understand?" The corner of his mouth twisted with exasperation.

An ultimatum! What gall! She clenched her fist. Nails bit into her palm, but she continued to stare into stormy, dark eyes.

"Why did you lie to me?" Deuce thundered.

"I didn't."

"Here we go again. You might not think you did, but those dimples tell another story."

"What do you want me to say? Confess? And to what exactly?" Her stomach knotted tighter, as she forced her gaze across the parking lot, searching for anyone lurking—anything to steer her attention away from Deuce's accusations.

"Don't take me for a fool," he said coolly.

"I've accused you of lots of things, but I can assure you it's never been being a fool."

"And that's supposed to clear things up? Just tell me what in the hell is going on. But first . . ." He reached across and snatched her keys from her hand. Firmly catching her by the elbow, he turned her around and headed for the stucco building. "We're going inside where we'll have some privacy—"

"Why? So you can handcuff me to those bars again?"

He stalked toward the entrance, half dragging, half lifting her along. "Don't tempt me, Rainey."

White-hot anger boiled inside of her.

Rainey double-timed it, taking two steps to his one, in order to keep up with his long strides. "Damn it to hell, Deuce Cowan, you can royally pi— royally water me off," she said breathlessly.

Once inside, he turned off the bellowing alarm and called his office. "Jessup, disregard the alarm at the depot. It's a false alarm." He pocketed her car keys and pulled over a straight-back chair for her. Turning one around for himself, he straddled the seat.

She jerked her chair back, separating them by a good two yards, then plopped down.

"Damn it, Rainey. You've put me in one hell of a position. I trusted you and all you've done is lie to me. What in the hell is going on? And don't tell me nothing. And don't lie. You *are* the deputy DA they were talking about on TV. There is *no* Edward Burlington Michaels. Not even an Edward Santa Fe Michaels. You *were* in New York for a short period of time, and I want to know why!"

"I don't need *you* or anyone else involved. It's *nothing*—"

"Damn it to hell . . . *nothing*!" He slammed his fist against the back of the chair, making her flinch. "It wasn't *nothing* that scared you out of your wits at the café."

"Go ahead. Arrest me." Rainey crossed her wrists and pushed her arms out to him. "Handcuff me. Lock me up."

"Oh, hell's bells!" Deuce jerked off his Stetson, ran his fingers through his hair, and crammed the hat back on his head.

She let out a deep audible breath, and dropped her hands in her lap. Her gaze followed. "I'd hoped to be gone before you came after me. One call to LA and you'll know the truth, so there's no reason not to tell you." She looked up and saw sharp, questioning eyes searching her face. "Yeah, Deuce, I'm in trouble. Big-time trouble. I just didn't want to bring you or anybody else into it. Where do you want me to start?"

"Begin by telling me what scared you at the café."

"There's a man that I prosecuted. A mad zealot that played mind games. Have you heard of the Stonehill murders?"

Deuce nodded. "An incestuous scumbag who branded nine or ten women and children like cattle before he murdered and stacked the bodies in a corner like sandbags, right?"

"Yes, nine to be exact," she said. "The crime scene was so disturbing that many of our veteran officers had to get counseling. I lived and breathed that case for nearly two years."

Deuce closed his eyes and grimaced. "Oh, God, Rai. I followed it for a while, but it was too gruesome for me."

"You are a trained professional and you still have no real idea what I went through. It's something you're not taught in law school. To prosecute him I had to get into his head. A place I don't ever want to go again." Realizing that her voice quivered, Rainey stopped and garnered a bit of coolheadedness before compiling more words. "There were lots of things not in the paper. The perp stalked me while he awaited trial, sending me threatening letters. Really weird, eerie stuff. Later he sent details about the murder scene written on pages from a Bible. Things only the murderer and people close to the DA's office knew."

"Oh, God—"

"He wanted to destroy me before I destroyed him. Hunter sat throughout the trial stoic, unreachable. Flat affect. That was until the verdict was read and he attacked me."

"He didn't hurt you, did he?"

"Not physically. A sociopath like him thought he could get by with murder. Literally."

"And of course they didn't have him in shackles." Deuce slammed a fist into his palm. "We don't want to infringe upon a murderer's rights by handcuffing him in the presence of the jury. To hell with putting everyone around him in danger. How did he get that close to you?"

"He had ankle shackles on, but they had rearranged the defense table to facilitate the cameras in the courtroom, so it was closer to our table than usual. And before you ask, the bailiff and deputies did their job. I don't blame them. The defendant was just too quick for them."

"Damn it to hell!" Deuce clenched his fist tighter. "They could have hinged his feet to the floor because of the seriousness of his crime."

"Deuce, they had no reason to. He'd been a model prisoner, and sat calmly during the whole trial barely even looking up. We fear that type of outcome every trial. It's part of being a prosecutor." She took a deep breath before going on. "I saw him back at the café looking in the window."

"You think he's in Kasota Springs?"

"I know he is. I only saw his face, but he has eyes that you'd never forget. Haunting, black, and murderous."

"Then why in the hell didn't you tell me right there and not rush out of the back door? You could have run right into him." His expression turned from showing immense anger to a semblance of sympathy.

"Deuce, I was just so scared that I couldn't even think straight." She fought back tears, refusing to allow him see her cry.

"This town is so small that when a person sneezes on North Main, they are blessed by someone on South Main. I haven't seen any strangers. Maybe it's someone who just looks like him?"

"No! It was him."

"He was convicted, so isn't he in custody?"

"Institutionalized at San Quentin." Rainey took in air to allow time to scrounge up enough intestinal fortitude to give Deuce as many of the details as she could stand to relive.

Tales of how the defendant's attorney used an insanity ploy to get the death penalty off the table resulting in Hunter's being incarcerated for the rest of his life spilled out.

After concluding, she felt drained, exhausted, and empty. She closed her eyes hoping to erase the images, knowing it never worked.

Rainey wasn't sure she could corral enough nerve to explain her nonexistent, yet dead husband, but she must.

And she did.

Once finished, she was as relieved as if she had shucked off a concrete overcoat. The truth really did set her free.

"Damn, Rai." Deuce clenched his fist again. "I'm furious at myself for not trusting you and forcing you to improvise such a cockamamie story."

"You didn't make me do anything. I did it myself. All I had to do was tell you the truth. I'm not a very good liar, am I?"

"Nope. Do you have a safe way to contact the DA?"

"She's the only one in LA that I can trust. But I agreed if she helped me I wouldn't bring her into my problem by making contact."

"Why didn't you go into the witness protection program?"

"And live the rest of my life fearing that every knock on the door will be a man handing me a new identity? Worry that every time I see a moving van, they're coming to take my things away? I won't live that way."

"But you're living a worse existence now," Deuce said, as more of a statement than a question. "We need to find out whether this man is still safely behind bars. I'll do that myself."

Deuce pushed his chair back and walked toward the exhausted woman. He pulled Rainey to her feet and scooped her into his arms. Smoothing her hair, he kissed the top of her head. "I can protect you, if you'll let me." He nuzzled his chin against her hair. "Don't leave. You need rest, so I'm taking you out to the ranch until I can check this man out. You'll be safe out there."

"I can't promise I'll stay, but I'm too emotionally drained to leave." Against her skin, his body felt hard and warm. She wound her arms inside his jacket and around his back, hugging him. Relaxing, she sank into his cushiony protective embrace. "I'm sorry I lied to you. I just didn't know who to trust, so I chose to trust no one."

"I wish I could say it's okay, that it doesn't matter to me, but it does. I shouldn't have had to pry it out of you. You should have trusted me as an officer of the law and your friend."

"I'm truly sorry." Rainey slid her hands from beneath his jacket and touched his face, lightly tracing the cleat scar above his lip with her fingertips, brushing against his dark stubbly jaw. "I wish I'd done things different, but, Deuce, I never meant—"

"We're not all perfect." He covered her hand with his and pressed it to his cheek. "Everyone has their secrets and it doesn't change how I feel."

"Danny, patrol the road to my place. Stay near the house, but make sure Rainey doesn't see you. I don't want anybody near the ranch who doesn't belong there. She doesn't need to be scared again." Deuce gave the chief deputy his location and, as an afterthought, said, "Didja ever get a haircut? You know you're pushing the envelope on county regs with your long hair."

Cramming his fingers in his Levi's pockets, he headed up the walk leading to the Kasota Springs Nursing and Rehab Center. Tonight was no different than the other three hundred and sixty-four nights of the year, but for some reason he dreaded this visit more.

Maybe it was leaving Rainey alone at the ranch when she needed him. Scared of what he would find when he returned. Or what he might not find. He had to trust her. Besides, she was too exhausted to run. Not tonight at least. Hopefully, she was snuggled up on the couch drinking the herbal tea he had fixed for her. Or, maybe stretched out, relaxing in the hot tub. Wearing a— uh, what? She probably didn't have a bathing suit, so she'd have to wear the obvious. Yep, the whole five feet of trouble would be lookin' good, really hot with nothing on but deep dimples and lots of charm.

He sighed. The truth was, he only half expected to find her there when he returned home; although he'd talked to his foreman and asked him to watch the house. Damn, Deuce wished he could have stayed and taken care of her.

Even lusty thoughts of Rainey running around naked couldn't chase away Deuce's apprehension about this visit to the nursing home. Maybe he was tired of being brave. One thing certain, of late his brain seemed to spend a lot of time crammed in his pants.

On the outside, Deuce Cowan tried to be a tough, unflappable hound dog like his father, but deep inside he knew he was little more than a Maltese. Even at that, he couldn't allow himself to feel the pain. To think. He had to remain in control, try to understand, and do what was necessary, regardless of how much it hurt. And, oh, God, did it ever hurt.

Pulling up to his full height, he jerked his hands from his pockets, opened the door, and entered the lobby. He removed his hat and headed for Unit B and the long walk to room B-16.

"Good evening, sheriff." A pocked-faced, male nurse-tech, not much older than eighteen, shuffled past.

Deuce returned the greeting. Nearing the nurses' station, he halted.

Smiling, a stately perfectly groomed lady dressed in ice blue walked in his direction. "Sheriff Cowan, good to see you."

"Thank you, ma'am. Any improvement?"

The administrator, Elaine, hugged her iPad as if it were a child and turned stern, yet caring eyes up to him. "No. I'm sorry."

"I was afraid of that."

"Deuce, come to my office. We need to talk." She escorted him to the third office on the left and closed the door behind them.

After taking a seat across from him, she eased into a reserved smile. "You have no idea how I've dreaded having this conversation, but we both knew it would eventually become necessary. It's time to move her."

Deuce dropped his eyes and studied the pattern on the carpet. Why would they choose purple and yellow for a nursing home? He never liked the colors anyway. He knew he couldn't avoid making a decision any better than he could determine why someone used such awful colors for floor covering.

He forced his eyes upward, and met Elaine's gaze.

"It's okay, Elaine. I knew when I brought her here that it'd only be a matter of time until she'd need the next level of care, but I thought maybe it wouldn't be so soon."

"I'm sorry. With Alzheimer's, no one can really determine how the disease will affect a patient ahead of time. Even on a daily basis, experts don't know what to expect. We knew she'd need more specialized care and the time came sooner than we anticipated." A cadence of beeps sounded and she checked her pager. "I've got to go, but there's a new patch on the market and the doctor has started it. Maybe we'll see some improvement before you have to decide where to move her, but most likely she's too far advanced now for the patch to help. I'll keep praying that'll help her."

Another peep came from her pager and she pushed a button. "She roamed away from the facility again today. She doesn't like the location bracelet, but at least it notifies us when she walks out a door. We can't take a chance on her endangering herself."

"Where was she headed this time?"

"To watch you play football, little league. Yesterday, it was to have lunch with your father, and the day before . . . I don't even remember. But today was different. She's been extremely agitated and has been talking about people she's never spoken of before. Regressing. If only our facilities were more geared toward her needs . . ."

"You've done everything you can."

"Thank you. We've tried, but even today she became belligerent to her favorite volunteer and we now have to find a replacement. Someone who has just a few minutes a day to visit with her. But it has to be a person she likes. Alzheimer's patients can be receptive to one person, while another can cause them to become disoriented."

"That disappoints me because she really liked her Pink Lady."

"She did and the volunteer feels she has failed her. Deuce, I've got to go, but our social worker is available to help with a placement for her."

"Maybe I need to move her back to Denton or even Amarillo."

"There are several good facilities in both towns. Do you want me to wait on contacting the worker?"

"Give me a few days to think through all of this. I know she's in good hands here."

"Sure. I know it's hard, but it'll be okay." She stood and patted him on the arm. "Take all the time you need to gather your thoughts before you go for your visit. Above all, it's so important that you stay positive, no matter how hard it gets. She can sense things and we don't know what will set her off and what won't. She simply cannot be upset, so please just stay positive."

Deuce stared into space and wondered when hospitals stopped painting their walls drab green and began using brighter colors. It didn't matter. Nothing mattered. He sat silently for a while, then rose and trudged toward unit B-16.

Tapping on the door before he entered, Deuce watched as a frail, delicate flowerlike woman with closely cropped blue-white hair stood over a dresser drawer sorting and resorting clothing. Haphazard, disorderly piles surrounded her.

"Don't just stand there, young man," she said, as she tossed a nightgown on a chair. "Come in and shut the door. You're letting out all of the cold air, and you know how it can run up the electric bill."

"Yes, ma'am." Deuce closed the door. "What are you doing, Mom?"

"Tah, tah." She wagged an arthritic finger at him. "Not everybody gets away with calling me that, you know?" She peered up at him with dull, emotionless brown eyes. "Just my husband and my son." She picked up the gown, examined it, and stuck the garment under the bed. "If I didn't enjoy our visits so much, young man, you wouldn't get by with it either."

She moved to the bedside table, opened the drawer, and dumped the contents onto the chenille bedspread. Fumbling through personal items, she removed the pillow from its case and tossed the things one by one into the pillow slip. Once finished, she closed the fabric with a clothespin and hid the bag under the bed.

That's when he noticed. He recognized the dainty pastel print of one of her favorite housedresses hanging low beneath a white, cotton slip. A fuchsia sweater he didn't recognize covered her shoulders and she wore fluffy, purple slippers with men's dress socks. She had dressed herself again.

"Stop ogling me," she reprimanded him.

At the sharpness of his mom's voice, Deuce jerked his head up.

"Do you like my new sweater?" She touched the hem.

"Yes. It's very nice. Where did you get it?"

"Oh . . ." She stopped and pondered. "From my closet. Yes, it was in my closet." She shrugged her shoulders in defeat. "It's gone."

"Mom, what's gone? What are you looking for?"

"You know!" she snapped, indignantly. Waving her hands through the air, she walked to the closet and jerked open the cabinet. "That thing! I have it every day after dinner."

Deuce pulled a Butterfinger from his coat pocket. "Is this what you're looking for?" He presented the candy bar to her.

"Oh, yes!" She grabbed the yellow-wrapped treat. "Yes . . . you are such a nice man." Tearing open the end of the paper, she took a bite. "So much like my son. He's a nice boy, too." She looked up with a vacant look in her eyes. "Have I ever told you about him?"

"Yes, ma'am, you've told me."

"He plays football for Texas A&M and I think the Steelers, too. Aren't they a college team?"

Not bothering to correct her, Deuce gave her a weak smile, remembering Elaine's warning about not upsetting her.

"That's why he can't come to see me. But he would if he could." She blinked up at him.

"I know he would." The words dug at Deuce's heart. "Mom, what happened between you and that nice Pink Lady you always talk about?"

"None of your business, young man."

"Maybe I could help. Did she upset you or something—"

"You are certainly nosey, but I have no intention of getting her in trouble. I just don't want to see her again. How do you like my new sweater?"

"It's really pretty."

"I got dressed up today because I'm going to have a visitor."

"And who would that be?"

"Well, uh, they haven't told me, but I hope it'll be my son."

Like an old wound that ached on a rainy day, Deuce forced back a lump in his throat. Would he ever get used to this? He watched her eyes brighten.

In a fragile, hesitant tone, his mother asked, "You know Deuce, don't you?"

Chapter Eight

Deuce drove what seemed like a hundred miles back to the Slippery Elm, feeling as though he had been kicked out of Sunday school because he didn't know the words to "Jesus Loves Me." Despair gnawed in his gut and truly wretched thoughts of what he might find, or worse, wouldn't find when he got home tore at his core. He couldn't stand another disappointment. Not tonight.

In the distance, the ranch house came into sight. Darkness permeated the house. Except for the steady drone of cicadas, the grounds shrieked of silence.

Deuce sighed in relief. The Malibu was in the driveway, but then that didn't mean Rainey was still there. Stubborn Miss Sassy-butt could have set out on foot and hiked cross-country to get away. To avoid what? Or who? Was it really Hunter who terrified her? Or could it be something else? Someone else?

Easing the county pickup to a stop behind the Chevy, the ring of his cellular phone quickly replaced the engine's hum. He glanced at the lighted screen. "Caller Unknown" flashed.

"Oh, hell," he mumbled before answering. "Sheriff Cowan."

To his surprise the Los Angeles County DA Judith Mason identified herself and without formalities began an interrogation, starting with the reason for his department's interest in the Alonzo Hunter case.

Seemingly satisfied the motives were strictly professional, she barged on. "So you're the Deuce Cowan that Maressa so fondly spoke of?"

"Miss Mason, I'm certain that if she spoke of me at all it wasn't fondly." If there was a feed yard within smelling distance, Deuce recognized bullshit, and he was already up to his hips in it.

"She spoke most highly of you, sheriff. But you sound much too young—"

"I can assure you that I am Deuce Cowan, but I'm sure she was speaking of my father."

"Oh, then you're the *other* one?"

Damn, he might as well be a two-headed rattler from her response.

Quit beating the devil around a stump, Cowan! After all, he had done very little for Rainey to talk positively about . . . except being positively the most knuckleheaded ass most of their school days.

"Yes, ma'am, I'm *the other one*. Dad was Denton County's sheriff, but died a few months back."

"I'm sorry," she rushed on, possibly embarrassed. "I apologize for calling so late, but it took awhile to talk to the warden at San Quentin—"

"And?"

"You can rest assured that Alonzo Hunter is still there. Safe and secure." She chuckled lightly. "Not all that sound I must admit, but certainly secure."

"But you didn't see him yourself?"

"Sheriff, the prison is north of San Francisco and it's seven hundred miles round trip. I can't drop things and rush off to reassure you that . . ." She methodically cleared her throat, corralling her obvious agitation. "I'm sorry, but I trust the warden."

Caution whispered, *Rainey doesn't know who to trust, so be careful, Cowan.* "Ma'am, I don't take a whole hell of a lot for granted, but I appreciate your efforts."

Shrugging off the lukewarm thank-you, she promptly changed the subject, rushing on. "Do you know anything about bonsais?"

"Those puny-looking scrappy trees?"

"That's certainly a unique way to view one. A word of caution, bonsais must be treated delicately; otherwise, they'll rebel and won't thrive. Give her a lot of TLC and be very careful not to suffocate her."

"You are talking about a bonsai, aren't you?"

"Of course," she said with a strange note to her voice. "I've become attached to a particular one over the years."

Deuce couldn't help but smile at the cryptic message in her words. "A bonsai can be a bit stubborn and a tad testy. Is that what you're telling me?"

"In more ways than you realize, sheriff, please take care of Mar—" Judith Mason halted in mid-sentence. "Uh, take care and have a good evening."

The phone went silent.

Deuce slipped the phone into his pocket.

Low light filtering from the upstairs guest bedroom caught his eye and kicked up his mood a notch.

Rainey was home.

Getting out of the car, he reached for his Stetson and in the process rammed his shoulder against the door frame.

"Sonofabitch!" Automatically, his hand massaged the tender area. Rain was on its way, as the tendonitis in his rotator cuff was more predictable than most meteorologists' forecasts.

A cold beer and the hot tub would help ease the pain.

Quiet welcomed him as he opened the front door. Deuce went into his office and slid the phone on the desk and locked up his service weapon. Hanging his Stetson on the coatrack by the staircase, he noted a stream of soft light escaping from beneath Rainey's bedroom door.

He grabbed his gray running shorts and Gold's Gym shirt from the dryer and changed in the laundry room.

From a bag of Meow Mix, he scooped up a serving. Deuce topped off the dish with an extra helping. Heck, Fat-Cat didn't get his name by drinking Slim Fast.

A pit stop at the fridge to pick up a Lone Star longneck, and he headed back to the front door.

"Here kitty, kitty," he called three times. "Damn it, Fat-Cat, where are you?"

Deuce refreshed the tom's water dish. *Didn't eat or drink much today. Guess you were off visiting the ladies*. Deuce chuckled and rounded the corner of the house.

At least one of them was getting some action.

Deuce seriously needed a visit with a special friend, too. He took a long draw from his beer, enjoying the cold liquid trickling down his throat. He strolled past a lilac bush bursting with sweetness.

Since getting the kind of workout he really needed wasn't liable to happen, Deuce would have to settle for some serious crunches. Exercise should ease the ache in his shoulder, as well as the one that seemed permanently implanted between his legs.

Flipping on the overhead light in the barn, he plopped down on the bench and aggressively began his routine.

Up one, down . . . hell, why bother keeping count? He'd work out until he was too exhausted to do anything but sleep. Besides he could use the time to think and sort out his feelings. And dang it if he didn't have plenty of new issues to work through.

Fat-Cat crossed his mind. It was unusual for that dern cat not to welcome him home. Where was he anyway?

Deuce winced. Holy crap, if Rainey tried to pick up the cantankerous bucket-of-lard, he'd scratch the daylights out of her perfect, satiny-smooth skin. Skin that smelled of lavender and vanilla. Skin ripe for a man's caresses just beckoning to be explored.

Sweet Jesus, corralling his testosterone had become a full-time job since Rainey's arrival.

That damn inner voice interrupted: *Hey, cowpoke! Remember, it ain't gonna happen.*

Up two, down—up three, down. He quickened his pace.

In the distance, as though challenged to match Deuce's increased tempo, the cadence of the cicadas' cry accelerated.

Deuce's mind wandered back to his evening with his mother and his conversation with the nursing home administrator, Elaine. Like a leech latched on to his heart, not letting go no matter how hard he tried, the pain was a permanent reminder of an uncertain future for his mother.

How long could he go on pretending that she was pretending not to know him? Surely somewhere deep inside she recognized him as her son? Surely she remembered giving birth to him? Protecting him? Surely?

Taking a deep breath, he curled tighter and faster.

It wasn't a pretense. The truth lay in her vacant stare, as she struggled to understand it herself. Eyes that asked questions. Pled for answers. Her illness was reality at its nastiest.

Deuce should be the child, letting his mother protect him . . . instead of the other way around.

Thank God, Deuce's father had taught him the need to be strong and to own up to his responsibilities. And never, never show fear.

But as his mother's illness dug in deeper, it had become more difficult to follow in his father's footsteps, fighting daily not to show how much he truly hurt.

He tucked his heartache away and tried to think of something more pleasant . . . the petite, pesky ray of sunshine that had waltzed into his life. Having Brainy Rainey to watch after felt kinda good, like finding a replacement for the hole in his heart that his mother's illness had plucked out. On the other hand, he didn't need a distraction. And boy-oh-boy, did Rainey ever distract him. Being around her was like trying to dance the do-si-do in a straitjacket.

A rambunctious libido had replaced logic. He had a job to do. To protect the woman, not bed her.

Once he was truly satisfied about Hunter's whereabouts, he could reassure Rainey of her safety and deposit her in her own little abode. Of course, he'd keep his promise and help her with the depot repairs. Once finished, he'd be free to send the little tart on her way. Then, except to tip his Stetson when he passed her on the street, he'd have no reason to be involved with her.

If Deuce really wanted her out of his life so badly, then why did his heart ache at the thought?

Soft music floated through the darkness. Deuce halted, listening before pulling into another crunch.

Through the serenity of the night, the sound of the door screen hitting the frame riddled his thoughts.

Deuce shot straight up.

What the hell! Was someone breaking into the house while he was holding a pity-party in his mind?

And Rainey was alone. Trapped in the upstairs bedroom.

In long strides, he hurried to the house.

A river of light flowed from the kitchen, shrouding a short, petite figure standing on the deck near the hot tub. No mistaking the slight woman with nothing on except tiny diamond stud earrings and an itty-bitty, flimsy swimming suit.

He squinted and took a second look. It wasn't a bikini at all, but sheer, clingy, flesh-colored underwear. The tiniest, laciest, and naughtiest bra and panties he'd ever laid eyes on, and brother, he'd seen his share of feminine, extremely sexy, and very arousing undergarments. Good Lord, what she wore was nothing short of something he'd expect to see in a Victoria's Secret catalogue.

Halting, Deuce stepped back into the shadows and justified his actions as not wishing to frighten the lady.

His brain had tee-totally gone on the fritz, and refused to signal his feet to move. His eyes feasted on her, as she lifted her arms above her head and stretched, exposing even more of her flat, silky-smooth abdomen. The delicate fabric tugged tightly against her breasts, causing them to plunge over the top of the bra in high mounds of delicate flesh.

Reality, Cowan. You like what you see! Dang, that tiny voice, probably his conscience, needed to go away and leave him alone. He was doing just fine without its interference.

Damn it, just as he scrounged up enough resolve to get the pint-size twerp out of his system, she did something to arouse his interest and draw him right back in. And there he was, a peeping tom, standing in the shadows, turned on, and gawking like a hypocrite hot-wired to smut. But it wasn't smut he watched, just a vision of yearning greater than anything he'd felt in a long time.

Rainey tested the water with her toes before stepping into the hot tub. Settling deep in the whirling water, she eased back and shut her eyes.

Deuce's heart jumped to his throat, causing him to gasp, not at the sight but at Fat-Cat who streaked out of the darkness and in one laborious leap landed on the edge of the hot tub.

The tomcat surprised Rainey, too. Her eyes shot open and she let out a giggle.

"Hi, big boy, I've been wondering where you were." She reached out and caressed the feline, causing him to extend his head to allow her full access to his chest.

Rainey exclaimed, "Enjoying that, huh?"

Deuce watched as the tomcat got his fill of scratching, and turned his attention to a bowl of something that looked pretty unappetizing, certainly not suitable for human consumption.

"I figured you'd be back for another treat." She spoke to him as one would talk to a small child. The animal stopped eating long enough to nestle the back of her neck with his nose in appreciation.

Man, if Deuce wouldn't like to be in that steamy, hot water with her, and it wasn't just his head he wanted to rub against her. But how in the heck did she tame the wild bad boy?

Damn, now more than his curiosity was aroused.

Judith Mason's words rang in his ear. ". . . but be careful not to suffocate her."

Giving Rainey privacy, he slipped from the shadows and made his way to the front of the house.

In his best police technique, Deuce crossed through the living room to the kitchen and gingerly opened the refrigerator door. After moving aside a Pyrex bowl of fried chicken livers, he snatched up another longneck.

Leaning against the sink, he took a long draw of beer and stared out the kitchen window. Just as he suspected, Rainey was hand-feeding the furry rascal that Deuce thought too barbarian for the likes of the lady.

Turning from the window, Deuce deposited his beer bottles in the trash basket and headed for the stairs, ripping off his T-shirt as he climbed. A hot shower would wash away the sweat. A cold shower would wash away his enthusiasm.

Thirty minutes later, Rainey silenced the TV when she heard Deuce's bedroom door close and his footsteps disappear down the stairwell.

When had he come home? What in the heck was that ornery Texan up to? She presumed he was out on a date. After all, a hunkster such as Sheriff Cowan would be a perfect candidate for an "all-nighter." She must admit that he was one hot cowboy and not even a blind woman could fail to see the way Mr. Testosterone swaggered in his confident fashion. The way taut denim hugged hard-bodied muscle, and his smile that was sure to leave a woman goggle-eyed, wanting to share more than a box of Junior Mints and a bag of popcorn with him. And she could only imagine what lay beneath those tight-fitting jeans.

If the mental pictures of Deuce didn't go to bed themselves, she wouldn't get a wink of sleep.

Slipping between the sheets, Rainey flipped between cable news channels before settling on one of the local TV stations.

Between the tranquility of the hot tub, a leisurely shower, and sinful fantasies about Deuce's, uh, hidden attributes, fierce flames smoldered deep in the pit of her stomach.

Deuce seemed comfortable about there being no strangers in town and had promised to verify the whereabouts of Alonzo Hunter. Considering there was nothing on the national news about a prison break, surely she could drift off to sleep. But first, the mental picture of the juicy hunk had to go away.

If only she could access the Internet, then she could find the answers about Hunter for herself. Tapping into the records systems that she was so familiar with would be easy. But her password would flag the transaction, and she'd be dead meat. There was no reason to take a chance of arousing suspicion. That is, if they hadn't already changed her password, which she had little doubt they had.

Let Deuce do his job.

Apparently, he hadn't confirmed Hunter's whereabouts or Deuce would have told her before he went out for the evening.

Until she knew for certain that the sadistic murderer was still behind bars, she would not totally let down her guard. She must presume the worst . . . he could be stalking her. Or worse yet, have someone on the outside do the dirty work as he had threatened when he was pulled out of the courtroom.

Suddenly, all the enchantment of the evening evaporated, quickly replaced with the troubled feeling that had become her constant companion.

Deuce was downstairs and she should go find out what he knew.

Recalling his disappointment because she hadn't trusted him when she first arrived in town, she recoiled.

No, she had given her word that she would trust him and that was exactly what she would do.

She had to trust him . . . but should she?

Chapter Nine

Wedged between a zillion fluffy, white sheep leaping an imaginary fence, visions of Rainey in her makeshift bathing suit kept Deuce awake. Fisting his pillow, he wadded it up and tucked the sucker beneath his head.

Sometimes the vixen was stark naked. Sometimes she wore a skimpy teddy with tiny, sheer panties. Sometimes the lingerie was hot pink; other times, passionate purple, but always sexy as hell and revealing a luscious, hot body.

He hadn't felt so primed in months, so why couldn't his urges cool their heels and patiently wait their turn? He had troubles that he had to resolve, beginning with deciding what to do about his mother, followed closely by Rainey's safety.

Dern it, thoughts of her crept up at the oddest times. But he still needed the lady in ways he couldn't explain.

Deciding sleep was impossible, he reached for the remote and switched on the TV, disturbing Fat-Cat—now known as The Traitor. Stretching out a country mile, the animal kicked up his purr a notch and curled closer to his master.

Deuce hadn't eaten. Maybe a glass of milk and some of the oatmeal-raisin cookies that he'd picked up at Winnie's Bakery would satisfy the empty hole in his stomach.

Rainey had turned off the lights and silenced the television hours ago, so he lay there imagining her cuddled deep into his comfy mattress. He questioned his intelligence by insisting that she sleep in his room while he took the guest quarters.

From the floor beside the bed, he seized his gray running shorts and tugged them on. Whether Rainey was asleep or awake, it probably wasn't a good idea to parade around in his skivvies which did little to disguise his aroused state just at the thought of her in his bed.

To hell with a shirt. It was his house after all.

Fat-Cat came alive and scampered toward the door. He entwined his furry body around Deuce's ankles, knocking him off balance.

Deuce found himself asking the tomcat why he wasn't sleeping with his new best friend. Beating his master down the stairs, the feline looked back as if to give Deuce the answer, "I'm hungry, too. Will you wake the lady and get me some liver?"

Deuce sauntered to the kitchen. Using the light of the refrigerator as a guide, he poured a tumbler of cold milk and retrieved three cookies from the tin. After wrapping the goodies in a napkin, he headed back upstairs.

As he stepped onto the landing, a soft, frightful cry came from Rainey's room.

The lawman in him sprang to life. He stopped to listen. Was she sobbing? A second louder moan called out in the night. Not a full-fledged cry but whimpering like a child dreaming about monsters under the bed.

Deuce eased the cracked bedroom door open. With the help of a full moon illuminating the room, he could clearly make out Rainey's silhouette on the bed. She tossed her head from side to side as though fighting a dream.

Fat-Cat shimmied past before Deuce could catch him, jumped on the foot of the bed, and with one cumbersome leap landed on the fretful woman's chest.

Surprised, she shrieked and shot straight up out of bed. The covers fell to her waist, exposing luscious, full, and oh, so tempting breasts with rosy nubs that immediately shot to attention.

Letting out a cry of relief, she picked up The Traitor, and nuzzled her face in his fur. "You scared the bejazus out of me, but you couldn't have come at a better time," she whispered in a broken voice, and began rubbing his head under her chin. "I could really use a friend right now." She clutched the cat closer.

That's when she saw Deuce in the doorway. "Deuce Cowan!" She tossed Fat-Cat aside and snatched the bedcovers over her bosom. "What do you think you're doing?"

"I, u-uh." Hesitantly, he shifted from one foot to the other realizing it wasn't just her nipples that stood erect. "Uh, here." He pushed the handful of cookies forward. "I brought you a bedtime snack."

"Will you throw me my top?" She motioned toward the ladder-back chair. "And, thanks for the cookies." Her voice sounded appreciative as she clutched the sheet tighter.

"Sure." Never taking his eyes from her, he eased toward the bedside table and set down the napkin and glass. Swaggering toward the chair, he retrieved his football jersey. "Here."

"Thanks." She caught the shirt in midair. "Turn around and close your eyes."

"Close them?" He turned his back and folded his arms across his chest. By damn, he'd keep his eyes open. So she wanted to play a game? To penalize him for making her shut hers when he disarmed the alarm in the depot.

Behind him sheets rustled and bedsprings squeaked.

"Okay. You can open them up and turn around." She flipped on the night light and eyed the cookies.

"What if I didn't close my eyes?" He faced her and wondered what she'd say if he mentioned that the thin fabric did nothing to camouflage her rigid peaks.

"What if I don't want any of your goodies?" She picked up a cookie and ran her stare from his chest to his knees and everywhere in-between.

"Then I'd have them all to myself." He had a difficult time dislodging his gaze from her breasts. But he did.

"Hum. Guess I'll beat you to it." Lazily, she traced her lips with her tongue before taking a slow, deliberate bite. Waiting until she swallowed, she said, "Thanks, it's been a long time since I've had cookies and milk in bed."

"Is everything okay?" Deuce wasn't sure where the conversation was heading, but obviously it wasn't toward Winnie's home-baked morsels.

"Why do you ask?" She took a sip of milk.

"I thought I heard you cry out."

"It wasn't a cry, it was— Well, I was watching an old movie." Tiny dimples at the corner of her mouth deepened, as she fiddled with the cookie.

"A silent movie?"

"I'd just turned off the TV." As any good lawyer would, she expertly shifted focus to another subject. "I thought you had dinner plans and wouldn't be coming home."

When she looked up into his eyes for the first time he noticed her swollen eyes and dry lips. He'd been schooled on PTSD and suddenly he recognized the symptoms. Why in the hell hadn't he seen the signs?

He forced his mind back to her question. So his being out for the evening gave her free rein to parade around in her underwear? And he was the one worrying about making her feel uncomfortable going downstairs half dressed?

"Something came up," he answered. *You waffle and I'll unwaffle, lady!* "So, what movie made you cry?"

"I wasn't crying. It was an old, uh, *Tarzan*. One with Ron Ely." She twisted the cookie between her fingers. "You know he went to school in Amarillo, don't you." It was more of a statement than a question.

"And the University of Texas, where you went." He would not let her change the subject. "Then you were able to relax, unwind, and enjoy a movie while I was gone?"

"Yes—yes, I did." Much as he suspected, she twisted the truth.

"Rainey, I have an update on your perp, Hunter."

She stiffened and returned the uneaten cookie to the lamp table. "Oh, God, I hope it's good news."

Business replaced their Me Tarzan—You Jane routine.

"I got confirmation that Hunter's still incarcerated in San Quentin."

"Thank goodness, Deuce." As though the words released her, she sprang off the bed, encircled her arms around his waist and hugged him tightly. "I'm so relieved."

Rainey released him temporarily only to gather him against her a second time. "I could kiss you right now."

"What's stopping you?" He squirmed and enjoyed her warm breasts rubbing against his arm.

Pushing up on her tippy-toes, she slipped her hands behind his head, and threaded her fingers through his hair, clinging to him, making him zestfully aware of her sensual body molded against his.

"Like this?" She pressed a fervent kiss to his lips.

For what seemed like an eon, he stood rooted in place. Without warning, impatient moans tore deep from his throat and he wrapped his arms around her waist, lifting her higher, tighter, deepening the kiss. She tasted of milk, cinnamon, and oh, so sweet sugar.

Every inch of her body melded against his. Desire fisted in his gut and boiled in his blood, intensifying the ache he already had way down south. Damn, he had to fight off the temptation to slip her a little tongue, wary that she'd whack it off with her snappy mouth and razor-sharp words.

Rainey's heart thudded out of control and then settled back to its natural rhythm. Shocked at her too eager response, delightful shivers circuited her body. She felt his arousal pressed against her leg. Hard, hot, and hungry.

Giving out a strange, almost sad little murmur of surrender, his tongue began a slow exploration, delving deeper, fuller, and searching.

Unprepared for the ripples of pleasure that radiated through her as he skillfully intensified his kiss, she locked herself in his embrace. Excitement sizzled along her nerve endings and she shut her eyes in a futile attempt to cope with the overload of sensation.

Drunk by his nearness, she felt his touch on her thigh as he eased the hem of her nightshirt out of the way to take possession of her yearning breasts, outlining the tips with his fingers.

In awe at the wonderful feel of his hands on her body, she opened her eyes. Heat washed up her neck and exploded in her cheeks as she found him staring at her.

Deuce's body was like molten rock against hers. She slipped her hands up his torso, running her fingers through the curly dark hair. Exploring, she stroked one nipple, then the other, until they stood in hard peaks against her palm, marveling how silk-over-steel solid he felt. She couldn't get enough of him . . . of his body. No more would she be a stranger to his thick shoulders, strappingly muscled chest, and flat belly.

He cupped her face in his hands and kissed her again and again until she was wrapped around him, her hands clutching his back, her legs twined with his, her hips drumming against him.

His breath, warm and moist, washed over her skin.

Releasing her, he held her gaze and slowly removed her nightshirt, dropping it to the floor. Cupping her breasts in his big, warm hands, he circled the rosy tips with his thumbs. She didn't want him to ever stop as she fell under his spell. He slid his mouth along her collar-bone, the motion brushing his cool, silky hair over her sensitized skin at the same time his clever fingers stroked her torso.

Instinctively, her body arched toward him.

Flesh against flesh.

Man against woman.

"Sophomore year, topsy-turvy dance." She enjoyed the way he rubbed the bare skin of her back and shoulders.

"What?"

"Sophomore year. Don't you remember the Sadie Hawkins Dance that you asked me to?"

"I certainly did nothing of the kind." She slid her fingers across the muscular chest wall ever so slowly. "I could hardly stand to talk to you much less dance with you in those days."

"Too bad about that because I would have gone, if you'd asked."

"Oh, yeah, you would have sandwiched me between you and ol' what's her name—"

"I can't remember." His hands were softer than she expected as he explored her waist and hips over her panties.

"Oh, but I do. Allura something or other," she whispered.

She watched as he lowered his dark, curly head and flicking his tongue on one and then the other breast. "If you say so," he mumbled.

Gasping, she arched her back as he suckled, gently at first and then with increasing pressure, the rhythmic pull and release caus-ing a corresponding throb that grew increasingly more difficult to ignore.

"Rainey, are you sure this is what you want?"

With her finger to his lips, she silenced any future question.

Without words, she answered with a kiss as challenging as it was rewarding.

He pulled away and raised a questioning eyebrow. "You're positive?"

"Tarzan doesn't like Jane?"

Deuce switched off the table lamp. "Oh, yeah, Tarzan likes Jane." He laid her back on the bed and covered her with his body.

"Show Jane, Tarzan." She teased his lip with tiny bites.

Pulling to his feet, standing over Rainey, Deuce thunder-pounded his chest with his fists. "Me, Tarzan. You, Jane." He leaped at her, pivoting his lean, rock solid body onto hers, but in the process accidentally tackled Fat-Cat, sending him into a frantic frenzy.

The cat bellowed louder than Tarzan and shot straight up, landing on Deuce's shoulder. The tomcat clung for dear life as Deuce sprang out of bed.

Fat-Cat clawed his way down Deuce's back and over his hip, landing with a thud on the ground. All four legs moved at once on the wooden floor, but the cat didn't move an inch. Finally getting traction, he fled for safety.

"Sonofabitch!" Deuce reached for the first thing he could get his hands on to throw at the critter, who hauled ass down the staircase. Rainey's sandal slammed against the door facing, slid across the hall and stopped at the wall.

Warm blood bubbled up along the jagged scratches.

"Holy cow, Deuce!" Rainey scrambled to her knees. "He got you good." Grabbing his arm, she turned him to her in one swift movement, checking for damages on his shoulder and back. And there were plenty of them. Blood trickled a path from the middle of his shoulder blades to his hip.

"Coward." Deuce bellowed in case the dern cat was in earshot. He ran his fingers over his shoulder and touched the thick, crimson mess.

"Don't yell at him." She grabbed his jersey and slipped it over her head. "You scared him."

"I scared him?"

"Yes, you did. You have a lot of claw marks, but nothing looks too deep," Rainey said, as though that made a difference.

"Damn cat." Deuce wiped his bloody fingers on his shorts. "Don't frown at me, they can be washed."

"Blood isn't easy to get out of cotton. Let's get to the bathroom and doctor you up."

"Forget the scratches." He reached for her hand and tugged her back toward the bed. "I'll live."

"And get an infection? No way. I've got plans for you, mister." She planted a row of kisses along his shoulder blade. "And it involves you on your back, so let's get the doctoring over with first."

"Peroxide's in the cabinet." He relented, following her into the hall, only to see Fat-Cat standing at the head of the stairs, quizzically peering up at him.

"You have some nerve," Deuce barked, causing the feline to scamper away. "Damn it to hell, I wish I didn't love that little bastard so much." Following Rainey into the bathroom, he continued. "In my line of duty I expected to get assaulted one day but never by my own cat."

Rainey dumped out a supply of cotton balls next to a brown bottle of peroxide, found a clean washcloth and went to work, dabbing away the blood with clear, soapy water.

Deuce jumped when the first shot of cold liquid hit him. Damn, the best chance of getting some uh, physical relief that he'd had in weeks, and then to be interrupted in such a libido-wrecking fashion by an animal. He wanted to be the only animal in Rainey's bed. And the worst part, he didn't dare tell anyone. What teasing he'd get. Jessup and Danny would be the worst. Nope! Way too embarrassing. Big tough sheriff whooped by his own kitty!

And to think it was only an hour earlier that he thought about taking a cold shower, but now, cold milk seemed much more appropriate. "Hey, let's go down to the kitchen and get some fresh cookies and milk."

"In a little bit. But now, I want to put some Corona ointment on the worst scratches. It'll slow up the bleeding."

She tended to a particularly nasty scratch on his chest and applied the medication liberally. *What a set of touchable, kissable, hard to take your eyes off pecs!*

Presenting a case in her mind, she argued against falling back in bed with this man. Although she had known him since play school, she really knew little about his adult years except his escapades as a football star. And casual sex wasn't her bailiwick. But then there wasn't much casual about how his body felt pressed against hers. On second thought, maybe casual sex wasn't such a bad idea. No promises. No commitment. No baggage.

Deuce interrupted her thoughts before she finished arguing her case against why she shouldn't go directly back to the lawman's bed. The jury was still out.

"You've cleaned and put salve on each scratch twice, so let's take up where we left off," Deuce said.

The verdict was in. She couldn't just jump in bed with Deuce again. Logic took over. "I've got to be at the depot early in the morning. Thanks, but I need to go to bed—alone."

"Rainey, you should know the rest of what the DA told me."

Chapter Ten

Deuce's words cut Rainey to the core. Cold chills ran up her spine and she was almost scared to find out what he'd learned.

She tossed the blood-soaked cotton balls into the trash can before she found the words to respond. "Please tell me that she went up to San Quentin."

"She didn't."

"Damn it to hell!" The revelation staggered her. She closed her eyes. In a couple of seconds she composed herself enough to propel the soiled washcloth into the hamper. "I was afraid of that. Then we can't be sure he's still there?"

"Rainey, she's so certain that I think you should trust her. But there's something else that's bothering me."

"What?"

"It's about the guy you saw at the café. Since Hunter seems accounted for, is there anyone else who might have it in for you?"

"I'm a prosecutor, Deuce. Fifty percent of San Quentin wants to see me dead and the other half wants to help."

"Point taken. I just wished the woman had confirmed it for herself."

"So do I. The whole nightmare makes me second-guess everyone around me. But Judith stood solid, even putting her job on the line for me. I have no reason to think she would lie to you. But do you think something went awry and the warden brushed off her inquiry?"

"You watch too much *Law and Order*. It's fiction, honey. Relax. There has to be someone around who just resembles Hunter." He tucked her close to him. "Let's make a pact. I'll worry about Hunter and you can concentrate on the good things. Your new business and plans for the future."

Her business. The future. Both sounded great to Rainey, although she wasn't all that sure that regardless of how hard she tried if she could put her worst nightmare behind her. She had no reason to think Hunter was not in prison and she could be happy with the possibilities of Deuce being a temporary—dern it, even a permanent fixture in her life.

Suddenly another thought stabbed her well-being. Hunter had threatened that he'd have someone on the outside do the dirty work for him. . . . She was not out of danger, even with the maniac in San Quentin.

Deuce took her arm and guided her to the living room.

Although it was late spring, the night was cool enough for a fire. In short order, he had orange flames dancing in the fireplace. Deuce settled next to Rainey on the couch and put his arm around her shoulders. "That'll cut the chill a bit."

She relaxed, sinking into his warm embrace. Having him nearby eased her worry some. "Deuce, just being able to talk to you about this nightmare is such a relief." Her hand rested on his thigh. "I feel so safe when I'm with you."

"I know where you could feel safer." He nibbled on her ear, planting a row of kisses down her neck.

"In your bed?"

"Good suggestion." He laughed just as his cell phone rang in the distance. "Damn it."

He kissed her lightly on the forehead and retrieved his iPhone. Checking the caller ID, he quietly said, "I have to take this," before answering. "Hey lady, I didn't expect to hear from you tonight. What's happenin' in Amarillo?" He ambled into the darkness of the kitchen.

Silence hung in the air as he obviously listened to the caller, before responding. "Sounds great, but I can't wait much longer. I've got to get some relief." He stopped to listen. "I've had things to deal with or you know I would have been there."

He moved deeper into the darkness, lowering his voice, but not to where Rainey couldn't hear. "As bad as I need it—" He quieted, apparently listening. "I know, but, sugar, I'll be okay until I can see you." Again he waited. "I know it's been weeks."

Again, silence from the kitchen.

Rainey tried to busy herself by fluffing a corduroy accent pillow and tried not to watch Deuce, but failed miserably.

"Allura, stop nagging. I'll be there as soon as I can fit you in and you know you're the only one who I trust—" His voice faded, losing its steely edge.

At hearing the name "Allura," Rainey's blood started to boil. Surely not *that* Allura! How many hot-to-trot ex-cheerleaders who spread her legs for more than a cheer were named Allura? And now she lived only sixty miles away in Amarillo.

Rainey closed her eyes and tried to check her fledgling feelings. Something clicked in her mind. Deuce had been playing with her, while thoughts of his ex-girlfriend controlled his cravings. No wonder the Sadie Hawkins dance memory came out of the blue. But then the man had always been drawn to the flirty-skirty bimbo like a weasel to a chicken coop.

The sound of Deuce at the refrigerator made Rainey open her eyes. She glanced in his direction, observing that he was listening to the person on the other end of the phone.

"Thanks, hon," Deuce finally said. "It's been way too long, and I'm definitely ready for one of your special treatments. Next time, promise I'll pay double." The light from the refrigerator cast a soft glow across the kitchen floor. "Yeah, I know you'd never charge me, but after all business is business."

Had the prettiest girl in the class, the one voted most likely to succeed, gone from being a dime tramp to a dollar hooker? And Rainey had nearly lost control and given herself to one of Allura's playthings.

Thank goodness for Fat-Cat, who saved her from making the biggest mistake of her life—having sex with a pretty playboy who seemed to have the philosophy that if he couldn't be with the one he loved, he'd love the one he was with.

Rainey rose from the couch and marched to the bookcase. Switching on the iPod, George Strait crooned through the speakers about all of his ex's living in Texas. She switched off the music and opened a bound volume of *The Outcasts of Poker Flat.*

"Did you ever read Bret Harte?" Deuce's voice called from behind.

Warm, needy lips seared a path down her neck, her shoulders. The harder she tried to ignore his caresses, the more insistent his kisses became, making it difficult to drag herself back to sensibility.

She clapped the book shut. "Sure, he's classic. Wrote about the rude, lawless Gold Rush days and wild-woolly women. . . ." She shelved the book. "Exactly what I'd expect to interest you."

"Come here." Deuce tantalized her shoulder with kisses, while slowing backing her across the room toward the couch. "I've been thinking."

"I have, too, Deuce." She slipped to the couch, putting a distance between them. "Upstairs you asked if I was positive about what we were doing and I said yes."

"It wasn't exactly in those words, but I got the idea—"

"I'm positive, but not like you think. I'm positive it'd be a big mistake."

"And now you tell me?"

"I'm not even sure if I should stay in Kasota Springs. I don't know where I'm going to find enough antiques to start up the business."

"Rainey, don't do this to us."

"Deuce, there is no *us*. We were on the verge of having a quickie under the cloak of darkness, and eventually we'd be sorry." She bit at her lip. "It'd ruin our friendship."

"I had no intention of it being a quickie, Rai." His meaning was unmistakable. "We can make it work."

"I'm not sure what I want, but a midnight interlude isn't it. Maybe I should go to Europe and be with my parents. I've got to have my space." She stared at the fire watching the flames leap and flicker.

"Before you go that far, give this some thought." Deuce went on to tell her that he had a friend that was selling out his hardware store in a nearby town and he could get his hands on some fixtures. "So all I have to do is give Robert a call and have the gondolas and display cabinets sent over here. He'll take pennies on the dollar. Then after we get the interior ready, we can focus on stock. I've got some ideas we can look at."

"There is no *we* in this deal. I don't need your help. And something else, since I have no other place to go at the moment, I want to pay my own way." She stopped and glared up at him. "What will you charge to rent your extra bedroom?"

"Damn it, Rainey!" His voice was rough with agitation. "I'm not charging you."

"Just like Allura isn't charging you." She yanked the throw pillow up and gripped it between her hands.

"You heard that?"

"I wasn't eavesdropping, if that's what you think."

"You've got it all wrong—"

"That hussy isn't the issue." She tossed the pillow aside. "You have every right to your private life and so do I. I will pay my way or won't stay." Crossing her arms, she continued, "And you can go your way and I'll go mine."

"This is stupid. One minute you're in my arms and the next you're as far away as the International Space Station."

"Let's get one thing straight, Cowan . . . if I stay, I'm your renter, *not* your girlfriend, *not* your lover, and certainly *not* a midnight fling," she said in a crystal-clear voice, hoping she'd made her point just as clear. "I want my privacy and nothing like what happened tonight will ever happen again. Understand?"

"That's the craziest thing I've ever heard of." He ran his fingers though his hair. "What in the hell did I do wrong?"

"If you don't agree, then I'm leaving." Defiantly, she came to her feet and took a threatening step toward him. "Tonight!"

"And just where will you go?"

"As much as I'd hate to do it, I'll go to Europe and spend time with my parents or I'll stay in the depot in my new sleeping bag."

"With no hot water and someone possibly after you?" He glared at her, but had a quirk at the corner of his mouth.

Without warning, Deuce stepped toward her. Clasping her to him, his mouth swooped down to capture hers, allowing passion within her to explode.

As abruptly as he took her into his arms, Deuce released her. "That can be the first month's rent—"

With his obviously quick responses, Deuce caught her wrist in one hand and avoided having the daylights slapped out of him.

"That's a low blow, Cowan." She tried to keep her voice calmer than she felt inside.

"Yeah, it was. Sorry." He stiffened as though she had struck him. "Have it your way." Shrugging, he continued, "You can stay under your terms."

Rainey settled back on the sofa next to Fat-Cat. "And one more thing."

"Geez!" He threw up his hands in defeat. "What?"

"I know you've got the ranch under surveillance."

"Affirmative and it is not open for compromise. A deputy stays— end of discussion." The look on his face made it clear that the issue was not up for debate. "There will be eyes on your every move, so get used to it." A muscle quivered at his jaw. "And you'll get all the room you need."

"Deuce, please understand. I just need to do this myself. I have to have space."

"If you want to be my roommate until the depot is habitable, then fine. It'll cost you fifty dollars a week. I prefer cash and if I'm not around when the rent comes due, leave it on the kitchen table. Or better yet—give it to the cat, since you seem to favor him over me." His tone was saturated with sarcasm. "By the way, the Fat-Cat eats Meow Mix, not chicken livers."

"Tell him that."

Hearing his name, Fat-Cat rolled onto his back, stretched a full two and a half feet and seemed to smile up at his owner.

Deuce snarled back at the animal, snatched up his iPhone, and furiously pressed in numbers.

"Allura, I know it's late but things have changed. I've got some vacation time coming and Danny can take up the slack." He leveled an icy stare at Rainey. "If you can fit me in, I'll be in Amarillo first thing in the morning." Although he spoke to Allura, it seemed that he directed his comments to Rainey. "I'll be on vacation, so I'm flexible."

Without taking his gaze from her, he added, "I have nothing holding me here." He put his phone on the table, and said directly to Rainey, "Not any longer."

Chapter Eleven

Rainey closed Deuce's laptop computer, thankful that he'd given her the code to the Internet, so she could check out prices for shelving and other things she'd need to set up her antiques store. She had just finished checking for locations of nearby flea markets and thrift stores.

Continuing to sit at the kitchen table sipping on a cup of coffee, she tried to stay focused on the positive while shucking off the negative thoughts, which seemed harder and harder to do the longer Deuce was gone.

Ever since he'd walked out, she'd gotten little sleep. All she seemed to do was toss and turn more than most major league baseball pitchers. Now she'd gone and done it. Forced Deuce into the arms of his ex-girlfriend because of . . . what?

Jealousy?

How could she be jealous of something she didn't own? The answer was simple—she'd been just too damn independent all of her life. And maybe a tad stubborn, too.

Deuce's last words the night he walked out, after he grabbed his Stetson, then retrieved his Glock pistol from the gun cabinet and stomped to the door, rang loud in her ears.

He had turned on his heels and his stony lava-dark eyes flashed. "You want room?" He plopped his hat on his head. "Then, by God, I'll give you space." Running his thumb along the brim as a salute, he added, "And keep the door locked. Don't let anybody, and I mean anybody, in the house, even if you know them!"

It'd already been four days since Deuce had walked out of his own house. Both his Lincoln Navigator and red Ford F-150 Texas Edition pickup were in the garage. She had seen no evidence that either had been driven and she certainly hadn't seen hide nor hair of the stubborn lawman. No doubt he'd been in the ranch house at least once, since she found a set of keys to the front and back doors, along with a twelve pack of Diet Dr Pepper on the kitchen table.

Still no sugar. Had he not even noticed she used it in her coffee? No sugar, yet he bought Butterfingers by the boxes and obviously someone was eating them based on the amount that had disappeared.

But the strangest items of all, he'd left plant food specially formulated for a bonsai plant and a package of raw chicken livers

She'd lost count of the times she'd driven by the sheriff's department trying to catch a glimpse of him, if he'd returned to town. The county's club-cab pickup was never there, and she didn't have the nerve to stop and ask about his whereabouts.

Her only solace was her work at the depot during the day, which kept her busy cleaning. The thought of the amount of work left to be done brought her out of her musing.

It was already eight o'clock and she hadn't even put on makeup. Other than forcing herself to get up and check Craig's List on the Internet for items she could use in the store, the only other thing she'd accomplished was drinking two cups of coffee with sugar. Sugar she had purchased from the little store downtown, along with a small supply of groceries. Just the thought of eating at the café turned her stomach, although she had stopped and picked up a pastry at Winnie's Bakery. The lady who owned it seemed very nice and didn't ask any questions. It was a quaint little place Rainey felt she could go to and drink a cup of coffee without being stared at.

In short order, she finished retrieving her things at the ranch, and pulled up into the empty parking lot at the depot, prepared for another laborious day of work. All the way in, she looked for signs about garage sales but concluded that Kasota Springs was so small that they didn't have a lot of them and she really wanted to stay with true antiques not junk. She had been trained by Deuce's mother to know the difference between knockoffs and real antiques when she worked for her in high school. Mrs. Cowan was one of the most intelligent and savvy businesswomen Rainey knew. She would really like to see her, but with Deuce temporarily out of the picture, she realized that wasn't about to happen. Rainey sure could use Mrs. Cowan's expertise, but would have to go it alone. At least temporarily.

On the negative side of her thoughts, she had spent several hundred dollars more at Gideon's hardware store on a mop and bucket, along with several carts filled with cleaning supplies. She felt ashamed of buying all but one bottle of window cleaner and a case of paper towels, not to mention almost his full supply of buckets with handles on them. Maybe what she purchased would make it necessary for his supplier to come earlier to replenish his stock, thus delivering her futon. If wishes were dirty dishes, she'd have to stay in the kitchen all night long.

Beads of perspiration ran down Rainey's face as she mopped the huge floor.

The shrill of the alarm system startled her. Someone had opened the front door. Her heart was still beating faster than she thought possible by the time she turned to see who had entered.

"I'm sorry I scared you by just coming in," Sylvie said, apparently noticing the fright that Rainey knew covered every inch of her face.

"Oh, no, it's fine." Rainey disarmed the alarm, but stayed behind the counter so she could hold on to the ledge until her shaky knees settled a bit.

"I knocked and you didn't answer. Since the door was unlocked I just came in," said Sylvie who was decked out today in an outfit that Annette Funicello or Sandra Dee would have truly appreciated.

"Since this is such a huge place, I can't hear anybody coming in, so I've been setting the alarm to alert me. I hope it didn't scare you."

"No, not really. That's a good idea though." Sylvie shifted from one foot to another, making Rainey think maybe the pointed toed shoes were hurting the postmistress. "Is this a good time for you?"

"Perfect. I have to let the floor dry back behind the counter and I need to sit down and take a little break anyway." She motioned towards the card table and chairs before continuing, "I don't have anything in the way of refreshments except for a couple of cans of Diet Dr Pepper, but they are cold. Want one?"

"Sure." Sylvie sat down in one of the folding chairs. "It's my lunch hour. You received a piece of mail and I thought it might be important, so I wanted to bring it over." She handed the letter in a regular business envelope to Rainey.

She accepted the piece of mail and thanked the woman. Without glancing at it, Rainey tossed the envelope on the counter. It couldn't be anything important, since nobody knew she was in town; not even her parents, who were still touring Europe. It was too early for utility bills to arrive and she got little if any unsolicited mail since her name was an alias.

After opening two cans of soda, Rainey took the seat across from her visitor. "What's going on around town?" Rainey asked knowing that if there was any town gossip, particularly about her, Miss 1950 would know it.

"About the only new thing is that the bypass crews are about to leave town because they're nearly finished." Sylvie accepted the soda.

Rainey deliberately made small talk. "So how is the bypass going to affect Kasota Springs?"

"That'll cut off all the through traffic. People like Gideon, Pumpkin's, and Winnie's really depend on travelers stopping by on their way through town. A petroleum company has already built a big truck stop north of town along the bypass. It's gonna take a chunk of business away from the locals." She took a sip of her drink. "Then you add the Green-Mart that's planning on building a store once they buy the land, and Kasota might well become a ghost town."

"I know I'm new to town and really don't have any right to express my opinion, but I can't see Kasota Springs doing anything but prospering. It's the biggest little town I've seen in a while. And Green-Mart would never build a store where the company didn't think they'd make a profit."

Sylvie seemed to think over Rainey's conclusion before saying, "Gideon's store has been in his family for nearly a hundred years. He'll be losing his monthly income from the government soon because they're building a new post office down on Main. All of this together will ruin him and other small businesses just like his." She ran her finger around the rim of the soda can.

Wanting to change the subject Rainey asked, "You mentioned the other day that you have a special friend. Is it serious?" She didn't know Sylvie well enough to ask such a personal question, but the town gossip sure seemed to know a lot about things that went on around town.

"He's really special, but sometimes I wonder if he even realizes how much I love him." A strange look came to Sylvie's eyes. It appeared she was about to cry as she looked up at Rainey. "Have you ever been in love?"

"No." Rainey caught herself, almost forgetting her lie about a dead husband. She took a deep breath to rid herself of some of the fright she felt at the miscue. "Well, I should have said nobody except my husband." Not wanting to dive deeper into the subject, she continued by asking, "Are you happy about having a new post office?"

"Not really. I'm very comfortable working out of Gideon's. It was a little hard for me to accept at first, but he made me feel better by reassuring me that we'll always be friends. He's really a good man. A little gruff sometimes, but someone I really admire and would do anything for."

"That's good." Rainey thought back to their conversation at the café the day of Judith's press conference and how Sylvie tended to Deuce, even pouring him tea and goggling him as much as he was looking at the T-bone steak on his plate. Could it be that Sylvie and Deuce were an item? Could he be cheating on her with Allura? Or could it be something else?

Since the postmistress was seemingly immature and out of touch with reality, it would be very easy for a man to take advantage of her. She reminded Rainey more of a teenage girl with an infatuation than a grown adult. Maybe the whole "have a serious relationship" was one-sided.

Rainey knew Deuce well enough to know he wasn't a player and even in high school, although all the girls wanted to be his girlfriend, he only had one at a time, and sometimes nobody at all. As an adult, she still couldn't imagine him playing two women against one another.

Deuce always welcomed a challenge, on and off the football field, so she couldn't see him having anything but a friendship or even a protective relationship with Sylvie.

"Tell me more about what keeps you busy besides being the

postmistress, which I know is very time consuming." Rainey stopped conjuring up thoughts that always seemed to involve Deuce. The lawyer in her knew to shine the spotlight on Sylvie and that would keep her from asking too many questions about Rainey. Questions she didn't want to answer.

"Before I forget, I overheard Gideon talking to your landlord and I got the impression that as soon as you get the depot cleaned up and open for business that he's going up on your rent." Sylvie fidgeted with the ring on her finger. "I just thought you should know."

"I signed a six-month lease, so he legally cannot do that prior to thirty days before its renewal or he'll be in breach of our contract," Rainey commented, although she was a little skeptical as to why Sylvie had come to visit in the first place.

"You're so educated and talk like those lawyers I see on TV—"

Rainey interrupted her. "I did graduate from college and my father is a judge, so I guess that's where I got it from. In college, my major was communications. Did it to please him." She tried to smile while bile made her stomach turn over again and again. Obviously, Sylvie still believed Rainey was the missing deputy DA. Could that be possible? She thought Deuce had put a stop to that theory back at the café by telling Sylvie that he'd known Rainey for a while and she wasn't an attorney at all. But what was she? She had to think fast to come up with an answer because she knew she was going to have to explain her life before Kasota Springs sooner or later.

A secretary.

That's it.

A legal secretary and she fell in love with her boss . . . the lawyer. Edward Burlington Michaels, Esquire, who died in New York City. She faced the issue straight on when she said, "I was a legal secretary by trade and my husband was a lawyer." Relief flooded over her.

"Oh, I see. You said your father is a judge. What did your mother do?"

Rainey wanted so badly to say that she was a trophy wife who thought the country club could substitute for Sunday school, and being featured in the society page was more important than being seen at the movies, but instead she simply said, "She's a housewife."

"That's good. I had one of those weird families and I didn't even know who . . ." She trailed off, changing the subject again. "I guess your mama had time to do a lot of volunteering."

"Yes. A whole lot. Do you do any?" Rainey scratched her palm becoming inpatient with the Q & A session.

"I volunteer at the local nursing home and rehab center." The question seemed to upset Sylvie or that's how Rainey saw her reluctance to talk about it. So far, she had never seen Miss 1950 be so short on words.

"That has to be rewarding."

"It is, but when you lose a patient, it breaks your heart."

Hearing the sadness in her voice, Rainey said, "I'm so sorry. I can only imagine how hard it is to get attached to someone in a nursing home and then have to let them go."

Sylvie shook her head. "It does hurt especially when . . ." She trailed off again, leaving her sentence unfinished as she took a sip of her soda. "I know you're busy trying to get the depot open, but if you ever want to help out at the nursing home, I can talk to them about you being a volunteer."

"I think I'd like that, but right now, as you can see I'm up to my ears in alligators and have no idea why I wanted to drain the swamp in the first place."

Both women shared a laugh.

"Never heard that one before," Sylvie said with a smile on her face. The first real one Rainey had seen all afternoon.

"Gideon said to tell you that if you need anything to just let him know."

"So you and Gideon must talk a lot since the post office is in his store." Rainey was on a fishing expedition and didn't feel the least bit bad about it.

"I share everything with him."

"Since you volunteer, what type of hobbies does Gideon have?"

"Stamps mainly. First-day issues. I think he has a set as far back as the 1800s. And, of course, he loves rare books and has many in his collection."

"I love books and have read all of my life. What's his favorite?"

"Fitzgerald, Shakespeare, Faulkner, and especially Edgar Allan Poe. You know, the classics."

Almost like she remembered something she had to do, Sylvie stood, picked up both empty soda cans, and deposited them in the trash. "I've got to go. I need to get back to work. Let me know if you decide to do some volunteering at the nursing home."

She rushed to the door and then suddenly turned around. "If you haven't heard, the Internet is down all over town and they aren't sure when it'll be back up. Might be days." Without saying even a good-bye, Sylvie walked out.

Sylvie's sudden change of mood hung heavily on Rainey's mind as she punched in the security code. She leaned on the counter. Being perplexed at the changes was an understatement. As an experienced prosecutor, she had been trained to read people's actions and facial expressions. There was little doubt in her mind that the postmistress had come by for more reasons than to leave a letter that probably wasn't even important enough to be placed in Rainey's post office box.

The words *"I share everything with him"* rolled around in Rainey's head like marbles on a sheet of glass.

Sylvie was hiding something . . . but what?

Rainey checked the bonsai, then watered and fed it. Then she worked the rest of the afternoon and into the early evening, cleaning and painting, which gave her a lot of time to think.

After carrying on a one-on-one talk with Sylie, it was apparent the airhead persona she used was exactly that—a façade. She was no dummy by any stretch of the imagination.

Now it was Rainey's job to figure out exactly what Sylvie wanted to know or exactly what she wanted Rainey to know.

One conclusion came to her over and over . . . the woman had used a piece of junk mail as an excuse to come see her. But what was the real reason? Sylvie never asked about Deuce, except to reinforce her special relationship with someone and Rainey presumed it could possibly be the sheriff. How special was special?

That jogged Rainey's memory that she should at least look at the envelope, although it was going directly into file thirteen under the counter.

Rainey picked it up and saw her name in care of general delivery in Kasota Spring. But it was the ever so familiar postmark that held her gaze: San Quentin, CA, 94964. With shaky hands she carefully examined the envelope. It was identical to the ones that were sent to her while she was the LA County Deputy DA containing threats on her life.

Her heart raced out of control and she buckled to her knees, as she stared at the postmark. She couldn't bear to open the envelope. In a spontaneous response, she threw the letter as far across the room as possible and put her head in her hands.

The only person sending her mail from San Quentin would be Alonzo Hunter. . . . He had found her.

But how?

Chapter Twelve

Tears blinded Rainey and choked her. Just the thought of what the envelope held sliced open a new wound in her heart. She wasn't sure how much more fear she would have to endure. Not certain her legs could hold her upright, she literally crawled across the floor like a baby just learning to maneuver around and finally reached the letter. With a pounding heart and shaky hands, she examined the envelope again. Hunter's CDC number on the return address glared up at her as if smiling at her pain. She checked the postmark again; it read "San Quentin, CA, 94964."

She had prayed once she left LA that she'd never have to see the number which was etched with indelible ink on her memory.

If only Deuce was there, she'd have him open the envelope—but he wasn't, so she had no choice but to do it herself, just like she'd done too many times before.

Finally pulling up into a sitting position, she stared at the envelope for what seemed like ages. Part of her wanted to tear it open and read what was inside; yet another part told her to destroy it without even opening the envelope. It was meant to upset and hurt her. To show her that Hunter could have someone get to her regardless of how many times she changed her name or relocated. He had warned that he had people on the outside to do his dirty work for him, and this was proof.

Logic set in. She realized that tearing the envelope open instead of using a sharp instrument to slice the top would compromise the integrity of the piece of mail. If there was any trace evidence, she couldn't take the chance of destroying it by opening the item with her bare hands. If he had sealed the envelope with his tongue, there could be saliva residue that could be used to test for his DNA. *What if? What if? What if?*

Rainey continued sitting until she stopped shaking and allowed some of the uncertainties the letter brought with it to pass. She then slowly, as if testing her legs, pulled to a stand and made her way over to the counter where she had both plastic gloves and a box cutter.

After putting on the gloves, as if she were unleashing an unknown creature, she carefully used a new straightedge razor blade to slice open the top of the envelope. She hesitated and took a deep breath before she unfolded the white piece of paper.

She gasped with disbelief, as she stared at the letter.

Hunter had changed his methods for antagonizing her. The words had been cut out of what appeared to be a newspaper or book of some sort and pasted on a regular piece of paper that could have come out of any paper supply.

As hard as she tried, she couldn't pry her gaze from the words, which she read again and again feeling more nauseated each time.

TRUE!—nervous—very, very dreadfully nervous I had been and am; but why will you say that I am mad? The disease had sharpened my senses—not destroyed—not dulled them. Above all was the sense of hearing acute. I heard all things in the heaven and in the earth. I heard many things in hell. How, then, am I mad since I found you . . . and you should leave town now to stay one step ahead of me, YOU BITCH!

> *With fond memories of your*
> *green fearful eyes, AFH*

Every inch of Rainey's being shook like it had never done before. Dreadful, fearful images blinded her. The thought that Alonzo Hunter had found her tore at her insides.

Bile formed and she rushed to the bathroom to throw up. After she washed her face, she sat on the toilet for what seemed like hours.

Once her mind cleared enough to think with even a tiny bit of rationality, she searched for the meaning in his words. More fear than she thought possible stabbed at her heart. The words sounded faintly familiar, but she couldn't place them. Possibly, they were from one of his previous letters, but the DA had them in her possession. Although Rainey had read each of them, this one seemed different. Maybe he had deteriorated mentally in prison to the point of no return. A true madman had written these words.

Damn, if only the Internet wasn't down she could do some research about the words.

She made her way back to the counter and stood staring at the envelope. The everyday sounds of life outside of the depot gushed in through the cracks around the doorframe and batted at her frail being. She felt vulnerable and exposed like a young fawn on the opening day of deer season.

Her pulse beat erratically and she thought her chest would burst open. It was becoming more and more difficult for her to keep her raw emotions in check, but she did.

Slowly, with gloved hands, she put the letter back in the envelope. From a roll of plastic she had purchased to protect the floor when she painted, she carefully cut a nice long piece to wrap the envelope in, and then put it under the counter.

She now had more questions than a seasoned interrogator, but the one that seemed to always surface to the top was how Hunter had found her. This threat still felt different from the others. He'd never sent anything with the words pasted together. Most of the ones she'd received while he waited trial had been handwritten on a number of odd items. One from a page from the Bible, which all inmates were allowed to have. One on a page from a pleading involving his case. One typed. Even at trial his behavior of sending threatening letters to the prosecutor was not brought up, so that detail was never presented to the jury nor released to the public.

How did he smuggle a letter like this one out of the institution?

How did it clear the mailroom?

Probably just like the others. Under the guise of sending something to help in his appeal.

But the biggest question she had was how did he find her? She had told nobody in LA except for Judith Mason, her boss and friend, about her decision to disappear. And the DA never knew the exact plan, just that Rainey planned to walk away from Los Angeles. She immediately discounted her friend, since Rainey had promised she'd never bring Judith into her deception.

Then of course Deuce knew her real name, as well as her alias, but whether it made her a fool or not, she trusted him to keep her secret . . . or at least the part she'd told him.

The only other person who knew her alias was . . .

Suddenly her knees felt like they were about to buckle again, so she slowly and deliberately slid to the cold concrete floor and leaned against the stucco wall.

It had to be the son-of-slime whom she had trusted to get her a new identity. He knew her alias, but how did he know her whereabouts? She hadn't used her fake social security number or credit cards since before settling temporarily in New York. She had paid cash for everything.

Slowly realization came to her. The bastard had to be working with Hunter.

She grabbed her purse from the bottom shelf and went through it looking for the piece of paper torn from a legal pad that had the car lot's address written on it. Pouring the contents out on the concrete, she searched item by item, knowing deep inside she hadn't seen it since the day she moved into the depot.

Think, Rainy, think!

All she could remember was that the used car lot had the name Los Angeles in it and was located in East LA, which was like looking for a man named Smith in a town that big.

The chances of ever finding him without bringing someone in from LA to help would be next to impossible. *No, totally impossible!*

The only person she wished would walk through the door was Deuce. To have him hold her in his strong arms would provide much needed comfort, but that was impossible. She had made a promise to herself that she would not interfere in his life. A day or two before, she had come to the conclusion that he was spending some time in Kasota Springs based on the items he left every day on the kitchen table at the ranch. He'd even left her favorite pastry from Winnie's Bakery. For someone who hadn't remembered she used sugar in her coffee, she found it strange that he knew her favorite pastry. Other than stopping by Winnie's for coffee and Gideon's hardware store, and of course the ranch, she had made a point to keep to herself. Her only visitor at the depot had been Sylvie.

If only Rainey could go to the ranch for its security. But she was too scared to take the chance of getting in her car and driving out there this late. She knew she'd be safe once she got to his place, since Deuce had made it clear that he'd have deputies posted at all times when she was on his property. For such a small town, with limited resources she suspected, she felt guilty having a detail posted for her, yet once she got over being angry at the idea, it made her feel secure.

Rainey heaved herself from the floor and checked the lock on the door twice, then double-checked the security system to make sure it was set. She even went to where the old freight doors once stood and checked that the locks were secure.

Pulling the sleeping bag into the corner, she lay down. Using her sweater for a pillow, she curled up and tightened into the fetal position. She lay there for hours wishing she would hear from Deuce. She made sure her cell phone was within arm's length and prayed he'd call, so she could tell him what had happened. That her fears were real. She needed to tell him the full story. All she had told him was about the threats Hunter had made in the courtroom. She hadn't confessed that she'd been receiving death threats from him through the prison system.

Comfort set in knowing Deuce would understand.

Morning light peered through the high windows of the depot, waking Rainey. She'd gotten little sleep and when she sat up, dizziness made her nauseated.

Rubbing her aching neck, she figured it'd be days before the pain from sleeping on the cold, hard floor would go away. The nightmares had come fast and furious, never allowing her to have a moment's peace. It was as if she had drunk a fifth of whiskey the way she felt. Probably not eating and drinking only a couple of cups of coffee and a Diet DP the day before contributed to her feeling so badly.

In the bathroom, she washed her face, knowing she had to do something besides lie in her own fright. She had always been a confident woman, so just the thought of spending the night curled up in a corner fearing for her life wasn't in her DNA. Her father would be furious with her for acting like a four-year-old afraid of the big bad wolf. The person looking back at her in the mirror certainly wasn't the self-assured, go where angels feared to tread woman she'd always been.

She would not allow some degenerate to frighten her to death, but how could she not? The unknown was scarier to her than Alonzo Hunter.

In the distance, she heard her cell phone ring. Rushing to retrieve it, she nearly tripped over a mop bucket but got there before the call reached her default voice mail. She looked at the caller ID. Trying to add confidence she didn't feel in her voice, she answered, "Hello."

To her surprise, Deuce bombarded questions at her like fireworks on the Fourth of July. "Are you okay? Where are you? Did you sleep at the depot instead of the ranch?"

"Mr. Sheriff, I know you have a detail on me, so they should have the answers," she replied wryly.

"Damn it to hell, for once just answer my question," he barked. Then he softened his voice a bit before saying, "If you're in the depot, let me in. I'm outside."

She hoped her relief at hearing from the sheriff didn't show in her voice because she didn't want to give him an advantage over her fragile thinking. "Give me time to turn off the alarm and I'll unlock the door."

In less than thirty seconds, she faced Deuce Cowan, who pushed past her as if he were the one making the lease payments on the building. She figured in true fairness, since he trusted her with his house on the ranch, he could barge in her business any time he pleased.

"You look like hell. And probably didn't get a wink of sleep by the look of your eyes." His mouth was tight and grim and a muscle flicked at his jaw. "I know you think because you're an attorney you can outwit anybody, but that doesn't happen every time. Tell me what is going on." His brows furrowed as if to say *I'll know if you are lying to me.* "There's something wrong, so don't even try to pull the wool over my eyes."

Rainey couldn't bear to see the stern look on Deuce's face another second, so she turned toward the card table. "Let's sit down. I have something to show you." She got the letter from the counter, along with two gloves, and placed them on the table. "This came yesterday."

After confirming that the letter hadn't arrived in the plastic wrap, Deuce picked up the envelope and looked at the return address and postmark through the plastic. He narrowed his eyes slightly and his jaw clenched tighter. "Damn it to hell, doesn't anybody at San Quentin censor his mail? I thought everything was read before it's mailed."

"Like any other business, they have a lot of inmates and with the state cutting costs they probably don't have enough mail room employees to do more than scan them. Inmates know how to circumvent the procedure using outside sources. That's how they determined the threatening letters I received got through the system." She took a deep breath. "Only mail sent to their attorney is confidential and cannot be read."

"Wait a minute." For a tanned, outdoorsy face, Deuce's turned somewhat pale. "You didn't tell me about any letters, just that he'd threatened you in the courtroom."

"Deuce, I didn't know who to trust, so I kept that to myself. I figured if someone brought up any of the contents, it'd give me a clue as to who on the outside was behind them." The next comment was hard for her to admit. "I think that his outside person might be the sonofabitch I got the car and my new ID from." She should have been ashamed of using unladylike profanity, but the words came out without her even realizing it. "Maybe when I had to get a replacement insurance card someone there notified him. I don't know what to think or who to trust."

"You know you can trust me." Deuce jerked off his hat and ran his fingers through his hair. "Don't you?"

She nodded.

Deuce plopped the hat back on as if gathering his thoughts. "So what else haven't you told me?"

"That's everything, Deuce. . . ." She trailed off, trying to decide whether to fess up about not being a widow, but decided this wasn't the time nor the place. She'd have plenty of opportunities to tell him later.

"Okay," Deuce said. "I need to digest this, so let's go to the ranch and I'll read the letter, but I've got a call to make first."

He eyed her in such a way that she figured he didn't believe her . . . and he had every right to do so. But she'd tell him the full truth at the ranch, not the depot.

"That's fine. Let me get my purse."

Deuce made a quick call to Danny at the sheriff's department and told him to come pick up Rainey's Chevy and put it in the impound yard, because she'd be riding with him out to the ranch and he didn't want it left at the depot.

After disconnecting, Deuce said, "As soon as Danny gets here, we'll leave, so if there's anything you need until we can figure this out, be sure to bring it." He looked at her with clear, observant eyes, while putting the letter in his pocket. "I'll keep this for the time being."

As much as Rainey hated being dictated to, she was comforted to have someone else making the decisions for her. Although she needed to work at the depot to get it ready so she could begin locating shelving and antiques, reality told her that the ranch was the safest place for her. At least for the time being.

A no-nonsense knock rattled the door.

"Must be Danny." Deuce motioned for her to give him her car keys. "I don't think you've met him."

Rainey followed the sheriff and stood beside him while the deputy identified himself and Deuce unlocked the door.

When she saw the deputy, panic worse than anything she'd experienced over the last twelve hours or so swept over her. She remembered screaming as Deuce caught her in his arms.

"What the hell," he said.

Steadied by the sheriff, once she caught her breath, she said, "That's him, Deuce." She had to force herself to open her eyes, scared to death of what she'd see, but she finally did. "He's the man who was watching me at the café."

"Rainey, that's my chief deputy, Danny Scott." He settled her in a chair, then turned to the deputy. "Damn it to hell, I've told you a dozen times to get that damn hair cut and a shave. You haven't been working undercover for weeks." His jaw clenched. "So get it done . . . now!"

Danny looked sheepish and a tad frightened of the sheriff at the same time. "Deuce, I'll have it off by tomorrow, if I have to cut it myself."

"You damn well better," said Deuce. "Don't let me see you lookin' that way again, you hear?" He obviously wasn't asking a question but making a strong statement to his deputy.

The deputy nodded.

"Hellfire and brimstone! Why in name's sake were you looking in the window of the café?" Deuce's clear as ice water words left no room for discussion.

The deputy turned to Rainey. "Ma'am, I didn't mean to scare you, but I'd helped Deuce out on some of the investigation on you, so I wanted to see you for myself." He looked up at his boss, then back at her. "I probably shouldn't have done it, but I threw on a hooded sweatshirt so if I ran into Deuce he wouldn't be too mad at me because I hadn't found time to get cleaned up. I started to come into the café, but when I saw Deuce, I backed out." He glanced back up at Deuce, as if to say he knew he'd been pushing the envelope on keeping his scraggly look, while at the same time asking for forgiveness.

So, Mr. Sheriff, you've been investigating me!

Obviously, he'd done so before he had seen the news conference on television. No wonder he was so quick to explain away who she was—or rather was not—the missing DA from Los Angeles.

She should be mad as a rattler with a toothache, but she couldn't find herself being angry with Deuce for doing his job. If he hadn't checked her out, then he wouldn't have been executing the law he'd sworn to uphold—protecting the town's citizens. Instead of being upset, she forced herself to admire him as a lawman.

Finally taking control of her thoughts, Rainey softly said, "What's done, is done. It's okay. Apology accepted. I shouldn't have overreacted." She looked straight into Deuce's face.

Deuce picked up the Chevy keys and tossed them to Danny. "It's to stay there until I personally release it. If anybody asks about it, just tell them to see me. End of discussion."

Rainey sensed a tad of rebellion coming from the look on the deputy's face, but he simply said, "Yes, sir."

As soon as Deputy Scott was out of earshot, Rainey lashed out at Deuce. "I know you didn't investigate me after you saw Judith's news conference, so that means you started when I first got in town. That's dirty pool," She said with easy defiance. "You asked me what other secrets I've kept from you . . . well, Mr. Lawman, I damn sure could ask you the same thing."

Chapter Thirteen

In short order, Deuce had gotten Rainey settled into his black-and-white, then drove by the sheriff's department impound lot to make sure her Malibu was there. To his surprise, Danny had almost hidden it from view. Smart deputy! He only wished the man were sharp enough to get the message about cutting his hair, but then credit where credit was due—he was certainly smart enough to serve on the special crimes task force.

They passed under Interstate 40 and caught the Farm to Market Road that would take them to the road leading onto Slippery Elm ranch land. To the east, a wind farm came in view, while to the west a herd of Herefords grazed in a lush green field.

Rainey was the first to break the silence. "Your deputy seems very nice."

"He is, but frustrates me at times." He shook his head. "Sorry you had to hear our exchange, but it's been weeks since he came off of an undercover assignment and I think he really just wanted to see how far he could push me with the hair." He glanced over at Rainey, knowing the truth was that he was simply furious with Danny for scaring the living hell out of her more than any haircut. "It really pissed me off when I found out he was the one who had scared you at the café."

"I was being sincere when I accepted his apology. I should have never been that edgy where he'd scared me in the first place. You said he'd just finished an undercover assignment. I would think in a town as small as Kasota Springs he couldn't pull it off without being made."

"It wasn't in Kasota, but he's on a multicounty major crimes task force, and with his naturally seedy-lookin' eyes, even when he's cleaned up, he's a natural for the job." Deuce chuckled. "Not to make light of it, but he fooled you."

For the first time in a lot of days, he heard her laugh like she was enjoying herself.

As they turned onto Deuce's ranch land, she asked, "You said the Jacks Bluff is on one side of you, so who owns the spread next to yours?"

"We're pretty much surrounded by the Jacks Bluff, but the Sullivan Ranch is on the other side of the road, although it winds around a little."

"I remember the Jacks Bluff as stock contractors. Everybody in Texas did. Is it still in the LeDoux family?"

"Yep, sure is. Five generations. Came about when this part of Texas was settled around 1875 or so." He kept his eyes on the road, watching for any wayward cattle that had broken through the fence, although he doubted he'd see any. His foreman was very good at his job, and Deuce was fortunate to have wrangled him away from a much bigger operation.

"I met a couple of the LeDoux girls, years ago. One was a Johnson I think, but can't remember her first name."

"McCall," Deuce added.

"That's right, and the other one was a LeDoux. I remember her name because it was so unusual. Mesa—Mesa LeDoux. What happened to them?"

"McCall married a rich dude out in California."

"A tycoon, he'd be called in Texas, huh?"

"Yeah, and that he is. Mesa is still single and lives on the ranch. She runs a horse rescue center out there, but they're out of the rough stock contracting business."

"I think I met them at the Fort Worth Stock Show and Rodeo. My father was a dignitary of some sort and introduced us. They were there with their grandmother. A genuine true Texas lady but with an

'I don't give a rusty rat's ass what others think' attitude." Again Rainey laughed and pleased Deuce that the small talk was relaxing her.

"Granny Johnson, as she's fondly known in these parts, is just that but it's their long-time housekeeper, Lola Ruth Hicks, who rules the roost on the Jacks Bluff."

"I think I remember some of the history. They're one of the biggest, if not the biggest, in the area. The founder Jack or was it John LeDoux—"

"Jack, I'm pretty sure."

"Then Jack won the ranch in a game of chance with four jacks and that's where it got its name."

"You're right as rain."

They passed alongside an arroyo before Deuce's house came into sight.

"We're home." He couldn't believe he said that as if they shared the house as a couple, instead of her being more of a person in protective custody.

Once inside, he locked up his Glock, then took the plastic wrapped envelope out of his pocket and put it in his desk drawer.

It's now evidence and nobody will touch it except me and the crime lab.

He gave Rainey time to settle in and then said, "I know it's early, but why don't you go take a nice long bath while I fix something to eat." He smiled at her, remembering his words to his deputy. "And this is not open for discussion."

"Yes, sir." She saluted. "For once I totally agree with you." She got up from the couch and headed towards the stairs. Looking back over her shoulder, she said, "And don't forget to fry up some of those livers in the fridge for Fat-Cat. I think he missed me fixin' them last night."

Deuce didn't respond. With his back to Rainey, he made a face at the big tomcat stretched out on the sofa where she had been sitting.

On his way to the kitchen, Deuce pulled out his phone and called the office.

Danny answered, but Deuce started to talk almost before the deputy finished identifying himself. "Do me a favor and make a quick call to the warden at San Quentin and verify that Alonzo F.

Hunter hasn't been moved." He waited for his chief deputy to respond, then added, "Text it to me, don't call. Just confirm and if need be use my name to get the information. Regardless of what you have to do, and you're a resourceful lawman, get the confirmation for me tonight." Deuce hesitated before adding, "And about your hair and beard. I know I've had you tied up with other stuff, and I realize if you get called out on another assignment a newly grown beard is a dead giveaway that you're working undercover, so just do what's best for you and the task force."

Deuce hung up and walked across the kitchen with the letter Rainey gave him heavy on his mind. After dinner, when he was calmer, he'd read it.

In some way, although he'd been thrown into some very uncomfortable, dangerous, and right out nasty situations in law enforcement, he wasn't certain he had what it took to read the letter, not just because it came from a deranged killer, but because he had seen for himself what it had done to Rainey. Even reading online the accounts of the murders Hunter had perpetrated had made Deuce sick to his stomach and he'd had trouble sleeping that night and the night afterwards. He couldn't even imagine what she'd gone through prosecuting the case.

Right now he'd best get his mind back to fixin' supper and taking care of Rainey and that dern tomcat. Almost having to hold his nose at the thought of cutting up and frying livers for an animal, Deuce went about the task of feeding the tom that seemed to be in Deuce's way every time he made a step.

In the refrigerator, he found a small casserole and a couple of plastic containers with food in them that had been left by his foreman's wife. The note taped on top stated the main dish was a King Ranch casserole and gave him cooking instructions. She had also left cooked broccoli and cauliflower in a cheese sauce and a small mixed salad.

He had just finished placing Fat-Cat's empty feeding dish in the sink when he smelled the light scent of lavender. Looking up, he saw Rainey standing in the doorway.

"Oh, does that ever smell good." With a sensual smile, she walked over to the stove and lifted the lid on the veggy dish. "Now don't tell me you cooked all of this yourself."

"I can't lie. I pay my foreman's wife extra to prepare a home-cooked meal a couple of times a week." He turned and eased into a smile. "Yesterday afternoon I picked up some of Granny's Special Cake for dessert. Does that count as cookin'?"

"It does in my book." She began to set the table with the plates and flatware he'd taken out of the cupboard. "I never really learned to cook. We had kitchen help and as busy as I was in the district attorney's office, I never found the need to learn. An In-N-Out burger was good enough for me." The warmth of her smile echoed in her voice. "There was a little deli down the street from our office that made really good pastries. I guess that's why I like Winnie's so much." She put the two plates in place. "By the way, how do you know what my favorite thing is from her bakery?"

"I stopped by and asked." He filled two glasses with ice and added tap water.

While they waited for the casserole to cook, they sat at the table and chatted about everything from the Dallas Cowboys to one of the funniest cases Deuce had ever seen nearly go to trial in Kasota Springs.

Rainey chuckled when he was finished. "So Mrs. Grooms's Chocolate Cake and Granny's Special Chocolate Cake are nonproprietary? They are one in the same?" Another full-hearted laugh rippled through the air.

"Yep. Winnie said her recipe was handed down generations and Clara said the same about hers. They each wanted the other one to stop baking it. When neither budged, Clara filed suit and asked for a cease and desist order."

"So what happened?"

"It wasn't until they took pretrial depositions that it was discovered that the exact same recipe was in a *Good Housekeeping* magazine back in the fifties, so it wasn't trademarked."

He thought Rainey was going to fall out of her chair in sheer joy at hearing about the story. "So I can alternate days in buying their cake and get the same thing each time." She shook her head.

"You got it."

Her eyes grew amused and she burst out laughing once again. He joined her, happy to see she had relaxed, but at the same time knowing it was only temporary because they had to talk. He had a couple of things to fess up to her about, and no doubt she hadn't told him everything, but he didn't want to ruin their friendly bantering.

Rainey broke into his thoughts. "You said your mother lives nearby. Is she still in Denton or here?"

The timer on the stove beeped. *Thank goodness, saved again!* "Time to eat. There are hot pot holders in the top left-hand drawer next to the fridge. If you'll put them on the table, I'll get the casserole out."

Deuce wasn't ready to discuss his mother. Not yet.

Ever since his visit with the nursing home administrator, Elaine, it'd been a hard choice but he'd decided not to tell Rainey his mother's whereabouts. Elaine was so emphatic that his mother was not to be upset and Rainey was in no shape to see his mama in her present condition.

When he thought the time was right, if he ever did, Rainey would need to be fully aware of his mama's condition and know what to expect. He'd give her his book on Alzheimer's disease to read.

Every night since he'd stormed out on Rainey, he'd gone to the nursing home. And every night his mama would ask if he knew her son, Deuce.

As soon as they could find a bed for her in another hospital more suited for her worsening condition, then he'd tell Rainey . . . if she was still around. He'd thought it before and now it seemed even more plausible she'd want to relocate, depending on what was in the letter. But he knew whatever was inside frightened her more than he'd ever seen.

He also needed to explain Allura because he had little doubt Rainey thought he was having an affair with her. He'd clear that up in due course, but right now he needed to keep Rainey calm, make her feel cared for, and give him time to handle the contents in the envelope with professionalism, not with his heart.

Supper was finally ready. He was glad to quit thinking and begin eating.

Deuce had seen a starved coyote tear into fresh kill, and that didn't hold a light to the way Rainey attacked her plate of food, only stopping a couple of times to say, "This is so good, Deuce. You have no idea how hungry I was."

It was obvious without her saying so but he agreed and enjoyed watching her eat for a change.

Once dinner was over, he helped her do the dishes by drying and putting them away. This time the small talk turned to the Los Angeles Angels. He was surprised at her knowledge of baseball.

"You know McCall Johnson's husband, Nick Dartmouth, owns or did own a farm team out in California, but I don't remember, if I ever knew, which one."

Obviously recognizing the name, she spouted off the team name and kept scrubbing the casserole dish until it was immaculate. He'd told her to put things in the dishwasher, but she refused, saying that washing by hand used less water.

Deuce tossed the wet dishtowel on the counter and said, "Done. Let's go to the living room." He reached for two glasses and poured them half full with wine.

She grabbed the wet towel and stretched it out on the counter to dry.

Once settled on the couch, Rainey pulled her feet underneath her and accepted a glass of wine. "I have something I need to tell you and hope you won't send me packing when you hear it." She bit her lip and panic settled on her face. She didn't wait for his response and rushed on. "First off, I'm furious that you investigated me, so I guess my confession isn't exactly news to you. I'm not a widow."

The anxious look on her face told him what he expected next.

"I've never even been married. I just made up a husband when you backed me into a corner wanting an explanation about my alias."

"And you don't think I know that." He was amazed that she gave him such little credit.

"I never expected you to check me out. I probably wouldn't have ever known it if Danny hadn't spilled the beans today. I thought you trusted me more than that."

"Trust you!" He shook his head. "What was I supposed to do?"

A sudden chill settled around them.

If she chewed on her lip any more she'd be drawing blood, but she stopped long enough to say, "You did exactly what you should have done." She offered him a slight smile, disarming him greatly.

"Is that what you really think?"

"Yes. You wouldn't be doing your job if you hadn't. It just took me a little bit to come to that realization. I'm sorry for getting angry about it." She laid her hand on his arm. "I'm really sorry, Deuce."

"Then I need to come clean with you." He wished telling her the truth included his mother's situation, but right now this was the closest to being honest with her that he could manage. "I let you think I was involved with Allura, but I'm not. Not really."

"Deuce, either you are involved or not. Regardless, it doesn't matter. I waltzed into town and although I didn't expect to find you, I did and turned around and inserted myself in your life. Whoever you are involved with is none of my business." Her voice was calm, matter-of-fact, but as silky as one of his mama's cashmere sweaters.

He kinda liked Rainey's groveling, and certainly enjoyed the feel of her soft hand on his arm, but he couldn't let his deception go on.

"Allura is a therapeutic chiropractor and I see her regularly for my shoulder injury." He stopped to watch the surprise that washed over Rainey's face. "The docs said I'll always have some trouble with it and they were right."

"I didn't know," she said very sheepishly.

"I wouldn't have expected you to. I've been so busy that I hadn't been keeping my appointments so she called to chew my butt out. That's what you overheard." He knew he shouldn't but he enjoyed just a little how uncomfortable Rainey had become. "And I bet you never thought that the girl who gave so freely of herself in high school would grow up to be successful at freely giving of herself, huh." He couldn't help but chuckle at the look on Rainey's face.

"No. No, I didn't. You honestly don't want to know what I thought." She lifted her head up and looked at the picture over the fireplace.

"I got several treatments and spent the nights at the office."

As much as he didn't want to address the issue, he decided he needed to read the letter. Deuce pulled to his feet and picked up the glasses. "I see your glass is empty." He moseyed to the kitchen to get some more wine.

Once he returned, he handed her the glass. He walked into his office and retrieved the envelope, along with a pair of plastic gloves.

Just seeing it in his hand caused Rainey's face to turn pale. The frightened expression he'd seen too much of had again surfaced. She pulled her feet from beneath her and looked like she was about to bolt.

He walked to her and pulled her to his side. "Don't be scared. If you want me to read it when you're not around, I understand."

"No. Go ahead. You've got to read it sooner or later."

"Let's sit back down." He pulled on the gloves and went through the process of carefully unwrapping the envelope. "You were smart to do this."

"I've seen many cases lost because of an improper handling of trace evidence," she said softly.

Rainey never stopped watching him as he opened the letter and began reading.

When he finished, he closed his eyes, afraid to even look at her as shock yielded quickly to fury. In short order, his anger turned to a rage like nothing he'd ever felt in his life. Without ever opening his eyes, he pulled her to him and nestled her as close to his side as humanly possible. He never wanted to let go of her, wishing he could take away her pain and shoulder it himself, but he knew that was impossible.

Rainey shook in his arms. He pulled her into his lap where she laid her head on his shoulder.

He kissed her forehead. "Rainey, this is a formal investigation as of this moment, and I'll do everything humanly possible to get the sonofabitch." He put his hand on her head, tucking her closer to him.

Within no time she relaxed completely and, by her steady breathing, he knew she'd finally fallen asleep.

Whispering to Fat-Cat, who snuggled against him, Deuce said, "I promise on Daddy's grave the bastard who sent this is gonna pay."

Chapter Fourteen

An awakening sun filtered through the windows in Deuce's bedroom. He opened his eyes and turned over to find himself alone in his big four-poster bed. He was certainly surprised Rainey had gotten out of bed without his knowing it. Obviously, she did and he was the lawman who should be aware of every movement made around him.

He remembered taking her to his bed after she fell sound asleep in his lap, but not until his legs finally went to sleep, too. It had felt too good having her in his arms, especially with her breasts settling against his chest.

When he laid her in his bed, she had awakened only long enough to ask him to stay.

Now he was there alone, having no idea when or how the spitfire had gotten not only out of bed but also past him without his knowing it.

Deuce lay there a few more minutes mulling over the night. He could still smell the light scent of lavender on her pillow.

He relived each moment—beginning with taking off her shoes, and as much as he wanted to he didn't go any further. He covered her and then laid his phone on the table before he sat down on the side of the bed and kicked off his shoes.

After he removed his jeans and shirt, his iPhone beeped indicating he had a text. The message from Danny read, "Confirmed 10-15."

Taking a deep breath he knew he'd sleep better knowing Hunter was still in custody. Now he had to worry if there was in fact someone on the outside doing the dirty work for the convict. He'd been behind bars for so long, no telling how many dangerous and horrifically deranged criminals he'd made contact with. Anyone from a gang member to the mob and in between would be willing to right what they saw as a wrong within their brotherhood . . . especially against the person who put Hunter behind bars in the first place.

Deuce typed in, "10-4," hit send and returned his phone to the nightstand. He slipped into bed beside Rainey. She rolled over right in his arms.

He had had a fretful night having her hot body next to his, but at the same time slept well, knowing she was safe.

Suddenly, a whiff of freshly brewed coffee filled the air. Now he knew where the five-foot-two, one hundred and ten pounds of dynamite was. Probably drinking coffee and feeding that dern cat.

Since he planned to work out before they left for Kasota Springs, he only washed his face and brushed his teeth. He stepped into running shorts and added shoes, and then stuffed his phone in his pocket. On his way down the hall, he pulled on a sleeveless tank.

After working out and catching a bite of breakfast, he'd take a shower and they'd head for town. He wanted to get the letter to Danny to be sent off to the state crime lab for testing. He could have his guys lift fingerprints, but no doubt they'd find dozens, including Sylvie's, and without a proper database to check them against, plus the inability to check for DNA, it'd be a waste of time.

He sighed. Once he finished at the department, then he'd help Rainey at the depot. After all, he was officially on vacation, although he didn't feel like it.

Deuce thought about the surprise he had for her and hoped it'd help put her at ease by getting her mind off of Hunter. Before he went downstairs, he wanted to confirm with his friend Bob, who was closing out one of his stores, that the merchandise Deuce had selected would arrive first thing Monday morning. He didn't want to tell her until he was sure the gondolas and shelving would be there on time. They'd have to do double-duty today, but with two people working they could finish the painting. On second thought, if he asked Sylvie, and maybe another trusted soul or two, they could get it done in half the time.

When he arrived in the kitchen, he discovered the coffee pot was still full, so whatever she was doing she didn't take time to even drink coffee. He rushed back upstairs to see if she'd moved to the guest bedroom, but there was no sign of her being there except for the clothes she'd worn the day before. He called her name as he descended the stairs.

With no answer, he walked quickly to the key rack. All keys were accounted for, so wherever she went she had walked.

His ringing phone startled him, but he quickly identified the caller as his foreman.

"Hey, Bran. What's up, man?"

"You told me to watch after your friend," his foreman said.

"Have you seen her this morning?" Deuce quickly asked.

"Yep. She's running like a hound dog chasin' a rabbit, but in an athletic sorta way."

"Where did you see her?"

"Down the road that runs cattywampus to the south pasture. I was out checking for any down fencing when I saw her. So that ol' plug I ride and I just stopped where I had a clear view and watched her for a while. She seemed to know what she's doin', but I thought you might wanna know."

Still on the phone, Deuce hit the door running in the direction of the pasture his foreman described. "Bran, would you ask Emily to prepare a meal each day except on Fridays, until I tell her other-wise?" It'd been a while since Deuce had been on a foot chase and never while on a phone but he increased his speed. "Of course, I'll triple what I'm paying her. But I don't need one tonight. Think I'll take the lady out to eat in town."

"Your lady?" A humorous tone was in Bran's voice. Not waiting for a response, he rushed on. "Sure, I'll have Emily fix some extra meals. I benefit in the long run since she'll be fixin' me a good dinner, too." He laughed.

"Thanks. If you need me, let me know—other than to sign a check, then send that to my accountant."

They shared a laugh. Deuce disconnected and slipped his phone in the pocket of his running shorts. He kicked his stride up a notch.

It seemed like he'd run two miles when Rainey came in sight. She looked over her shoulder and apparently decided to increase her speed.

They went from a comfortable cross-country pace to full-fledged to the finish line sprints. He thought he was in shape but obviously she hadn't lost her cross-country running skills from high school.

He rather enjoyed lagging back a bit because he got pleasure from watching her long legs, strong shoulders, and nice butt as she ran ahead of him. The only thing better would be if he was ahead of her and running backwards to see her sweet, taut bosom. For a small woman, she sure had long legs and nice, firm, very appealing breasts.

Laughing as he ran, Deuce imagined his stepping in a hole and killing himself trying to run backwards. *What a way to go with those images in his head!*

Deuce increased his stride to catch up with her and in short order did so.

"You really meant it when you said you'd keep a detail on me all of the time but I didn't realize it'd include you having to run to keep up with me," she said dryly and a little winded.

"I keep my promises." Deuce jogged alongside her, noticing that she had slowed considerably. "Plus, I have something to tell you."

"If you're going to tell me the difference between a bull and a steer, I already know that, so make sure it's something I don't know." She flashed him a mischievous smile.

"I can guarantee you don't know this."

"Shoot away." She slowed to a fast walk.

"How about that Danny talked to the warden and confirmed that Alonzo Hunter is still securely tucked away behind bars. No transfers of any sort."

Rainey stopped dead in her tracks and leaned over and put her hands on her knees. Taking a deep breath, she pulled upright. "That's a huge relief, but don't forget that Hunter said he'd have someone on the outside do his dirty work and get to me." She looked up at him and he couldn't escape seeing the fear in her eyes.

"Not with me around they won't." He spoke the words with confidence that deep inside he didn't feel. "Let's get back to the house and drink some coffee, then head for town. I want to get that letter off to the state crime lab today—"

"No!" she said in a choked voice.

"Why not? It's evidence and the sooner we get it to Austin, the sooner we'll get the results and know what we're dealing with."

Rainey bit on her lip. "I'm just . . . just not sure if it's a good idea. It will let more people know my alias. And they might put two and two together, causing trouble for Judith. Plus, we already know it's from Hunter." Her tone was firm yet he heard the apprehension in it.

"No, Rainey, we don't. There's something odd about the whole letter. The words don't seem right. Kinda contrived to throw you off and anybody else who you shared it with. particularly the officials at San Quentin." He took a deep breath. "I just wish to hell the Internet would get fixed, so we could do some checking on the language. Maybe it means something."

It didn't take her long to answer. "You're right. Let's sit on that tree trunk for a minute and rest."

After getting as comfortable as possible on the ancient cotton-wood, she continued. "I know the words in my head somewhere but they aren't ones that he's previously written to me. I've been wrack-ing my brain trying to see how it all fits together. The part about my green eyes and the fear in them is right, but the rest seems out of place, and I can't put my finger on it."

"More of a reason to send it to Austin. They're professionals and they won't be lookin' to investigate you. They'll be performing tests to find out who sent the letter."

"Deuce, there's probably so many sets of prints on it that they'll never be able to match whatever they find intact enough to ID with anybody in the national data bank."

"But if we don't send it, we'll never know. Right?"

She nodded, as false bravery settled on her face.

"Plus, there's always the chance that whoever sent it left their DNA if they were careless enough to lick the envelope to seal it."

After seeing the uncertainty on her face, he added, "Come here." He put his arm around her shoulder and pulled her closer to him. "I know you're still scared but I'll keep you safe. To get to you they've got to get through me first."

Hesitating for a moment, as though giving it more thought, she finally said, "You're right." She lifted her head and kissed him lightly on his cheek. "Thank you."

Deuce felt a stirring deep inside, and he couldn't resist tipping her chin and brushing his thumb along her jaw. "You don't have to thank me. Only trust me."

Just the touch of her skin made the burning inside worse. She was so soft, with the faint scent of lavender mixed with a spring day in the country making him want to gather her in his arms and kiss her the way she deserved and not stop until he'd erased away all the hurt.

Slowly, deliberately, he stroked her soft cheek, which glimmered with perspiration before again lifting her chin so they were eye to eye. Courage and fear laced with a look of serenity shone from her deep green eyes. It was hard for him to believe that he'd known her for so many years, yet only really got to know her over the last few weeks. A regular man could live a lifetime waiting for a woman like her. So why was he so hesitant in taking advantage of her coming back into his life?

Desire fisted in his gut and his blood was near the boiling point as he continued to look at her. He wanted to taste her fully . . . and now, to see if she was everything he had been dreaming about. Everything he didn't see in her growing up, except for a big heart. He'd always recognized that.

Damn, it took every bit of courage he could conjure up to keep from taking her in his arms and kissing her deep and hard, but instead he kissed her lightly on the forehead. Then he told her they needed to go back to the house, have some coffee, and get ready to get to the depot.

In record speed Deuce and Rainey had downed a quick cup of coffee, showered, and were ready to leave for town.

"You're not dressed for work," she said when he came downstairs.

He looked up and noticed she was dressed to do some serious work at the depot.

"No uniform," he said. "Remember, I'm on vacation and plan on helping you today."

A thoughtful smile curved her mouth and her left eyebrow rose a fraction. "You look a little like John Wayne with your holster, gun, and badge. But his badge would have been on his vest, not his belt." She reached over and pinched at his cheek like a mama might do a small child. "You look so cute."

When she turned to pick up her purse, he almost patted her on her cute butt, although he caught himself in time.

Enjoying the smell of fresh cut hay he drove them into town.

Stopping in front of the sheriff's department, he called and had Danny meet him outside, where he could keep an eye on Rainey, who remained in the car.

After he gave his chief deputy the letter, he raised an eyebrow at the clean-shaven man and said, "Nice job and I'm puttin' money on the fact you didn't do it yourself."

"You'd win," Danny said and went back inside.

Once Deuce and Rainey arrived at the depot, she quickly unlocked the door and rushed behind the counter to disarm the security system. "Want a drink?" she hollered.

"Sure."

Something on the floor caught his eye . . . an envelope. He picked it up and with Rainey busy getting them canned drinks, he had a chance to look it over.

Deuce's stomach tightened in knots.

Quickly he grabbed a quart-size zip-top bag Rainey had bought for paintbrushes and slipped the envelope inside. Folding the plastic bag in half, he stuck it in the waistband of his jeans and pulled his T-shirt back in place.

Afraid to breathe, he closed his eyes, but could still see the envelope in his mind.

Identical to the first one . . . postmarked San Quentin, California, 94964.

Chapter Fifteen

Deuce took a deep breath and hoped he could get the letter in his chief deputy's hands before Rainey discovered the bulge in his pants . . . not anything like the one he seemed to be having way too often.

Rainey placed two cans of soft drinks on the cabinet. "Sorry it took me so long, but I went to the back and got some plastic to cover the floor. The paint is premixed and Gideon said that if we use it right away it won't have to be stirred again." She stopped and stared at the high vaulted ceiling. "I wish we could paint up there, too."

"And lose its historical value? No way. This is a decades-old train station and those ceiling tiles should be preserved." Deuce found himself folding his arms across his stomach whenever he talked with her, so she couldn't see the outline of the envelope, which had slipped farther down inside his Levi's.

"You're right. It'd be a shame to ruin them. So many places have destroyed landmarks when with only a little work they could be saved." She squatted down, moved two paint pans near a gallon of paint and picked up a church key to open the container. "Plus, I'd have to hire a paint contractor who has special equipment to do the job."

Man, did he ever enjoy watching her firm, and oh, so touchable butt again, although that was farther down his list of problems than he would like. Right now his priority was to figure out a way to get to his office without Rainey being suspicious. Leaving her alone was out of the question, so he needed someone he trusted to watch over her without her knowledge.

"While you're doing that I need to make a call." He hoped she'd presume he was checking in at the department.

Meandering out of earshot, he placed a call to the first person he thought of and one who had befriended Rainey. The post office closed at noon on Saturday, so hopefully Sylvie would be free to lend a hand without asking why.

It didn't take much persuasion to get the postmistress to agree to help paint as soon as she got off work. He then lowered his voice almost to a whisper. "Sylvie, did you deliver any mail to the depot?"

"Yes. And why are you whispering?"

"I'm not. I guess it's the paint fumes. What kind of mail?" He kept one eye peeled for Rainey.

"A regular business envelope and a piece of mail addressed to current occupant. I knew she'd want the envelope since it was like the one she got a couple of days ago. When her car wasn't there, I just slipped it under the door. Got a customer. See you in a little while." She hung up without saying anything further.

Deuce glanced towards the entrance and sure enough in all his haste in getting the envelope from San Quentin out of sight he'd over-looked a piece of junk mail. He'd continue to ignore it for the time being.

Footsteps coming his way gave him sufficient warning to put on his game face and he tried to, the best he knew how.

"Are you going to help or stand around pretending to be one of the huge pillars, thinking I wouldn't notice?" Her smile deepened into laughter, as she stood there with a paint tray filled with light taupe paint threatening to overflow in her hands and two paint rollers tucked under her arm.

"Okay, so you caught me." He put his phone on the counter and picked up a plastic tarp. "Which wall first?"

"Let's start behind the counter since there's already some plastic on the floor." She put down the tray and both rollers and eyed the swatch she'd made on the wall earlier. "They called this 'buckskin,' but I'd call it 'butt naked.'" She laughed again and he swore it made her look ten years younger.

"You mean 'buck naked.'"

"No, butt naked." She shot him a look that smoldered with fire.

Deuce joined in on her jovial mood. "Okay, then the paint is hereby officially known as 'butt-naked tan.'"

She gave the paint sample another look. "Come here, butt naked," she addressed the paint on her roller and began working on the lower part of the wall.

"I'm going to put down a tarp on the south side so we don't get in each other's way." He grabbed another package of plastic and opened it. He couldn't help but think back to the night she stood beside the hot tub, the closest to being buck naked that he'd ever seen a woman who was fully clothed.

Taking the loose end of the tarp, he whipped it through the air to unfold like he'd seen his mother do every time she put fresh sheets on the bed.

The sound echoed off the nearly empty rotunda similar to an unexpected clap of thunder.

A scream came from Rainey and echoed through the air much like the whip of the plastic had done.

Deuce rushed to her. He gathered her into his arms and rested his chin on the top of her head. "I didn't mean to scare you. Promise." She shook as if a bolt of lightning had just hit her.

He pulled her closer to him and she hid her face in his shoulder. Once she stopped shaking, she pulled her head back and he saw eyes rimmed with tears. With his thumb he wiped away a single tear that rolled over her cheek.

"I'm the one to apologize, not you." She sniffed lightly. "I was so engrossed in what I was doing and wondering if the color was right that the noise caught me off guard."

"Come on." He took her hand and guided her to one of the folding chairs. "I need to talk to you about something. Have you thought about the possibility that you're suffering from PTSD with everything you've gone through?" He watched carefully for any response and saw what he interpreted as relief come over her face.

Although he'd considered the possibility that she had been experiencing post-traumatic stress disorder, saying the words out loud caused a cold knot to form in his stomach.

He didn't even realize he held his breath until he exhaled.

To his dismay her voice broke slightly as she answered. "I have."

She laid her hands flat on the table. "As an ADA, I had to attend a course on PTSD. Actually, it was a requirement after the Hunter trial."

"From what I saw that was a good call. I read in the newspaper that they had counselors on the scene of the murders for the first responders."

"They did." She looked up at him and he knew full well that the memories were flooding back to her.

"We've taken courses, too. I've witnessed you dealing with what they're calling re-experiencing of the traumatic event. The memories, flashbacks, nightmares, and even now a simple loud noise made you jump out of your skin, scaring you to death. I've seen you avoid people, try to turn inside of yourself." He took her hand in his, forcing her to look up at him. "I've seen or heard all of it, but it's the other things that I couldn't hear or see that scares the hell out of me."

Rainey looked him squarely in the eyes. "You're very astute and know how to read people very well." She turned her hand over and gripped his. "Sometimes I think my heart is going to pound out of my chest and I sweat for no reason, especially when the memories flood back. I have been avoiding interaction with people, letting mistrust and anger be my norm. I hate to admit it but I know I've been depressed and let the guilt and shame rule me."

"Will you do me a favor, just to patronize me if nothing else, but let me ask Allura for the name of a therapist that specializes in PTSD? I don't have to tell her who I'm wantin' it for because it could be for a number of people in my line of duty."

She bit her lip and took a long time before answering. "Yes. I'll do it for you." Suddenly, as if a good memory surfaced, an almost hopeful glint came to her eyes. "The only thing I've found that makes me happy is you so I can't say no."

"You're making me happy by allowing me the privilege of helping you."

Deuce slipped his hand out of hers, stood, and walked around the table where he took both of her hands in his and brought her up to meet him, planning on giving her a supporting hug.

In a soft whisper she said, "Kiss me, Deuce."

Not waiting for a second invitation, his mouth crashed down on hers. He kissed her deep, hard, and fast with all the hunger that had been building inside of him since the moment he stopped her for speeding on Main Street. Rainey parted her lips and he drove deeper still. Her lips were softer than he had imagined. He knew he'd never get enough of her sweetness. He thought he'd go crazy when her tongue began to tangle with his, and he let out a soft groan. He felt as if his heart had just opened and she had walked in. Although he knew they were treading water, he couldn't stop himself. He pulled away and asked, "Are you sure?"

"As sure as this." She left no question in her answer when she pressed her mouth against his.

Her kiss was slower than his, like that of a seductress with a hunger that made him wish he'd never called Sylvie. But that thought was quickly replaced with Rainey moving her tongue slowly along his lower lip.

The heat from her body pressed against him made him lose all of his determination as savage heat and hunger ravaged his body. He wanted her and wanted her here and now . . . not tonight but in the depot in the middle of the day.

As much as he hated it, he had no choice but to pull away and put her at arm's length. He couldn't take the chance of her discovering the letter stuck in his waistband.

Having to stop gave him another reason to despise the callous bastard sending her the letters.

"Sweetheart, this isn't the time or place." He pressed a kiss to her waiting lips. "I want our first time together to be something special." Eying the orange sleeping bag in the corner he continued, "And a sleeping bag on concrete isn't special."

Kissing her on both cheeks, he stepped back about the same time as knocking began on the front door.

Rainey grabbed the neck of her blouse and Deuce wished he had an apron on to cover his arousal.

"This isn't over," Rainey whispered as she rushed to the front door, leaving Deuce to decide whether he should hide behind the counter for a few minutes until his need wasn't as visual or to stand there and let Sylvie know his less-than-honorable intentions. Not to mention he'd lose his help for the day because the town crier would run, not walk from business to business alerting them to his condition.

He quickly turned to the wall, picked up the paintbrush and began to work.

Behind him he heard multiple footsteps and turned to see Sylvie leading a band of citizens through the door. So far he'd counted Sylvie, Gideon, Winnie, and Clara, but suspected there might be more behind them. Each carried a covered dish, tea jugs, and both Clara and Winnie had a cake carrier in their arms. He could bet a dollar to a donut that each toted a chocolate cake. Behind them, Winnie's husband, Stanley, pushed a cart loaded with plates, cups, a huge bucket of ice, and a tub filled with flatware and condiments. An employee of the catering business brought in a six-foot-long table and set it up.

Sylvie placed her serving dish on the card table before speaking. "We heard you needed help to finish painting so I called in reinforcements."

Winnie was next to speak. "When Stan and I heard about it, I called Clara and we decided to fix lunch for everybody. Nothing's too good for our newest resident." She turned to Rainey. "And one of my best customers." She placed her Tupperware cake carrier on the table. "And here's my famous Mrs. Grooms's Chocolate Cake."

Clara sidled up next to her. "And here's my Pumpkin's Famous Chocolate Cake."

No doubt Clara and Winnie were staking their territories just like the Hatfields and the McCoys. There was always the chance of a smack down whenever those two women got together.

"We brought barbeque, potato salad, and cole slaw," Clara added.

"I came to paint," Stan said as he picked up a brush and began to work.

"Me, too," Clara said.

Giving Rainey a light kiss on the forehead Deuce whispered, "Now that you've got plenty of help, I'm going over to my office and check on things."

"You're on vacation," she whispered back.

"Never on a real one unless I leave town." He grabbed his phone from the counter. "I promise we'll finish what we started when this place is ready for shelves and gondolas."

"You promise if Clara and Winnie start a fistfight over their cakes you'll send someone immediately?" She laughed and gave him an amused wink.

"Just call 911. Jessup will answer. Say 'cake' and my whole office will empty out to get over here to see if there's any left." He laughed and touched her lightly on the nose with his finger.

He slipped out the door, relieved to get out without Rainey discovering the letter. He was lucky to have a T-shirt on or the plastic would have stuck to him like chewing gum dropped on a sidewalk during the heat of summer.

When Deuce entered the sheriff's office at the town hall, Danny looked up with a puzzled expression on his face. "I thought you were helping your lady friend."

Deuce deliberately shot him a frown. "Got something I've got to do first." He opened the door to his office and shot over his shoulder, "I'm not here if anybody asks."

Within minutes, the sheriff had taken all the precautions to preserve any fingerprints or other trace evidence on the envelope and read its contents.

I've been counting the days since I last saw your fearful green eyes, so I can ask you why will you say that I am mad? It is impossible to say how first the idea entered my brain; but once conceived, it haunted me day and night. Object there was none. Passion there was none. I kill because I like to see the expression on their faces when they know they are about to die.

With fond memories of your
green fearful eyes, AFH

Fury replaced the numbness Deuce felt after he finished reading the words a second time. During his years in law enforcement he'd seen and heard things that upset him beyond words, but this topped the list, second to the first letter.

He got up and walked to the window that looked out into the town square. Putting his hands on each side of the window facing, he leaned into the glass. Because of the air conditioning it felt cool against his forehead.

What was he to do?

The first thing, of course, just like with the other letter, was to send this one to the crime lab. But not until the next time Federal Express was scheduled to be in Kasota Springs, and that wouldn't be until Monday.

Thoughts of not telling Rainey about the second letter weighed heavily on Deuce's mind. He knew it wasn't fair, but for the first time since she'd arrived in town, he had witnessed her interacting with the town folks seemingly without being skeptical that they were out to get her.

Thinking this through, he sat back down in his chair and looked at the wall covered with diplomas. They didn't help him an iota where his heart was involved. Knowing he needed to get back down to the depot so Rainey wouldn't suspect anything, he drew himself to his feet and ambled to the door. Opening it, he asked Danny to come in.

"Deuce, I promise I sent that off this morning. How'd you get ahold of it?" Danny began almost before he got through the threshold. "I promise—"

"I know you did." Deuce turned the letter in a protective envelope around towards his chief deputy. "Take a look at this. I found it at the depot this morning."

Danny turned pale as he read. "Damn it, Deuce. Exactly the same, but only with different words." He turned the protective sleeve over. "Same paper and the letters look like they were cut from the same publication. And there's something else." He continued to study the letter. "Look at the last sentence. It's different. A much more educated person wrote it, not a lunatic. The other words are literary, like the writer has been trained in journalism."

Frowning as he reread the words, Danny finally asked, "Want me to get it ready for the crime lab? No need to wait until Monday for pickup. This ups the ante a bunch, doesn't it?" Without waiting for a response he continued. "Since FedEx already came today and I've got to go over to Amarillo to meet Brody VanZant this evening, I can drop it off at their offices. No need to wait until Monday."

Deuce nodded. "Is there something new happening with the task force?"

"Same ol' thing. We got a BOLO for a shipment of meth coming out of California crossing our counties this evening or early tomorrow morning so we'll all be on duty, along with the DPS guys, until we get the bastards in custody."

Deuce shook his head, wishing every drug dealer would fade away like a buffalo wallow in a drought, but he knew that wasn't gonna happen. But without guys like Danny and Brody out there doing their job, there'd be even more drugs on the streets.

Danny gathered up the letter and turned to leave.

"Thanks," Deuce said to his deputy. "And be sure to make a copy of this one, just like the other one before you leave." He felt the tightness that radiated through him subside when he forced himself to relax. "Hey, I owe you, man."

"Then the next time I'm undercover you won't stay on my ass about getting a haircut?"

"Not going that far." Deuce sat back down in his chair. "Another thing. I don't want Rainey to know about the second letter. You hear?"

"Yes, sir." Danny raised an eyebrow. "Makes me feel better to know that I can hold intercepting federal mail without a warrant over your head." The chief deputy quickly closed the door before Deuce could be tempted to throw his shoe at him.

Deuce took a deep breath, trying to prepare to return to the depot and act like nothing was wrong.

Might be easier said than done but he'd make it happen . . . to protect the woman he knew he was falling in love with.

Chapter Sixteen

The next morning Rainey sat in her car in the parking lot of the Kasota Springs Nursing Home waiting on Sylvie. She stared at the sign and the throngs of people going inside and thought back over the last twenty-four hours. She'd totally forgotten just how much she had missed over the last several years while putting one hundred and fifty percent of herself into being a deputy district attorney. What all had she missed?

For starters, a love life of any sorts. She had gone on an occasional date, if those were what she could call a date, generally with an associate who talked business during the whole evening. Although most were handsome, intelligent men, she'd gotten very little satisfaction out of any of her dates except for good food and decent company. She always went home filled but not fulfilled and went to bed alone, not even settling for casual sex, with few kisses to be remembered. She couldn't place all the blame on the men because if they weren't talking about their cases, she was thinking about hers. That left little room for sweet talk much less pillow talk.

Now she had someone in her life who rarely discussed business and seemed more into her and her project at the ol' Rock Island Depot than anything else.

She checked the time. Sylvie should have been there by now. Rainey smiled thinking about how easy it was to get Deuce to let her have her car back once he heard she was taking his advice and spending the afternoon with Sylvie. He never asked what they were doing, and she presumed he thought there wasn't much happening in Kasota to get a Miss 1950 Prom Queen impersonator and a workaholic in too much trouble.

Rainey felt exhausted but happy with all the work that had gotten done the day before. Almost all of the painting was finished. She had the bathroom to do, but things were coming together nicely. Even Gideon had helped paint and wash windows.

By the time she and Deuce had gotten back to his ranch house after working all day, it was way past midnight. They immediately headed for the showers. Wrapped in each other's arms afterward, they drifted off to sleep like two babies who had spent the day at a family reunion.

The smell of coffee had awoken her long before daybreak. She couldn't resist the temptation to have coffee with Deuce, so she got up, pulled on a robe and trotted barefooted downstairs.

Finding him sitting at the table, she filled her cup and joined him. After typical morning chit-chat, particularly about how the work was going at the depot, she had the opportunity to thank him again for having the courage to bring up PTSD with her and it made her feel not so alone. He seemed pleased when she told him that she'd taken his advice and had accepted an invitation to spend the day with Sylvie.

Deuce told her how happy he was that she'd taken her first step to get outside her comfort zone. He kidded her about Sylvie being the perfect companion and had said that he needed to take care of some out-of-town business and wouldn't be home until late.

He never said where his out-of-town business was and she hadn't asked. It was likely connected to his job or he would have offered an explanation.

Glancing at the clock again, she began to get worried about Sylvie being so late. Of course, it being Sunday, and the fact they were going to a Mother's Day Tea, she probably needed extra time to get ready. Rainey smiled, thinking that Sylvie would likely show up wearing a hat and gloves just like Rainey remembered her mother doing when she was a little girl.

Thoughts about her mother caused an ache to settle in Rainey's heart. She'd tried to reach her to wish her a happy Mother's Day but got her voice mail instead. She had tried several more times over the morning before calling her father and receiving his voice mail.

Maybe her mother didn't want to be remembered on Mother's Day. Not wanting to be reminded she was a mother because she'd then have to admit she was the much younger woman who broke up Rainey's father's first marriage by getting pregnant.

Rainey took a deep breath and repeated the words she so frequently thought to herself.

She's my only mother and I'm her only daughter and that will never change.

Rainey's cell phone rang and brought her back to the late spring day.

"Hello, Sylvie. You running late?" she asked.

"I'm so sorry but I've come down with a sour stomach and need to stay home. I'm so sorry. I'll make it up to you, I promise." Sylvie's voice rang of true sorrow at missing the event. "The administrator's name is Elaine. She's expecting you, so go see her."

"Please don't feel bad about not being able to come. There are some things you can't help. Just take care of yourself." Rainey checked the rearview mirror to make sure she still had enough lipstick on. "Thanks for Elaine's name. I need to get to know more people and this is a good start."

After another half dozen "I'm sorry's" from Sylvie, Rainey disconnected, turned the ringer off, and placed her phone in the inside pocket of her purse.

When she got to the entrance, she was immediately met by a woman who welcomed her and told her to help herself to the refreshments. "Enjoy your Mother's Day. If you or your mother need anything, please let me know," the willowy woman said before turning to the next arrival.

Rainey felt sure that if the woman knew how the words only added to Rainey missing her own mother, the greeter would have never presumed Rainey had come to visit her.

A professionally dressed lady in heels, about the age of forty, whom Rainey pegged as the administrator walked up to her. "Hi, I'm Elaine and I don't believe I've met you before." She extended her hand and Rainey reciprocated, giving the lady her name.

"You're opening an antique shop in the ol' Rock Island Depot, aren't you?"

"Yes, I am."

"Sylvie told me all about you. Let me introduce you around." She turned back to Rainey and said, "I understand you'd like to volunteer some and we can sure use your help. But if Sylvie hasn't told you, we do have a number of residents who are suffering from dementia and Kasota Springs is fortunate to have an Alzheimer's unit. Although, when they reach the latter stages of the disease, we don't have the manpower it takes to handle them, so most have to be moved to a bigger facility." Elaine never took a breath during her whole spiel.

Rainey watched the residents interact with everyone around them.

Four ladies sat at a game table playing Monopoly. Others laughed with their loved ones, obviously enjoying the day. Several sat all alone or with people who were staff, based on how they were dressed.

Elaine went on to explain that if Rainey wasn't familiar with Alzheimer's that it was paramount that the residents not be upset or confused any more than they already were. She went on to say that there are various stages of the disease, but it was also hard to distinguish which stage they might be in because of their erratic behavior.

"I know very little about it," Rainey admitted, opening the door for Elaine to continue her explanation.

"You'll find some who are confused about what day it is and don't know significant details about themselves or their families. Just go along with them and don't try to pressure them for details. Remember they are in a world only they know and it's kinda like channel surfing to them. The scenario changes. Being suspicious and delusional is fairly common at all stages. They don't see the world as we do. Just mingle and let them enjoy you being here." Elaine touched her on the shoulder. "We're so happy you're willing to volunteer. We have a couple of classes you'll need to attend to become a regular volunteer, but today especially, we're thrilled to have you. We're so shorthanded, as you can see." A sadness came to her eyes as she looked around the room.

This is the perfect place for me to volunteer! I need them as much as they need me!

"I'd like to introduce you to a couple of volunteers and wish I could spend more time with you, but can't. I hope and pray you'll find this a good fit for you and you can come back and visit. I can see the kindness in your face, so please consider it." Elaine kept a watchful eye on first one, then another resident. She was obviously good at her job, and Rainey suspected that Elaine loved her patients as if they were her own family.

"I can already tell this is what I want to do. Now, until I get the antique store opened, I'll be limited on time. But maybe I can come one or two days a week."

"Mrs. Michaels, even an hour a week is more than some of our people get. Please excuse me, but I can see that Mr. Simpson needs to make a trip to the bathroom."

Rainey followed her gaze to an elderly man sitting in a wheelchair who obviously hadn't asked for assistance soon enough. "I'll warn you now that incontinence is a serious problem for many of our residents. I need to get a nurse's aid to get him cleaned up."

"Ma'am," an elderly voice called from behind. "Ma'am."

Rainey turned and walked directly to the man who looked lonely sitting by himself. "May I sit next to you?" she asked.

"Yes, ma'am. I don't reckon I've met you before," he said with a rather strong voice for his obvious advanced age.

For what seemed like only fifteen minutes, but by glancing at the wall clock, she realized it'd been nearly an hour, she listened to the veteran, who had introduced himself as Captain Chalmers. He proudly shared his stories about World War II and the Korean War.

As another elderly man joined them, she learned that the ninety-two-year-old gentleman wasn't telling stories but true tales from a much decorated veteran. She felt happy that she'd spent time with the man, but while he and his friend talked on, she couldn't keep her eyes off a lady probably in her late seventies who sat alone in the corner shredding one tissue after another. When she was finished with one, she'd put it in her pocket and get another tissue and the process began all over again.

Although Rainey had never met the woman, her gaze kept returning to her because she looked so familiar. So far nobody had come to visit with her. Whether she knew her or not, Rainey felt that she had to spend some time with the elderly lady.

Suddenly, someone came to mind and she took a breath of relief finally remembering who the woman reminded her of: Marie Cowan, Deuce's mother. But could that be possible? Although she had brought up the subject of his mother several times, Deuce had avoided giving her any information. Rainey had come to the conclusion that it had to be for one of two reasons—either she had passed away and he didn't want Rainey to know, or they had had a falling out, which she couldn't imagine. The other possibility, of course, was that she still lived in Denton and had a life of her own that didn't necessarily involve Deuce.

Anger rose inside of Rainey because she'd been so wrapped up in her own feelings of despair and guilt, coupled with being afraid of everybody she came in contact with, that she hadn't pressed Deuce on the issue.

As the men talked on, she kept a watchful eye on the woman, who by now had ripped up at least a dozen tissues, each time placing them in her pocket.

The more Rainey watched the woman, the more she came to the realization that she couldn't be Deuce's mother because Rainey remembered her as being almost as tall as her son. A proud, stout lady with shoulder-length, raven hair, while the woman tearing up Kleenex had short, gray hair, probably didn't weigh a hundred pounds soaking wet, and slumped down in her chair making her look about as short as Rainey.

No—no way could this be the same woman, although she did have dark brown eyes just the color of Deuce's.

Rainey had to remind herself that there were a million people in the world who had brown eyes, not just Marie and Deuce Cowan.

Rainey excused herself from the two men, telling them how much she enjoyed visiting with them, although she hadn't gotten a word in edgewise.

"I hope you'll come back and see me," Captain Chalmers said, giving her a toothless grin and a wink.

"I'd be honored to, sir." She patted his hand. "I really enjoyed visiting with both of you." She smiled at one, then the other before walking in the direction of the woman in the corner.

"Hi, I'm Rainey Michaels and I'm new here," she said to the woman, who looked up at Rainey with vacant, sad eyes.

"I don't know you," the resident said in a no-nonsense way. "But you look nice."

"How about me getting us some punch and I'll sit and visit with you?"

"That'd be nice. But I don't want to drink very much because my son will be here soon and he'll want to have some, too." She tore another strip off the tissue in her hand. "That is, if he can make it today, but if not, that nice young man who comes every day will be here."

"Let me get some punch and maybe a cookie." Rainey rushed off to the refreshment table.

She tried not to make something out of nothing but the lady did say she had a son.

Returning with what tasted like fruit punch and an assortment of cookies, she set the small plate of refreshments along with the drinks on the table between them and then pulled her chair around to face the woman.

"I told you my name, but I don't know yours." Rainey took the tissues out of the lady's hand and asked, "Is it okay if I hold these for you so you can drink your punch?"

The woman nodded. "Now, what is your name, young lady?"

"Rainey Michaels, and what is yours?"

"I need to drink this while it's still cold. I like milk. Do you?"

"Yes, I like milk. Particularly chocolate." Rainey thought about the many times she and Marie Cowan had slipped out of the antiques store and purchased for each of them a pint of chocolate milk and drank their fill.

"Oh, I don't like chocolate but sometimes they'll put the strawberry stuff, you know the stuff that makes the milk turn pink." Her hands began to shake. "You know the stuff—"

"Oh, strawberry syrup. Like the Hershey syrup," said Rainey, feeling sorry for the woman who had become so upset over not being able to remember the word "syrup." "I like strawberry, too. But let's drink our punch. It's pink like strawberry milk." Her smile was met with one from the person sitting across from her.

The two new friends enjoyed their refreshments in silence.

"I don't believe you told me your name but mine is Lydia Dunivan."

Rainey almost cried out when she heard the name and could barely say, "Donovan. D-O-N-O-V-A-N?"

"Oh, no, it's Lydia Dunivan. Dunivan. Like a divan. Dunivan."

"I see. How about me just calling you Lydia and you can call me Rainey."

"That's a nice name. I like it." Lydia reached in her pocket and got out some shreds of tissue. "If you need some of these I've got plenty more." She extended her hand out to Rainey.

"Thanks. That's good to know." She accepted the Kleenex pieces.

"I like your necklace," Lydia said touching her bare neckline.

Rainey reached for the antique necklace she wore. "I do, too, but here." She unhooked the piece of jewelry, then walked behind Lydia to put it around her neck. "I think we can share it. One day you can wear it and the next I will. Okay?"

Lydia clutched the sterling silver and mother-of-pearl piece. "I'll keep it safe." She lowered her voice. "You know there are a lot of people here who you can't trust. I had a very nice lady that came every day to see me, but she stole something very valuable from me and she doesn't come anymore." She stopped and thought for a long time. "And there's a very nice young man who comes, but I have to watch him now because sometimes he takes my clothes. If he wasn't such a nice young man I'd turn him in."

She extended her hand with another bunch of Kleenex. "You might need these. If you could come back tomorrow I'll have more. I think I see my son coming so I've got to go right now."

"Lydia, I promise to come back tomorrow if I can. If not, I promise it'll be soon. Real soon." She took her hand and without thinking leaned down and gave her a hug. "Promise."

Rainey looked up and saw a short, middle-aged man wearing khaki walking shorts and a Hawaiian shirt walk through the door and head their way . . . and he was no Deuce Cowan.

* * *

After finishing his business in Denton, Deuce drove as fast as the law allowed to make the four-hour trip back to the Kasota Springs Nursing Home and Rehab Center before the Mother's Day festivities were over.

He didn't want to miss spending time with his mother on Mother's Day, but wasn't too disappointed that he missed the tea. It always aggravated him how some children rarely showed their faces around the facility but always managed to make a big deal out of special events, such as Mother's Day. In his opinion, it was more important that he see his mother daily than to wait for a special day. He didn't make it in to see her every day, but he missed very few.

Deuce had been relieved when Rainey stopped asking questions about his mother. He didn't mean to deceive Rainey but had to abide by the recommendations of the administrator by making sure his mother wasn't upset. He knew since she loved Rainey like a daughter that her sudden appearance might confuse the elderly Cowan even more. Yet he couldn't come right out and tell Rainey that he didn't want her to see his mother either.

Rainey was in a bad place of her own. Hopefully, once she received some professional help and with as much TLC as he could give her, he'd eventually be able to tell her about his mother's condition. It'd be a happy day when he could come clean with Rainey and let her know the truth—even take her to see his mother—her old friend.

Finding a parking place in the crowded lot in front of the nursing home, Deuce mentally scratched his head. Even in the shadows of late evening, he could swear he saw Rainey's car leaving the parking lot out of the farthest exit south, but then if there was one, there were a hundred white Chevy Malibus in the area. Plus, being Mother's Day, there'd be a lot of visitors coming into town.

After being greeted by several workers, he saw his mother sitting in her favorite chair in the corner with two other women, nibbling on a cookie and sipping punch. He was pleased to see her looking so relaxed. Something he hadn't seen for a long time.

Elaine came up from behind and said, "She's having a good day, sheriff."

"I was just watching her. She seems less agitated than I've seen her in a while."

"It could be nothing but her having a good day with a lot of people around, so please don't get too encouraged that we won't still have to move her. But I'm hoping we don't, because she's such a lovely patient." She smiled up at him, then said, "I felt bad about Sylvie not being able to come back, but sometimes things occur between a volunteer and a patient that nobody can explain. That seems to be what happened. Sylvie was too upset to talk about it. I think her feelings were hurt more than anything. She hasn't been back to volunteer since the day she walked out."

"Thanks for the update, Elaine. I'm encouraged but won't read too much into Mother doing better."

"By the way, she decided on a new name today."

"And what's it now?" Deuce couldn't keep track of all the names she'd given herself.

"Today she's Lydia Dunivan." She raised an eyebrow.

"Donovan, like my given name?"

"No, Dunivan and she spells it out to make sure everybody knows exactly how it's pronounced. Like divan, she tells them. Although, I have to admit she rarely spells it the same way. Tomorrow it will probably be something else but call her Lydia today, please. I've got to check on Mr. Chalmers. Enjoy your visit." She touched Deuce on the arm and walked off towards Captain Chalmers and another man Deuce didn't recognize.

Deuce picked up a couple of cookies in a napkin and put them in his pocket, before he reached his mother.

"Hi, Lydia," he said, aching inside because he couldn't call her "Mama."

She looked up with a smile and said to the other women, "I knew he'd come. When my son can't make it, this young man always comes to see me. Isn't he a nice man?"

They all nodded and hustled away as if scared off by Deuce.

"Let's go to your room so we can visit before bedtime," Deuce said.

He helped her pull to a full stance and he slid her walker in front of her. "You're such a nice man," she said. Then she continued. "There's something I need to talk to you about."

As they walked down the B wing hallway on the way to B-16, she chatted away about how much she enjoyed the tea and about the nice lady who had sat and talked to her.

"I think she was Mr. Chalmers's wife, because she talked with him for a long time."

Deuce knew Captain Chalmers didn't have a wife, but just walked behind his mother listening, trying to keep up with her disjointed details of the day.

When they reached her small two-room unit, he made sure she was comfortable in the overstuffed chair his father had always sat in when he was alive before Deuce settled in the blue wing back chair across from her.

They shared the cookies he pulled from his pocket.

She didn't seem to want to get off the subject of the woman who visited her. "She was so nice. You would have liked her. She brought me punch and cookies, too, and stayed a long time. I think she's Mr. Chalmers's wife. Did I mention that?" She looked up at him with brown eyes identical to his.

"Yes, ma'am, you did. What was her name?"

Mrs. Cowan stopped and thought for a long time. "I think it was . . . yes, Mrs. Chalmers, I'm sure. She gave me this necklace." She touched her new piece of jewelry. "She said she'd come back to see me tomorrow."

Deuce wondered about the woman and made a mental note to check with the administrator to see if she knew who had befriended his mother. He knew they were very careful about who came around the residents but, as a son, her welfare was his number-one priority.

As late as it was, Elaine probably had already left for the day but he'd ask her the next time he saw her. He wanted to make certain the necklace was a gift, not some other resident's piece of missing jewelry.

"That's lovely. Do you recall the lady's name who gave it to you?" he asked for the second time, not really expecting an answer.

She looked perplexed, then said, "Young man, I can't remember every visitor's name. Plus, I have a problem I need solving."

Patronizing her, he said, "I'll try, but first I brought you something for Mother's Day." He retrieved the small jewelry box from his pocket and gave it to her.

After she opened the gift, she admired the bracelet inside and told him how much she liked it, then said, "It's this one that bothers me." She touched the location bracelet they had put on her because of her wandering off. "Will you tell them to take this one off so I can wear the new one?"

"I'll ask but I'm not sure they will." He smiled at her pleasure with his gift. "Why not wear both of them until I can find out." Deuce got up and helped her slip the new, inexpensive gold-and-pearl bracelet on her wrist.

"Young man, they will if you tell them to." Determination echoed through the room. She softened her voice and said, "But what I want to talk to you about is that someone stole my football games where my son, Deuce . . ." She trailed off and looked up at him. "I've told you about him, haven't I?"

The question stabbed at his heart. "Yes, ma'am, you have."

"I thought he'd be here because it's—it's, well, it's a special day but if he's playing football he can't come. That's why I knew he'd be playing on television, but someone stole my football game." She stopped to think a minute. "I know he would have been here if he could." She stopped again before she continued. "You know, he has to play ball, so I watch him on TV." She touched the bracelet Deuce had given her, then reached for a Kleenex, which she began shredding into little strips.

Deuce could only watch her. The hurt deep inside became more than he thought he could endure. But every time he came, he always left feeling the same way . . . abandoned and helpless. If he could change places with her, he'd do it in a heartbeat, because he knew if he was the one living in a world only he knew, his mother would be the first to take his place.

Suddenly, she said, "But I don't think I've seen my son for a while." She looked into his eyes and pleaded, "Would you see if you can find out why they took football off my TV? Without it, I can't watch him play." She shredded more tissues. "I think it was the Pink Lady who used to come see me who did it. She told them I didn't need to watch so much football. I'm going to see if it was her." She tried to get up and Deuce rushed to her side to help her.

"Mama—I mean, Lydia, I'll go right now and check with the administrator and see what they're doing about it." A knife twisted in his gut as he opened the door.

"You'll see that it was that Pink Lady because she stopped coming to visit me. But I trust you to do something about it because you're such a nice young man. You remind me of my son, Deuce." The faraway look crossed her face again. "Have I told you about him?"

"Yes, ma'am, you did. I'll see you tomorrow. Okay?"

"Well, where is it?" His mother's stern eyes flashed.

"It?"

"You know what I'm talking about, young man. Don't try to fool me."

"This." Deuce pulled a Butterfinger out of his pocket and handed it to her knowing she didn't know the name of the candy bar and likely couldn't remember the word "candy." Another ache attacked his heart.

"Thank you, young man."

Although Deuce was prepared to help her back to her chair, she sat down without any trouble, opened the candy bar and took a healthy bite.

"I'll bring you another one tomorrow."

She set her candy aside, picked up a Kleenex, and began shredding it. "I gave the nice lady today some of my pieces I'm tearing apart to make a new quilt." She looked up with haunting eyes. "I hope she takes care of them."

Deuce got into his pickup and tried to keep his focus on some of the great Mother's Days he'd had with his mother, and he quickly found himself thinking that the good thoughts had to outweigh the bad ones. The last thing Rainey needed was for him to show up at the ranch upset. Also, not being able to spend the day with her own mother had probably saddened her on top of things.

He'd told Rainey that he'd be late returning to the ranch so she wouldn't be expecting him any time soon. He hoped she'd had a nice day with Sylvie, whatever they had ended up doing.

Deuce walked into one of two bars in town, The Wagon Wheel,

and ordered a Lone Star longneck and took a big swig. The county's club-cab pickup was parked over at the sheriff's department and he'd taken his personal F-150 pickup to Denton because his original plans were to go through some of his mother's packed-up antiques to see if there were enough to help Rainey get started. To his surprise, there were more than he remembered, so he spent most of his time sorting them and then made arrangements for Bob to bring them, along with the fixtures from his store, the following day. It might be a good start, but she'd still have to find a regular supply for collecting the antiques. He suspected garage and estate sales in Amarillo would be her best sources.

Although Rainey was heavy on his mind, his thoughts kept wandering back to his mother. It had been a particularly trying day, yet he felt a sense of encouragement seeing that she was less aggravated than usual.

Maybe her feeling happier had something to do with the woman who had visited her. But who would have brought her a gift besides him? He hadn't seen any wrapping paper or a gift bag. Regardless, the necklace came from a very caring and wonderful lady.

Right or wrong, other than the employees of the nursing home, few people in Kasota Springs even knew his mother was a resident there. He wanted her protected and having anyone remind her of the death of her husband in the line of duty could mean a nasty setback for her. Deuce wasn't willing to take that chance.

In his book, the more fictional names she made up for herself, the better.

After ordering another beer, he listened to the band The Wagon Masters play a song co-written by an Amarillo guy who grew up there in the sixties, Terry Stafford: *"Amarillo by morning, up from San Antone,"* the lead guitarist sang.

Deuce smiled as he listened. Although the song wasn't released until the seventies, no doubt Sylvie knew every word.

Suddenly he missed Rainey and wanted to see her, hold her in his arms.

Tossing down some cash to cover his tab and a generous tip, Deuce headed out the door.

The ringing of his phone could barely be heard over the loud hum of the cicadas.

The nursing home's night nurse began speaking almost before Deuce answered. "Sheriff Cowan, we have a problem with your mother. She says you know all about whatever is bothering her and won't go to bed. It's already way past bedtime, but she is just sitting in front of the TV saying that she will only talk to the nice young man who comes to visit when her son can't. Of course, we know it's you. Something about someone stealing her football."

"I know what she's talking about. I'll be there as soon as I can get out to the ranch and pick up a DVD player and some videos." He shut his eyes and listened to the cicadas. "Tell her you've called me and I'm on the way, but I want her to go to bed until I can get there."

"Just knowing that you're coming generally settles her down and she'll go to bed. I knew you'd want to know what is going on with her, sir. By tomorrow, she'll probably forget all about the TV problem."

Deuce stared into the night. "If she doesn't settle down, call me immediately and I'll be right over."

"Yes, sir. And good night," the night nurse said before the phone went dead.

Although Deuce didn't expect to have a good night, he wanted to get back to the ranch . . . back to Rainey.

Chapter Seventeen

Sunlight filtered through the curtains in Deuce's bedroom and settled across Rainey's face, making her come alive much like the morning sun. She rolled over expecting to find Deuce but he wasn't there . . . not any longer, but she knew he'd come in and remembered nestling against him during the night. She touched her lips, definitely recalling the good night kiss he had given her after settling in bed. It must have been late because she barely woke long enough to return his kiss and say good night.

Feeling more rejuvenated than she had in weeks—no, more like months—she was eager to begin a new week.

Eager to tell Deuce about her visit to the nursing home and the people she met.

Eager to hear about his Sunday.

She sighed. Most likely he'd spent yesterday in Amarillo dealing with the case he'd only mentioned in passing: trafficking small bags of methamphetamine tablets known on the streets as "bags of ice." She suspected he'd mentioned it because it would have been a no-brainer that she had prosecuted a zillion cases of meth coming into California from Mexico.

Applying some mascara, she couldn't help but think about the amount of self-discipline Deuce had had to enforce upon himself in order to keep his business and personal life separated, especially when under any other circumstances she would be considered a colleague.

Quickly she dressed in work clothes and went downstairs eager to see Deuce only to find half a pot of coffee. Disappointment washed over her when she didn't find him sitting at the table to help her welcome the morning. He must have gotten up early, although it was only six-thirty. She'd set the alarm on her phone so she could get to the depot and paint the bathroom.

Fat-Cat was nowhere in sight.

It didn't take a law professor to tell her that the extensive amount of time Deuce had spent with her working at the depot had taken him away from his responsibilities as sheriff. A job he was elected to by the citizens—people who expected him to earn his paycheck, although most probably didn't consider the fact he worked for them 24/7, not just eight hours a day.

Rainey walked out to her Chevy listening to the cheerful song of a multitude of birds, many gathered around birdseed that had fallen from several feeders. Smiling again, she thought to herself that today was the first time in years that she'd even taken the time to appreciate the sounds of the outdoors. With a renewed excitement about life, she decided that henceforth it'd be new beginnings and all the negatives of the past would be cloaked by the contentment she felt.

Fat-Cat crouched under a bush watching the birds feed.

When she got into town, she noticed Deuce's personal red F-150 Ford pickup parked outside the building housing the sheriff's department, but the county's club-cab he usually drove wasn't there.

Three hours later, Rainey finished rinsing out the paint roller and pan, setting them aside to dry. She scrutinized the walls of the bathroom and decided that her choice of Wedgwood blue for the room was perfect. While painting, she had thought of a zillion ways to decorate around the color.

Before she grabbed some lunch, she wanted to get the hardware on the cabinets because tomorrow she would have the depot in shape to seriously begin shopping for fixtures. She couldn't wait to see the antique glass she had ordered online. Hopefully, she could purchase some fixtures before they arrived.

After locating a screwdriver, Rainey sat on the bathroom floor and began taking off the old hardware, preparing for new knobs and pulls.

She sighed trying not to remember her disappointment at being unable to reach her mother to wish her a happy Mother's Day, although she'd made two more calls after going back to the depot and working until she couldn't put one foot in front of the other. Her final message to her mother before she went to bed had ended with, "I hope you're having fun. Love you."

As she screwed on another knob she remembered one more thing she was eager to talk to Deuce about. Maybe when he was in Amarillo he'd been able to talk with Allura and hopefully she had recommended a therapist. Just making the decision to seek help, coupled with Deuce's tenderness, she already felt better. Much of it had to do with visiting the nursing home and the time spent with Lydia. She could hardly wait to tell Deuce all about it.

A cowbell sounded its distinctive clap as someone opened the front door to the depot. She rushed from the bathroom to the front eager to see who had come to visit.

"Sylvie sent me over with this package that just came in." Gideon held a medium-sized box that Rainey presumed contained some of the items she'd ordered online. "Where do you want me to put it?"

"Any place is fine and thanks." She moved her arm in a semicircle around the huge, bare room. "As you can see I've got plenty of space."

He joined her in laughter.

"Where'd you get the bell over the door?" Gideon asked.

"Deuce installed it for me so I didn't have to set the alarm when I'm here alone," she answered before asking if he'd like a drink.

Once she got two cold bottles of water, they took seats at the card table. She sensed he had something on his mind because she couldn't see him volunteering for much of anything, much less making a delivery for the post office, whether he was friends with Sylvie or not.

"I'm glad you came by, Gideon. I needed the rest." She twisted the cap off her water bottle.

"I've been wanting to come talk with you about something but thought it'd be best if I came when there wasn't a bunch of folks around." He didn't look her in the eye and his body language screamed that what he had to say wasn't going to be good.

"It's just something that I think as a friend I should tell you."

Fear girded her insides. She held her breath knowing that he was about to tell her that Sylvie and Deuce were lovers, based on the tidbits Sylvie had dropped about having someone special in her life and that she wondered if he was as crazy about her as she was about him. Thinking about the day before, maybe that was why Sylvie had come up with an excuse not to come to the Mother's Day tea. Deuce said he wouldn't be home until late. She braced herself for the worst.

"I wouldn't put any more money into this place because Wilson isn't planning on renewing your lease. He is really doing everything he can to make sure you don't get open. Says the place is draining him and the little bit you're paying him doesn't even cover what he had to pay to have new water pipes put in." He looked at her over his glasses.

"Well, that's kinda between him and me. I appreciate you letting me know, but we've got a contract and he can't just kick me out." She wanted to say that she'd buy the place, but that was out of the question, since Rainey Michaels barely had a background, much less a credit history. "Maybe it qualifies to be in the national or state historical register."

"No. He'd never go for that. He wants to get rid of it, even tearing it down if he can't find a buyer. He thinks it's worth a whole lot more than it is. I've been trying to buy it from him but he wants too much. Before you put more money into the building I thought you should know. Even if he waits out whatever agreement you have, he isn't going to renew. He's a hateful, nasty man who's only lookin' out for himself."

"How do you know this?" It wasn't the first time she'd heard that her landlord wanted to break the lease agreement.

"Just around town. He's like that. Untrustworthy and gossips a lot. That old battleaxe who works for him is as bad as him." He cupped his plastic bottle with the palms of his hands. "I'm doing this as a favor. If I were you, I'd just walk away and save yourself a lot of money and hard work, plus there aren't five people in this town interested in antiques. You'll go out of business before you get started." He stared her straight in her eyes with a look that made her feel he was issuing a warning. "Just get out before you get hurt."

He laughed in a cynical fashion. "I don't mean physically, just financially." He tossed his full bottle of water in the trash and got up. "I've got to get back to the store. I don't like to leave my business in Sylvie's hands any longer than I have to." He stopped and his gaze moved around the depot as if taking in every detail. "You know she's got problems, don't you?"

Taking a deep breath, Rainey decided to step into uncharted territory and tested the waters a bit. "I thought you and Sylvie are . . ." She chose her next words carefully. "You know, she really admires you and I took it that you two are in a relationship."

Gideon shot her a dark, unnerving smile. "She thinks that. Pesters me all of the time, but she's harmless. See, that's what I mean. I've got to go." He rushed to the door without saying good-bye, then suddenly turned back in Rainey's direction and said, "Take my advice about Wilson and get out while you can."

"Do me a favor, as a friend. If you see Mr. Wilson, tell him I'm here to stay and there's nothing he can do about it." She hoped the tone in her voice portrayed her stubbornness on the subject.

The thud of the bell echoed through the tomb of the ol' depot. Rainey stared at the door as it closed.

What a way to ruin an otherwise great day!

The bell clapped again. This time Deuce walked through the threshold.

Rainey rushed to him and threw her arms around his neck, whispering, "I'm so glad to see you." She was afraid he could feel her heart beating out of control. "So glad." She kissed him on the lips.

Over his shoulder, she saw four men who all had surprised yet bemused looks on their faces. She quickly pulled away and whispered, "I'm sorry."

"I'm not." Deuce kissed her lightly on the forehead. "I thought I was the one giving you a surprise but it seems it's the other way around." He put her at arm's length and studied her. "Although I'm happy about the kiss, you have a strange look on your face."

"It's just . . ." She tried to think up an excuse. "There's men at the door and I wasn't exactly expecting—"

"I know. They're part of my surprise. This is my friend Bob and some of his guys. They're delivering the fixtures from one of his stores that he's closing." He turned and introduced each man to Rainey.

"Well, let's get busy." He turned to Rainey. "We've got gondolas, peg boards and hooks, and shelves. A couple of glass cabinets." He smiled down at her. "And I hope you'll be happy with my other surprise. Sunday I drove over to Denton and went through some of the things at the old house that were left over from Mama's antique days. Bob and the guys brought over a bunch of glass to get you started."

Her heart leaped in her chest. All the misgivings she'd had about Gideon's visit vanished and she thought she might just kiss Deuce again.

"Then your mother is—"

Her voice was drowned out by the racket of metal shelving hitting the concrete floor. One set whacked Bob on the head as it fell.

"Hey, guys, be careful." Deuce rushed over and checked on Bob first, then with his help pulled the shelving upright. "Rainey, tell the guys where you want the stuff 'cause I don't think Bob wants to come back and move them later." He and his old buddy laughed and Bob gave Deuce a high-five.

Around four o'clock, Rainey and Deuce stood at the door and waved farewell to his friends, whom she now added to her list of friends, too. The thoughts of Gideon Duncan's visit resurfaced. There was just something not right about him dropping by.

"Deuce, I can't thank you enough." Once again she put her hands around his neck, locking her fingers behind.

His arms circled her waist and he pulled her tightly against his rock-hard body.

Their gazes locked. His eyes brimmed with tenderness and passion, as he leaned down and kissed her. A kiss that began whisper-soft and tender, but quickly became intense with yearning, sending spirals of ecstasy throughout her body.

Rainey pulled away, but not before she pressed her lips to his, caressing his mouth more than kissing it. "Unless you want to try out that orange sleeping bag—"

"Or a cot in one of our empty jail cells." He planted a tantalizing kiss in the hollow of her neck. "We'd better stop because right now that sleeping bag is lookin' pretty damn good to me." He kissed the top of her head. "Plus, I have another surprise for you."

"What did I do to get so many surprises?" As much as she didn't want to, she tugged him with both hands over to a chair so they could sit down.

"Just being yourself and coming into my life when I really needed you." He gave her a smile that set her heart racing. "I decided you need a surveillance system so you don't have to set the alarm every time you're here alone. Between the bell and a monitor or two, you'll be able to see who comes and goes."

She wanted to kiss him again, but knew that if they did most likely neither would be able to stop this time.

"I have a couple of monitors, so you can put one at the counter with the cash register and another one some place else where you can see the whole store. There are several cameras with this system and I can get more if you want them."

"You make me so happy." She took his hand and kissed it. Surely that wouldn't start something that neither wanted stopped. "Let's get busy. If you'll unwrap, I'll start putting the glassware on the shelves. I can place them where they belong later. I'm so eager to see what you have here." She unwrapped the first piece of Depression glass, a golden topaz six-inch plate. "Oh, Deuce, I hope there's a lot of this here." She held the piece up to the light. "These are fairly rare and the best I remember were put in oat boxes back in the thirties. Isn't it beautiful?"

"It is and I know there's more here, but if you stop to admire every piece, you won't have this place open until Thanksgiving." He chuckled and unwrapped another piece of glassware and put it on a shelf. "I'm going to my truck and get the ladder and then I'm installing the surveillance system tonight."

They both began working at each of their jobs. But not being within hearing distance of one another, they worked in silence until Deuce decided to take a breather.

Wiping his forehead with his shirtsleeve, he said, "I put one monitor out of sight over at the ticket master's cage." He looked up at her. "Oops, I mean counter. And where do you want the other one?"

"Maybe in the area I've blocked off as a workstation. I can see pretty much all of the store and it'll help me monitor the front door, which I can't see."

"Done." He stepped forward and gave her a kiss on the forehead.

"I think they hold about ten days of recording. Then you'll have to save it or the device will begin recording on top of the old footage."

Other than taking a short break to eat hamburgers and fries that Deuce had picked up from Pumpkin's Café, they worked all evening, late into the night. He finished the surveillance system and she stocked the shelves.

He came up from behind her and put his hands around her waist and pulled her into him. She enjoyed the feel of his strong arms around her . . . something she'd become accustomed to.

Spying the box Gideon had brought by, she pulled away and said, "I forgot about the delivery Gideon made earlier today for Sylvie." She rushed to the package that was turned upside down. "I'm sure it's some pieces that I ordered online."

"Do you need help?" Deuce asked.

"I've got it. It's not as heavy as I thought it'd be." She took it over to the table. Ripping the tape from the bottom, she pulled back the cardboard. Her back became ramrod straight and she wasn't sure she could get enough breath to call out to Deuce, as she spied the familiar turquoise-and-gray paisley printed Prada handbag exactly like the one she'd tossed behind the trash receptacle a few blocks away from her offices in Los Angeles.

She steadied herself on the edges of the table and leaned forward until her lightheadedness began to subside. Had she gone mad? Had she ordered the same handbag and forgotten about it? Not in a million years.

In a voice as weak and unsteady as her legs, she managed to call for Deuce.

"What's wrong?" He grabbed her and looked down at the package. "Isn't it what you ordered?"

Tears welled in her eyes and she swallowed hard before she looked up at him. "Turn the box over and see where it was mailed from."

He did as she requested. She didn't have to look at the mailing label. She could tell by Deuce's face, along with the way the muscle in his jaw quivered, her suspicions were right.

With an odd yet gentle tone, he said, "San Quentin."

She closed her eyes and in a broken whisper said, "Look inside of the purse and see if there's a red ink stain about the size of a dime on the bottom lining."

"Let me get some gloves. Are they still in the workbox?"

She nodded, opened her eyes and stared at the mailing label. Just like the death threats . . . San Quentin, CA, 94964.

When Deuce finished examining the purse, he looked up at her. She didn't need words to know he'd found the ink spot.

"Who would send a purse from San Quentin?" Deuce bellowed, probably not realizing how loudly his voice resonated through the air.

"A very sick, deranged murderer," Rainey managed to whisper. "Someone who has made it his mission to try to make me become as mad as he is." She leaned into Deuce, who had her tucked into his side. "Someone doing a favor for Alonzo Hunter."

Chapter Eighteen

Tuesday morning, Deuce sat at the kitchen table and thought back over the prior evening. He hated like hell having to leave Rainey's car parked at the depot, but she was too upset to drive out to the ranch.

Without asking her for more information, it was obvious that the purse held a huge significance, not just the fact that it had come from Hunter.

What did it mean to her? All the way to the ranch, he wanted so badly to ask her about the purse, but there was no doubt in his mind that it somehow had to do with her planned disappearance from LA. Her tone had chilled his blood when she said, *Someone doing a favor for Alonzo Hunter.*

They drove home in total silence. He asked no questions and she offered no explanation. He knew she'd talk about it when she was ready. He'd found himself trusting her, although he wished the same could be said of her. He'd been holding back personal matters, plus the arrival of the second letter. And he hoped when she learned the truth, it wouldn't ruin what they had found with each other.

When they reached the ranch, he asked if she wanted to talk and told her he had a bottle of wine waiting in the kitchen. She had thanked him and said she needed a hot bath and to go to bed. She'd kissed him lightly on the cheek and said good night.

He'd drunk two bottles of beer and had gone upstairs to take his shower and crawl into bed with hopes he could pull her to him and provide her some comfort.

When he opened the door to his bedroom, to his surprise, Rainey wasn't there.

Slowly, he had walked across the hall and quietly opened the door to the guest room. Still in her work clothes but without her shoes, he found her curled up in a fetal position on top of the bedspread.

Not wanting to wake her, he eased one of his mother's quilts from the rocking chair in the corner and spread it over Rainey. He stood there for a while watching her sleep before he went down on his knees and pulled her hair back from her cheek. After kissing her lightly, he had quietly retreated with his heart breaking for her.

Suddenly, it occurred to him that she had become more important to him than he even realized. And they had had such a good day . . . until she had opened the package from San Quentin and had found the purse.

He glanced up at the clock on the wall. Nearly nine o'clock. He thought back to the package. Putting his lawman's hat on, the significance of the purse was secondary to the fact that it had been mailed from a man behind bars. A man whose every movement was monitored. Every visitor scrutinized. Every piece of mail read except for anything coming from or going to his attorney of record.

So how in the living hell had a high-security inmate such as Hunter gotten a purse to someone on the outside?

Deuce smelled Rainey before he saw her. The familiar freshness of lavender mingled with the scent of fresh brewed coffee and wafted through the air.

Looking up, he noticed she was dressed in clean work clothes, which meant she planned to go into the depot.

"Good morning," Rainey said as she poured a cup of coffee. "I owe you an apology for the way I acted last night." She put her cup on the table and took the seat across from him. "An apology and a lot of answers to questions I'm sure you have. But before we start, thank you for putting covers over me, and for respecting my privacy. I'm not sure I deserved it."

"I'm just glad I could be there for you." He took her hands and looked into her emerald eyes. "You don't owe me an apology. Sometimes we all need the space to digest things. In my line of work, I know I do. There are times that you haven't asked questions about a case when I know you wanted to."

"I have." She squeezed his hands before pulling hers back and reaching for the sugar bowl.

"I know you were upset when I took the box and purse to my office to be sent off to the state crime lab. I sensed you didn't want to talk about it and probably don't today, but I need to know about it so Danny can tell the crime lab what we're looking for."

"I know. If you haven't already figured it out, it was the one I was carrying when I walked away from the DA's office. I left a few dollars inside, my identification and tossed it behind a trash can, thinking somebody would come along, dump the contents, take the money and it'd look like nothing more than a snatch and grab."

"Can you give me any idea who might have found it and who knows your alias and where to locate you?" His gut tightened just at the thought that he was interrogating her right at his kitchen table. "You got your new ID from someone. Who was it?"

As Rainey stirred, her spoon hit the sides of her coffee cup again and again before she answered. "Some guy my friend Judith recommended. I thought I had all of my bases covered."

After giving him what he could only presume to be every detail about her plan, something she'd not told him before, he found himself thinking that obviously she hadn't woken one day and decided she'd disappear. It was a well-made plan. Over the weeks he'd thought up dozens of possible scenarios, but transferring from terminal to terminal using several different modes of transportation at the Los Angeles International Airport before going to the car lot certainly wasn't one of them.

"Then the only person who knows your alias was the guy at the car lot and your boss gave you his name." Deuce took a sip of his now cold coffee to give himself more time to think through things. "How'd she get his name and know he could be trusted?"

"Judith was close friends with an undercover cop, so I figured the guy at the used car lot was one of the LAPD's informants." She bit her lip. "I've wanted so many times to contact Judith but I promised her that, unless it was life or death, I wouldn't."

Deuce tensed his jaw in frustration because he wanted to tell her that this might well now be life or death, but he didn't want to speak the words out loud he knew she was also thinking.

"When I was in town last night, I told them that I wouldn't be in until late. That I was working on a case. And I am, so let me fix us something to eat." He tried to lift her spirits a little by adding, "I don't want to take the chance on you burning my house down fixin' breakfast." He pointed a finger at her. "I know because you already told me you can't cook. Why do you think I have Emily prepare meals for us?" He raised a questioning eyebrow.

"Thanks." She continued to stir her coffee. "I probably need to eat. Maybe it'll settle my stomach down a little bit."

Deuce set about cooking bacon, eggs, and toast, by pulling a cast-iron skillet from underneath the cabinet. Shortly, the smell of bacon frying filled the air.

"I have good news for you."

"I can use some." She spoke in a soft voice, but her words were stiff.

Deuce wasn't sure if this was the best time to bring up Allura's giving him the name of a doctor for PTSD, but he knew Rainey needed more help than he could give her right now. She needed a professional since the discovery of the purse had led to such a setback for Rainey.

Another big concern was he still hadn't told her about the second letter. By now, the state crime lab was probably ignoring Danny's daily calls to see if they had preliminary results on the letters.

Deuce turned slices of bacon and wondered how well Rainey was going to take having a second letter sprung upon her. As mad as a calf being branded probably wouldn't compare to what he expected Rainey's response would be. But he felt justified in keeping the knowledge from her to protect her.

After giving it a second thought, he decided to bring up Allura's recommendation.

"Allura called and gave me the name of a therapist that specializes in PTSD." He pulled two pieces of paper towel off the roll and put them on a plate for the bacon. "I've got his name in my billfold."

"Thanks." Again, another bland, distant response.

Think, Deuce, think . . . surely there's something I can say that will make her smile!

The sound of a jaybird's call filtered through the open screen door.

"Since you got to town I've been thinking about our school days together. Do you realize that if you hadn't stayed on my ass to keep my grades up that I'd have never made All-American and certainly not have made it to the pros?" He didn't expect an answer, so he went on. "Hell, I wouldn't have even gotten into college."

He looked at her and sad, vacant eyes stared up at him.

"You probably didn't know how many times I thanked you. My Brainy Rainey, I think I played every game for you."

"And I have to admit that I crushed on you a bit." A slight smile curved the corner of her mouth.

"Crushed on me?"

"That's what I hear the kids say now—they crush on someone." For the first time since she'd walked into the kitchen her voice didn't sound fragile and shaky.

"Hey." Deuce walked to her and stood behind. Putting a hand on each shoulder, he leaned down and whispered, "You know what, I think I'm crushin' on you now."

Rainey put her hands on each of his. "That's good, 'cause I've never stopped crushin' on you." Looking deep into his eyes, she asked, "I've got a question and if you don't want to answer, then you don't have to."

"Shoot away."

She took a deep breath as if having to gather up courage. "Our senior year, you left the impression that you planned to ask me to the homecoming dance. Why didn't you?"

Her question stirred something deep inside as he recalled his conversation with her father. He thought twice about giving her an honest answer but decided he'd kept too many things from her already. Finally, he answered, "Rainey, I called but your father told me basically that I wasn't good enough for you and never to call again. So I didn't."

"That explains a lot." She bit on her lip.

He kissed the top of her head. Deciding nothing else needed to be said, he went back to the stove and changed the subject. "Scrambled, I hope because if you order anything else I can promise they'll be scrambled."

"Then scrambled it'll be." She got up and poured her coffee out and refilled both of their cups as if she'd heard nothing she hadn't heard before. "Can I make the toast?"

"Sure."

Relief flooded over Deuce just at the thought that maybe her knowing he had tried to call her all those years ago helped get her mind off the purse that had come in the mail. Whether she was willing away her bad memories or the thoughts of a good breakfast was doing it, he could care less as long as she was feeling better.

Over breakfast they talked mainly about the things he'd brought her for her shop and her mood lightened. More than once she thanked him for the fixtures and fussed at him because he refused to tell her how much he'd paid for them.

"I probably should go into my office today, so why don't you stay out here and rest?" Deuce took both of their plates to the sink and scraped them.

"And you'll have someone sitting on the doorstep all day long?" she said matter-of-factly.

"No. I haven't had a 24/7 detail on you since the mysterious stranger staring at you through the window ended up being one of my finest."

She eased up next to him. "Thank you." Rainey slid her arm around his waist. "You've been so understanding and I've acted so ungrateful to you."

Turning, he took her in his arms and said, "I know a way you can show me how thankful you are of me." His lips pressed against hers, then gently covered her mouth. Raising his mouth from hers, he gazed into her eyes and was happy to see sadness replaced with yearning, passion.

Standing on her tiptoes, she touched her lips to his, welcoming another deep, searing kiss that was disturbed by the sound of his iPhone.

"Damn it." He brushed a gentle kiss across her forehead. "I've got to take this."

"I know." She began to run water in the sink, obviously still refusing to use the automatic dishwasher.

"Danny, you got any news?" Deuce had been told that the state crime lab might have a prelim report for them sometime today. He'd said a dozen prayers that it would come in soon because he was worried about Rainey. Whoever Hunter had on the outside doing his dirty work for him seemed more deranged than the mass murderer himself.

After hearing that once again Danny had been assured that the prelim test results could be in as early as tomorrow, Deuce said, "Stay after them, man. Did you get the purse and box off?"

Danny reassured him that he'd taken the package to Federal Express in Amarillo himself and had just gotten back and knew he'd want the update on the letters.

"We really need at least a prelim report on the two letters. I'd bet my bottom dollar that whatever trace they find on the letters they'll find on the box. Keep me posted."

Pressing the end icon, Deuce looked up into eyes that brimmed with fire and ice, but her words were colder yet. "What do you mean 'two letters'?"

Deuce's first thought was to deny there being a second letter because just within the last hour she had turned the corner back to normality. The reality . . . she didn't need justification not to trust him, although the omission of the second letter might well give her enough reason.

"Don't you dare lie to me, Deuce Cowan." Her brows drew downward in a frown. "I mean it, don't lie to me. Was there a second letter?"

"Come sit down," he said.

"No, Deuce. Every time you have bad news for me you want me to come sit down like it'll make telling me easier. I want the truth and now." Her words came out hard and very pointed.

"Yes, there was a second letter." He began to walk toward his office, half expecting her to pull him back by the nape of the neck like his mother used to do when he was caught doing something she didn't like. "Come to my office. I have a copy."

Rushing past him, she stopped his progress forward. "Why in the hell didn't you tell me? I thought I could trust you." She spat the words out like someone had washed her mouth out with soap.

"Because you were in a good place. You'd just gotten settled down after receiving the first one. I know I should have told you, but just couldn't." The look of disbelief on her face made him ashamed of his actions, but if being intent on saving her could be used as a reason maybe she'd understand.

"It wasn't your decision to make." She turned and stomped to his study with him closely behind.

After he logged on to his laptop, he pulled up the file with the two copies side by side. "Not to justify my actions, but this one came just a day or two after the first one. I wanted to get it off to Austin for examination as quickly as possible."

"Let me see it." She sat down in his desk chair and stared at the words, without saying anything for the longest time. "There's something not right about the second one. The words are so familiar, yet aren't modern. Did you notice this?" She ran her fingers along the words: "*I kill because I like to see the expression on their faces when they know they are about to die.*"

"Rainey, I've read each letter until I've memorized them, trying to figure out what they mean."

"It's a mixture of classic writing and modern day. These words aren't like the others. The syntax is different. There's something I can't put my finger on." She minimized the screen and tried to log on to the Internet. "Damn, it's still not connecting. Well, I thought maybe I'd find something there, but guess not. It's going to eat me alive until I can remember where the words came from." She looked up at Deuce. "And, I'm not mad at you. I was at first, but I realize you were doing what was in my best interest. I really do love you for taking care of me."

Putting his hands on her shoulders, he squatted down and kissed her on one side of her neck, then turned his attention to the other side. "I love you, too," he whispered, then pulled up to his full height.

"Let me try to access the Internet one more time. Maybe I put in the wrong code." She sat down and got immediate access. "I think I was just too upset and put in the wrong password."

Deuce watched as she typed in several words, each connected with the plus sign.

The screen flashed up with numerous links that included the words.

"'The Tell-Tale Heart' by Edgar Allan Poe!" she almost screamed. "We had to read it in high school. Don't you remember?" She stood up and threw her arms around his neck and gave him a long, lingering kiss.

Damn, he didn't want to admit that he couldn't remember reading the story but if he had, after all these years, the words didn't sound familiar to him. But if it took suddenly remembering to get another kiss, he could make himself recall each and every word vividly.

"Oh, I remember now." He kissed her long and hard. Whether he wanted to release her or not, he had to take care of business and then he could go back to kissing.

"Got to call Danny." He stepped away and picked up his phone and punched in his chief deputy's number and hardly waited for his answer before he began, "Part of the letters came from 'The Tell-Tale Heart.'"

He stopped to listen to Danny say, "By Edgar Allan Poe?"

"Yeah. Rainey and I had to read it in high school, but to be honest with you, she was the one who remembered the words. Got a job for you."

It took Deuce a few minutes to give Danny his assignment and to reiterate that he was to tell the warden at San Quentin that they were investigating a case and needed the information on Hunter posthaste.

"Let's go sit on the couch." This time it was Rainey who made the suggestion.

"So they're going to check to see whether Hunter has access to anything by Poe."

He nodded. "Particularly in his cell. I know you heard but I want his visitor's log. Do you remember the name of the lawyer handling his appeal?"

"No. He hadn't been assigned one when I left town. There certainly weren't any clamoring to get the case, so I'm sure he had to wait for some unwitting lawyer to surface to the top of the pro bono list and get assigned the appeal. Or some lawyer who thinks he can make a name for himself by accepting the case came crawling forward."

"There's nothing we can do now but wait. Tell you what. Let's make a couple of sandwiches, take a blanket and blow off this day. Go down by the stream and sit under one of those big ol' cotton-woods," Deuce said.

"Sounds well and good to me, but then your phone will ring and that'll be the end of blowing off the rest of the day."

He tried on his best smile. "It'll take Danny a while since it's two hours earlier in California. I'll leave my phone here and promise to work extra hard tomorrow to make up for it." Since his smile didn't work, he put up his little finger and said, "Pinky swear."

Rainey rested her chin on her hand. A bemused smile touched her lips. "That's so girlish, it isn't even funny."

Compared to the look on her face when she came downstairs he saw a hopeful glint in her eyes along with her smile.

Taking his phone out of his pocket, he laid it on the end table, got up, and pulled her to her feet. "Turkey or ham?"

"Turkey."

They walked hand in hand into the kitchen.

While Rainey changed her shoes, Deuce made a quick call to the nursing home to check on his mother and let them know he wouldn't be by until later in the day with the VCR and tapes if she was still upset over football. To his surprise, the clerk for Unit B wanted him to talk with the administrator, Elaine. While he waited for her, his heart pounded out of control thinking that something was wrong and they hadn't called him.

"Sheriff Cowan, I'm so glad you called. I had hoped to be able to talk to you today. I know you were so upset the other night when you were called. Your mother is doing so much better. The doctor is really amazed. Not that the disease is in remission or anything like that because Alzheimer's doesn't take a break, but if we can keep the patients comfortable and as happy as possible, we consider it progress. She hasn't even mentioned not being able to watch you on TV."

"What do you attribute her improvement to?"

"I think increasing your visits to twice a day has helped. And she's been a whole lot more content since Mother's Day. But as you know she's not letting go of being called Lydia Dunivan. She also talks about the nice lady who spends so much time with her. The one who brings her strawberry milk."

Before Deuce could ask more about the new volunteer his mother liked so much, he heard voices arguing in the background of the nursing home.

"I've got to go, Deuce, but I wanted to let you know."

He looked up just in time to see Rainey shutting the door of the guest bedroom.

Barely saying good-bye, Deuce returned his phone to the end table when Rainey started down the stairs. Apparently, she hadn't heard any of his conversation.

An hour later, Deuce and Rainey lay on one of Deuce's mother's quilts beneath an ancient cottonwood tree that shielded them from the afternoon sun. They enjoyed the birds as they fluttered around singing their songs of late spring.

Lying on her back, Rainey tucked her arms behind her head and obliviously studied the clouds.

"I see an elephant," she said.

"An elephant? Anyone can see an elephant in the clouds. What about that coyote over there?" He pointed toward the east.

Elephants turned to castles and melted into lions. Damn it if he wasn't becoming painfully aware of the magnetism drawing him to Rainey . . . the love of his life.

Deuce lifted up on an elbow and watched the rise and fall of her breast. Pebble hard peaks fought the restraint of her thin yet service-able blouse. He made no attempt to hide the fact he watched her. There was no need.

Gently, almost hesitantly, Deuce lowered himself toward her, pressed his lips against hers, then slowly covered her mouth with a soft kiss, as she'd fallen asleep.

Putting his arms behind his head, he stared up into the clouds, enjoying the quiet of the prairie. He thought about what it would have been like to live on the Slippery Elm when it was established a hundred-plus years ago. Slowly his eyes closed.

He was awakened by shrill, ear-piercing calls of two scrub jays as they staked their territory. By her color, apparently the female had a nest in the tree and wanted to make sure it wasn't bothered. Just another woman protecting what was hers. He smiled to himself.

Rainey rolled over and slid her arms around his waist and kissed him full on the lips, then whispered, "I'm hungry, so let's go back to the house and see what Emily left in the fridge for us today."

"I'd rather stay here and kiss you." His lips brushed against hers as he spoke.

She buried her face in his neck and breathed a kiss there. "But it's nearing sunset and unless you have a flashlight, I think we'd better get back to the house."

"You're right." He got up and began packing the picnic basket while Rainey folded the quilt.

Back home, Deuce had barely set the picnic basket on the kitchen cabinet when his iPhone rang. He decided whoever was calling could wait until he put the extra unopened drinks in the refrigerator. He knew it wasn't anybody from the sheriff's department because he'd assigned their calls with a different ring from others.

When his phone when off a second time, he rushed to retrieve it.

The caller ID pulled him immediately into his professional mode. "Sheriff Cowan," he answered.

After ending the call, he yelled at Rainey to hurry as they had to get to town, while he unlocked his gun cabinet.

"What's wrong?" Rainey said as she rushed down the stairs.

"There's a fire at the depot." He buckled his gun belt.

"How serious is it?"

"I don't know. The fire chief didn't say. Just said to get down there and asked if anybody was inside. I told him no."

They rushed to Deuce's county vehicle and ran hot, with lights flashing, as fast as he could without endangering them.

Once at the depot, they were met with the chief of the volunteer fire department and together they walked to the back of the depot where huge lights lit the area. "Glad you guys got here so fast," the chief said.

"I see it's out. Where did it begin?" Deuce shot off the question to the chief.

"Right here at the back between the tracks and the building. Looks like tumbleweeds blew against the ol' wooden freight doors and apparently something caused them to catch fire." He sighed. "Pretty sure I smelled gasoline but it's still too hot to really begin our investigation. Did you store anything combustible out here for any reason? Cleaning supplies even?" He addressed the last two questions to Rainey.

"No," Rainey answered softly. "Thank you and the other firemen for putting it out so quickly."

"Has Harold Wilson been notified?" Deuce asked.

One of the volunteer firemen stepped up to answer. "I called his cell phone and his wife answered. I didn't talk to him directly. She relayed the message to him and I heard him with my own ears say that he was sorry that we got the fire put out because if the place burnt to the ground, it'd save him the trouble of tearing it down himself."

"Very suspicious for a man who used to love the building more than life," the fire chief remarked.

"Something else, sheriff. I think the fire was deliberately started."

"What makes you think that?" Deuce asked. "Besides the smell of gasoline, which is enough in itself."

"For one thing, when I was here a while back with my day job with the water department, all the tumbleweeds were removed so the plumbing company could lay down new lines."

"They probably blew back in since it's been so dry," Rainey interjected.

Deuce's jaw tightened and he clenched his fist, knowing what he had to say was only going to upset Rainey. "No. I was out here when I put in the new surveillance system and there were no weeds." He took a deep breath. "And keep that under your hat. I don't want it to be common knowledge that I installed a system or Mayor Humphries will skin me alive for not going through hoops to get a permit." He raised an eyebrow.

The fire chief seemed to be thinking things over, and then asked, "Deuce, when have you ever known tumbleweeds to still be around in the Panhandle this late in the spring?"

"Usually they've blown all the way to the Rio Grande by now."

"That's right, except for the ones that have blown across a field and gotten all tangled together before gettin' piled up in the corner of a fenced pasture."

"These had to be deliberately placed here. A few could never be high enough to reach the freight doors. When we got here, the stack was still pretty high, although it'd burned down a bunch."

"The worst damage is definitely the ol' freight doors, so, sheriff, I've got to put this on the records as an arson investigation."

"And our lead suspect is Harold Wilson," Deuce said.

"From the things he's been spouting around town and what he said over the phone, it looks that way to me, too," the fire chief said.

Rainey took an audibly deep breath. "Gideon Duncan came by and said he had something to tell me as a friend. Without all the detail—"

Deuce cut her off. "I'll need everything you can remember."

"I know. But basically he said that Wilson wants me out of the depot because it's costing him too much money to maintain."

"Damn it." Fury ran through Deuce. "You should have told me, Rainey."

"I didn't think it was important but he did contradict himself."

"How?" Deuce could kick himself twice again over for flaring up at her, but at the moment she wasn't the woman he cared about and loved, but a victim.

"Gideon said that Wilson wanted this place condemned and it wasn't worth me putting any money into. But then he said something about Wilson wanting too much money for the depot or he, Gideon, would buy it himself. I just found that strange. Why would Gideon want to buy an old building when Wilson had already told him it drained him financially? Just seemed an odd statement to me. Then he left like his tail was on fire . . . no pun intended."

"Good question," Deuce said.

Danny walked up and the sheriff said, "Don't think you heard but we've got an arson and a suspect. Go pick up Harold Wilson for questioning."

"Sheriff, I can't. He broke a hip last night. I heard Jessup when he took the 9-1-1 call. It was a hit and run. Wilson was out walking his dog, but didn't see who hit him. No witnesses. The last I heard he's in ICU under heavy sedation."

"If it wasn't Wilson, then who in the hell tried to burn the place down?" Deuce said aloud, knowing that Rainey had just given him another suspect, but he didn't want to act upon his intuition at the moment. He knew Rainey was likely thinking the same thing he was . . . someone hired by Alonzo Hunter.

Whoever was trying to get Rainey out of the depot would try something again.

But the next time they'd have to deal with Donovan Cowan, *the Deuce*, as his daddy always called him, swearing he'd won him in a card game with four deuces.

Chapter Nineteen

Hours turned into days, days into weeks without any suspects being arrested for trying to torch the depot. Rainey had as many questions as an inquisitive kindergartner. Not just who had sent the letters but the culprit responsible for the purse. Then add the fire at the depot, which if it hadn't been noticed by Winnie's husband walking his dog, could have destroyed the historic building. Who was trying to run Rainey out of town?

As much as she didn't want to consider the idea, could it be someone hired by Hunter?

Rainey folded clothes with the help of Fat-Cat, who seemed to think the thick bath towels, separated from the regular laundry and thrown in a big wicker basket, were just the answer to a warm place for the tomcat to curl up for a nap.

She was still amazed that Deuce hadn't asked her to drop the whole idea of opening an antiques store, but she hoped that meant he realized she didn't accept being dictated to very well. Another thing she couldn't believe was that it'd been nearly two weeks since the fire.

With Deuce at her side, she wasn't terrified at every turn. She continued to spend her mornings preparing for the depot's grand opening, which meant trips every Friday and Saturday to Amarillo's garage and estate sales. Sometimes she'd stop at a house she'd discovered on one of her trips that was similar to the one in Denton where she'd grown up. She tried to think about the good times but her thoughts never lasted very long. It'd been nearly a month since her multitude of calls on Mother's Day and she had not received a return call from either her mother or father. No doubt she had disappointed both of them to the point that their relationship might never be repaired.

"Move, Fat-Cat," she told the ol' tom as she gently lifted him from the wicker basket. "I've got to get finished so I can go visit Lydia."

She felt happy inside thinking about getting to see Lydia Dunivan, who was always waiting for her in the recreation area shredding Kleenex. Rainey could see Lydia's pleasant smile as she tried to look behind Rainey's back to find the Dairy Queen strawberry shake Rainey always brought her. So far Rainey hadn't missed a day going to the nursing home, even those when she felt anxious because she could depend on Lydia to cheer her up. A funny feeling came over Rainey that she was the one who was supposed to cheer up Lydia, but instead it was the other way around.

Rainey folded another towel. She had told Deuce the night before, as he was falling asleep on his feet after a long and likely stressful day, just how much better she was feeling since seeking treatment from the therapist Allura recommended. In the same way Rainey had felt a sense of relief when Deuce brought up the possibility she was experiencing PTSD. It made her feel better sharing it with a professional who was honest with her, telling her that the symptoms wouldn't go away overnight but she could learn techniques to help her deal with the disorder. She was trying to work on facing and feeling her memories and emotions so she could move on with her life and be happy again.

No doubt the case Deuce was working on was a humdinger. It seemed to have consumed him as he stayed at the sheriff's department later than he had since she'd arrived in town and came home exhausted. Most evenings he didn't come upstairs until long after she had gone to bed; but every morning she woke up in his arms feeling his comfort surrounding her.

Neither of them had taken much time for themselves, or for each other for that matter, but they tried to catch lunch at Pumpkin's Café or Winnie's together as many days as possible. Most evenings she warmed up the meal Emily prepared for them and ate alone. Occasionally, he'd make it home in time to share a meal.

Deuce laughed one night when he told her that he thought his foreman had put on weight because of Emily's cooking.

Eagerly putting away the folded clothes, Rainey looked at the clock. She had to hurry. Deuce had said he'd be home early for "Date Night." They finally had an evening together. She almost laughed out loud at his statement, "Don't cook. I'll bring dinner." As if she could cook!

"If tranquility had a name it'd be Deuce Cowan," she whispered to herself as she stripped down and showered. After putting on one of her best outfits, she added gold hoop earrings. She had just sprayed herself lightly with perfume when she heard the door open downstairs.

Rushing down the stairs she launched herself into Deuce's arms. He kissed her like he hadn't seen her in a month. Breaking loose, she asked, "What did you bring for dinner? It smells so good."

"Winnie's barbeque with all the fixin's." He handed her the bag and kissed her again. "Let me lock up my gun and change clothes. Then I'll come in and prepare dinner."

"Oh, no, you don't." She laughed as she hid the sack behind her back. "It's my turn to cook. Take your time and I'll have supper on the table in no time." She stood on her tiptoes and kissed him with a hunger that sent the pit of her stomach into a wild swirl. "I know you're hungry."

"I'm hungry okay, but it isn't Winnie's barbeque that I'm wantin' right now." He put his arms around her waist, almost knocking the sack out of her hand, and pulled her up to meet his lips. He moved his mouth over hers leaving her with a burning desire, an aching need for another kiss. He obliged.

Setting her down on her feet he said, "Now go fix dinner."

As she turned, he patted her on the fanny and she heard his hearty laugh fade into his study.

An hour later, they sat on the sofa with two glasses of wine. She leaned against Deuce enjoying every second with him.

"I'm so glad you planned a special night for us." She nibbled on his earlobe.

"I am, too." He set down his wineglass and turned to her. "I think we've become close enough that I can ask you a very personal question and if you don't want to answer, all you have to say is well, nothing. I'll understand."

"There's nothing I won't share with you, Deuce." She also set down her glass and looked him squarely in the eyes. "I know at first I kept secrets from you, but I thought I had to for my own safety. But now there isn't any question I won't answer." She deliberately shot him an open, friendly smile. "I love you that much."

"And I love you, too." He laid his hand on her knee. "Why didn't you go to your parents when you felt you were in danger? Why devise such an elaborate scheme when, with the political power your father has, he could see that you were protected?"

"They were out of town. They have their life to live and expect me to take care of my own."

"Don't give me the runaround, Rainey." His dark eyebrows slanted in a frown. "They weren't out of town all that long. And what I can remember from growing up together is nothing was good enough for their little girl."

"That was the way it probably looked to others, but my father is a judgmental, overbearing politician. He wanted me to be the perfect child and when I wasn't, then I was just a big disappointment to him. His first was that he wanted a son to follow in his footsteps and when I was born, he pretty much rejected me, leaving me to get what love I got from my mother, only if it didn't interfere with one of her social gatherings or a game of tennis at the country club."

"I'm sorry I asked." He squeezed her knee and kissed her temple. "But that does explain why he didn't even bother to tell you that I called to ask you to the homecoming dance. He truly didn't think I was good enough for his little girl."

Rainey found herself staring at the picture over the fireplace, while the memories flooded back to her. She'd never spoken of her life as a child and it felt good to tell the person she cared about more than anyone in the world.

"He treated me like a hole-in-one at the golf course. I was little more than a coveted achievement he could brag about when I excelled and make an excuse for me when I didn't meet his expectations. The trial was one of those times." She took a deep breath, feeling free for the first time in her life when it came to discussing her upbringing.

"He called me every day, sometimes twice during preparation for the trial to see if I was following his advice. When I didn't, I'd lie to him and tell him I was. You'd think as a judge he knew that I had a boss who was pulling the political strings and a slew of co-counsels to work with. Being lead counsel didn't make me the lord of all of the prosecutors. Plus, Judith was up for reelection and had to play politics."

She suddenly felt ill-equipped to continue telling Deuce about her family life, yet at the same time she felt a need to tell all of it so she continued. "You have no idea the humiliation I felt when I was forced to take the death penalty off the table. None of my co-counsels wanted it either, but we knew if we didn't that there was a good chance Hunter would get off because of his mental state. To protect the citizens, we wanted him under lock and key and that's what we got."

"Your father was a renowned judge and should have known that you can't always get the verdict you want but what is dealt you."

"You know what he told me when we had to change our strategy?"

Deuce shook his head, and squeezed her hand.

"His exact words were 'I'd rather see you dead than a failure.'" She looked up at Deuce. "He even laughed at his own sordid humor. So when Hunter threatened me when the verdict came in, I felt as if I should have gone to the rooftop of the courthouse and shouted: 'Well, Dad, I fulfilled your wishes!' And I haven't heard from either Mother or Father since."

"Come on." Deuce stood and pulled her with him. "I brought home a couple of slices of Mrs. Grooms's Special Chocolate cake."

"I didn't see them."

"I hid them before I let you know I was home so I could surprise you."

"No, that wasn't it. You knew I'd eat 'em up before dinner."

They shared a jovial laugh setting Rainey's bad memories aside.

After pulling a takeout box from the cabinet, he put slices of cake on two saucers and placed them on the table. Rainey got the forks and filled two glasses with milk.

"Well, we finally got a preliminary report on the letters, but not on the purse." He sat in the chair across from her.

Rainey's heart jumped in her throat. "It took them long enough. They were expected two weeks ago at least."

"The state crime lab is backed up, but—"

"Not anything like the ones I had to deal with in LA. At least we've got answers now." She softly asked, with her heart skipping every other beat, "So what did the report tell us?"

"As we expected, lots of fingerprints. Of course, there were Sylvie's and a dozen they could match in the federal database, but that only eliminated the obvious. Whoever deposited the letters used gloves because there were no unidentified fingerprints on either of the envelopes, but Hunter's were on the letters."

"How can that be? There's no way they would have gotten through San Quentin's internal post office." She shivered at the thought. "They have their own post office so it would have had to have come through there." The raw sores of an aching heart seemed to open up and pull out all of the happiness Rainey had found inside. "What else did they find?"

"The paper was regular ol' laser printer paper that could have come from a million places. The words were cut out and attached using a glue stick that could be purchased anywhere from a truck stop to an office supply store. But the words were cut from a government document. Again, something easily obtainable and certainly available to someone behind bars.

"We're not getting the cooperation I would have thought I'd be gettin' from San Quentin, so I called in a favor from a guy I know in the Bay Area. He's a very thorough private investigator and I know he'll get the information we need to fill in the holes." Deuce pushed back his plate and took her hands again. "Trust me. Look at me, Rainey."

She raised her head to meet Deuce's sharp assessing eyes.

"I do, Deuce. I do."

Deuce's phone rang. "I've got to take this, but we'll have our answers soon. I promise." As he passed, he kissed her on the top of the head.

"Sheriff Cowan," he said and walked towards his study.

Rainey's phone rang and she rushed to get it.

"Hello," she answered. The lady on the other end began immediately. "Mrs. Michaels, I'm a volunteer at the Kasota Springs Nursing

Home and was asked to call you. I apologize for bothering you so late and doubly sorry that I don't have all the details, but the lady you bring the strawberry shake to every day has walked away from the facility. She was asking for you and said she was going to come find you. That's the last time we've seen her. They are notifying her son, but they wanted me to call you so you can be on the lookout for her. They wanted me to ask if she knows where you live."

Rainey's heart beat out of control. "No. No she doesn't know where I live. I'm on my way to the nursing home now."

She pressed the end icon, grabbed her purse off the stool and rushed to Deuce, who was just coming out of his study.

"I've got to go to town."

"I've got to go in, too." He had his gun belt in one hand and kissed her on the forehead before buckling it around his waist. "I hope I won't be gone long."

They rushed to their automobiles. By the time Rainey reached the gate leading to the Farm to Market Road connecting the Slippery Elm to town, Deuce was at least a mile ahead of her.

Something had upset him . . . and upset him terribly.

Deuce skidded to a stop in front of the Kasota Springs Nursing Home and rushed inside to find the administrator waiting for him.

"I'm so sorry, Deuce." A worried look covered the woman's face. "I don't know exactly what happened. She was a bit upset today after you left. The lady who usually comes to visit her every day and brings her a strawberry shake didn't come and that seemed to upset her."

Before Deuce could ask any questions, Elaine rushed on. "Your mother said she didn't want to stay here any longer and that she was going to find either you or the lady."

"Did she have her location bracelet on?" He knew it wasn't Elaine's fault but the worry for his mother's safety overshadowed his professionalism. "She damn well better have."

"She's tried taking it off a number of times but as far as we know she has it on. I've got someone checking the GPS right now."

"Who is the volunteer who brings her strawberry milkshakes?" He took off his hat and ran his fingers through his hair and without giving Elaine a chance to answer, he demanded, "Who is she?"

"Deuce." He heard Rainey's voice behind him and turned in her direction. "Deuce, I bring Lydia a strawberry milkshake every day but didn't today."

Rage ignited within Deuce like a wildfire blowback. "*You* have been coming to visit *my* mother behind my back."

Immediately, he could tell by the confusion on Rainey's face that something was wrong. "I, I . . . oh, Deuce, I didn't know Lydia was your mother. She told me that she had a son, but he never came to see her so I had no way of knowing she was your mother."

Tears welled in her eyes. A single one ran down her face. "I would have told you if I'd known." She flinched and retreated backwards. "I'm sorry, Deuce, it's my fault. I should have come today."

He swallowed hard trying not to reveal his mounting anger but reality set in. "We've got to find her. She could be anywhere." He tried to control his temper, but it was getting harder and harder. He wasn't sure whom he was madder at, Rainey for keeping it a secret that she volunteered at the nursing home or him for not telling Rainey the truth about his mother. But being angry wasn't going to locate his mother.

The administrator put her arms around Rainey and handed her a Kleenex.

Deuce jerked the phone from his pocket and called the office. "Put an APB out on my mother. She's walked away from the nursing home and we've got to find her. I want every available unit out on the streets and don't come back in until she's located." He ended without even saying good-bye.

A young man appeared from the doorway to Deuce's left and said, "I've got a track on Mrs. Cowan. She's in the area of the ol' Rock Island Depot." He disappeared as quickly as he appeared.

"Let's go." Without thinking, Deuce grabbed Rainey's hand, then turned back to the administrator. "Elaine, it's not your fault. We'll find her and I'll let you know as soon as we do."

"You're dragging me," Rainey said.

"Get in the car," he said, but slowed his step. The last thing he wanted was to hurt her.

Once they were in his county vehicle, he leaned his head against the steering wheel. "Rainey, I'm sorry that I yelled at you but I was upset."

"I know you are. But, Deuce, you know that I would have been thrilled to be working with your mother, if I knew it was her. But she told me she was Lydia Dunivan and she doesn't look like the same woman I knew fifteen years ago."

He headed down Main Street towards the depot. "She isn't the same woman and I shouldn't have expected you to have recognized her."

"I'm so sorry." Tears streamed down her face. "I'm so scared."

Deuce took his hand off the wheel long enough to grab hers and squeeze it. "I know. So am I. I should have told you about her but she was in such a delicate place. I was just trying to follow the advice of her doctors and the staff. I'm really sorry."

As they neared the depot, Deuce drove slowly with each of them watching for any sight of his mother.

"I don't want to scare her with my lights, so look as carefully as you can."

Deuce's iPhone rang. He snatched it up and activated the speaker-phone. "Did you find her?"

"No, sir, but she's definitely around the depot and hasn't moved out of position but has been walking around."

Deuce presumed it was the young man from the nursing home since the caller ID was from there.

When they reached the depot, Deuce turned off the lights and drove up as silently as possible. "The front doors are open." The law-man in him kicked in. He punched a button on his radio and said, "Need backup at the Rock Island Depot."

"Ten-four, units on their way," Jessup said.

"You stay here," he ordered.

"Shouldn't you wait on backup?" Rainey grabbed his arm.

Deuce didn't answer but drew his service pistol.

"Then I'm going with you."

Before he could catch her, she had bailed out of the passenger-side door. He didn't have time to wait.

"I said stay in the car."

"I said I'm going in with you."

He silently entered the depot after announcing, "Sheriff. Hold your hands where I can see them."

In the middle of what looked like a glass shop hit by a tornado his mother sat on the floor with her hands held above her head.

Deuce took a deep breath and hoped his heart would stop racing so badly. "Mother, what happened?" He was afraid of her answer. "How did you get in here?"

Then he noticed the tears in her vacant eyes. "Young man, put away that gun." She may have had tears in her eyes but her voice was strong. "I don't appreciate it in the least."

"Yes, ma'am." He holstered his Glock. "Do you want to tell me what happened?" He gingerly approached her so he wouldn't scare her any more than she already was.

"And you tell those young men behind you that they need to put away their guns, too."

Deuce turned to see Danny and two of his deputies holstering their guns.

"Guys go back to your units. We're fine here," Deuce ordered.

Deuce's mother pulled to her feet and used the corner of the counter for leverage. He took her walker to her and pulled up a chair for her.

"Tell me what happened?" He tried to keep calm and speak with a softer than usual voice because he knew she was scared.

"I don't want to talk to you. I want to talk with the nice lady behind you."

Rainey stepped forward and squatted down to Deuce's mother's level. "Yes, Lydia. Would you tell me what happened?"

"This is no way to run an antiques shop. You didn't bring me my strawberry milk today, so I came to find you."

"How did you know where I worked?"

"I don't know, but it took me a long time and I had to ask a lot of people. I knew you were Mr. Chalmers's wife and she owned the depot, so I followed the railroad tracks." She looked from Rainey to Deuce and back. "You don't think I did this, do you?"

"Of course not, Lydia." Rainey reached for her hand. "You would have never broken any of the glass because I remember how much you loved each and every piece."

The truth hit Deuce between the eyes and everything fell into place when his mother said that Rainey was Mr. Chalmers's wife. She had told him about Rainey and that she brought her strawberry milk every day, but he never put two and two together. And he was an investigator!

Rainey continued to hold Deuce's mother's hand. "Why don't you let this nice young man take you to the Dairy Queen and get some strawberry milk and then you can go back home and go to bed. Miss Elaine is worried about you."

His mother nodded her head. "You know my son was supposed to come today but he had to play football. I saw him on television." She looked past Rainey where Deuce was standing and said, "I've told you about my son, haven't I?"

"Yes, ma'am." Deuce wasn't sure how much heartbreak he was supposed to take, but seeing the gentleness Rainey exhibited and how well his mother accepted her made it a whole bunch easier.

"Deuce, just ask them to make a milkshake very thin. They'll do it." Rainey looked at him, still with tears in her eyes. "I need to sweep up some of the glass so you won't get cut."

Rainey stood and grabbed the broom from the corner and swept her way to the door.

"Let's go, uh, Lydia." He helped his mother from the chair and held her arm as she walked towards the exit. "Wait just a minute. Can you hold on to your walker for a second?"

"Young man, you know I can." She straightened her shoulders.

Deuce walked back to Rainey and put his arms around her. Pulling her tightly to him, he whispered, "Thank you. I'll be back as quickly as possible." He wiped a tear from her cheek and kissed her lightly.

No response. She picked up what remained of the bonsai plant, threw it in the trash. and began sweeping glass into piles.

It took Deuce a while longer than he'd anticipated to buy the milk shake and get his mother settled in her room at the nursing home. He was tired and felt about as drained as he'd ever felt in his life. What a fool he'd made of himself. He should have told Rainey about his mother as soon as he knew Rainey was determined to stay in town. It was his fault and if Rainey walked out on him, he deserved it.

What bothered him the most was that he'd been so angry and upset that he'd taken it out on Rainey. But when they got to the depot, as foolish as it had been, she was willing to put her life on the line for his mother.

If only . . . if frogs had holsters they could just shoot the flies. He smiled thinking about how his father used to say that when Deuce was a kid.

He got out of the county's pickup with a sinking feeling that although Rainey hadn't pulled away from him when he kissed her that she might well kick his butt from the Panhandle to the Rockies and back . . . but he deserved it.

When he got to the door, she said, "Be careful. There's still shards of glass everywhere."

Deuce went over to her and took the broom out of her hands. "Let me do the rest of the cleanup. After all it's my mother who caused the damage. Why don't you let me take you to your car and you go to the ranch and get some rest. I know this has been a grueling day for you."

"No." She took him by the arm and stopped his sweeping. "I've got something to show you. I couldn't imagine your mother being capable of doing this much damage, not to mention why she would do it. Surely not over me not bringing her a shake today. Did you notice the alarm wasn't going off when we got here and there's no way she would have known the code?"

A spark of interest hit Deuce. "I should have but I was so glad to find her safe." He took a deep breath. "Rainey, I'm sorry but I was reacting like a son, not as the sheriff."

"You acted the way any son should." She smiled up at him. "The alarm not being triggered didn't occur to me either until you left."

Walking behind the counter, she flipped the rewind button on the surveillance monitor. "Look at this."

Deuce studied the tape, frame by frame.

"Damn it to hell." Anger resurfaced all over Deuce. "I should have known."

Switching back into full sheriff mode, he dialed the office. "Jessup, tell Danny and his team to go pick up both Sylvie Dewey and Gideon Duncan. And he knows the routine—keep them in separate interrogation rooms until I get there. I'm at the depot so it won't take long."

He hung up. "Let's get this place locked up for the night and if you want, you can watch the interrogation. I don't know why they tore this place up, but I have a feeling that they also had something to do with the fire."

"Deuce, I know Sylvie was manipulated. I just know it. Couldn't you see the fear on her face? Her body language on the security video screamed of being scared to death. She didn't touch anything. I think she was forced by Gideon to participate," Rainey said softly.

Deuce wasn't sure how Gideon and Sylvie fit into the picture, but he sure as hell was going to find out.

Chapter Twenty

Sun was coming to life in the east when Deuce and Rainey walked into the ranch house the following morning. They had spent the whole night at the sheriff's department, but had learned nothing except Sylvie and Gideon didn't have anything to say. To both Rainey's and Deuce's shock, neither asked for a lawyer.

Rainey made two cups of chamomile tea while Deuce locked up his Glock.

By the time the tea was steeped, Deuce returned and they sat at the kitchen table trying to unwind from their grueling night.

"I don't need to tell you that I can hold them forty-eight hours without charging them with anything." Deuce took a sip of his tea.

"I still think Sylvie was forced by Gideon to be there. You told me the first time that I met her that she couldn't hurt a fly. She's being manipulated by him. I just know it."

"Then why didn't she turn on him to save herself?"

"Because I think he's made her think he's in love with her and she'd never give up the man she loves," Rainey said. "As a lawyer, I can tell you that the DA has the latitude of charging them with a number of things," Rainey said wearily. "If I find out Gideon is behind this, I promise you that I'll ask the DA to drop the charges against Sylvie, unless there are other circumstances we don't know about."

"You might be right." He rubbed his neck. "I can't imagine Sylvie's involvement either."

"I'm going to take a shower and lay down for a few minutes. Then

I want to go back to town, pick up my car, and visit Lydia—I mean Marie."

"Sounds like a plan. We both need some sleep," Deuce said.

Wearily, they climbed the stairs. With the mid-morning sun flooding the bedroom, when Rainey saw the bed her shower was forgotten.

Fully dressed they laid side by side determined to get a little bit of rest.

What seemed like only minutes later, Rainey woke to the sound of Deuce's phone going off in the distance. She knew it was someone from the department because of the distinctive ring.

"Wake up." She punched him and he sat straight up. "Your phone is ringing."

While Deuce took the call, she went to the bathroom and splashed water on her face, then brushed her teeth. After hanging up the towel, she walked back into the bedroom and saw Deuce sitting on the side of the bed with his face in his hands.

She sat down beside him scared of the news he had received. "What's wrong?"

"I can't believe I'm such a fool." He threw his phone against the pillow. "I don't deserve being sheriff if I can't even figure out such a simple plan by that bastard Gideon Duncan." He slammed his fist into the pillow.

"What plan?"

"Sylvie turned on him finally. There'll be so many charges filed against him that he'll be in prison for a long time, but that doesn't get her out of hot water over the damage done to your property."

"Don't worry about my stuff. I won't press charges against her. Just tell me what he had against me."

"It wasn't against you personally. Just as you suspected, that son-ofabitch Gideon Duncan used Sylvie to do his dirty work. Let her think he was in love with her so she'd spread rumors around town."

"I don't see what rumors have to do with it."

"You know there've been men in town from the Green-Mart Corp checking on property to buy to build a store here, right?"

"I think I heard about that the first day I got into town. But what does that have to do with wanting me out of town?" She could see anger written all over Deuce's face so she didn't want to push him. She just let him tell the story the way he wanted.

"Gideon owns the warehouse next to the depot and he was trying to force Wilson to sell the depot to him because he knew Green-Mart needed to build in that location. One plot of land wasn't any good without the other. That's when he apparently decided to use Sylvie's vulnerability by making her think he was in love with her. He wrapped her around his little finger and told her things that he knew she was going to tell others."

Rainey raised an eyebrow and took a deep breath.

"Apparently, when she couldn't scare you away but ended up befriending you, he took the plan to another level."

"That's why he came and talked to me as a friend. Telling me to get out before I got hurt. Then he laughed and corrected himself by saying he didn't mean physically hurt but financially hurt."

"I'm sure. I think the department solved another case. Pending further investigation, my guys found blood on the fender of Gideon's black sedan. Bet anything it belongs to Wilson. According to Sylvie, when he didn't kill Wilson, he tried to burn the depot, thinking it being of no value would make Wilson sell to him but that didn't work. Then as you could see on the surveillance tape, he broke in through the freight doors and wrecked the place, thinking you'd pull up stakes and leave, thus giving Wilson no income and an incentive for him to sell to Gideon, who in turn would sell both properties to the Green-Mart folks. I doubt Sylvie knew of his plan until after the fact."

"Then Wilson didn't know the Green-Mart people wanted to buy the depot along with the warehouse Gideon owns next door?" Rainey said.

"Apparently not. According to Sylvie, Gideon represented to them that he was the owner, not Wilson. He set the rumor mill in action when he told everybody that the Green-Mart was going to be built out near the truck stop off I-40 to throw them off."

"Deuce, I lost count of the charges that'll be filed against Gideon Duncan and, unfortunately, Sylvie for being an accomplice." Rainey thought a minute, and then said, "Unless she turned state evidence against him."

"You know, I think Danny said he told her that he'd see what he could do to keep her out of trouble, if she'd tell him everything she knew about Gideon." He quirked a grin at her. "That's the best way I know to get a girl to roll over on the man she loves."

"Not the very best way to get a girl to roll over on the man she loves, but it is when they are both facing prison time." She kissed him lightly. "Anything Sylvie gave up will only help the state's case, so I know they will go easy on her. She's just a naive woman, but I have to admit she isn't as dumb as she wants people to think. And rolling over on Gideon shows that. Let me know when bail is set because I plan to bail her out, if she doesn't have enough money herself."

"After everything that happened, you'd bail her out?"

"I'm totally convinced Gideon used her, Deuce."

"Tell you what, if you'll rub my neck, I'll help raise the money for her bail," Deuce said.

"Deal." Rainey willingly massaged his back while thinking that if only the results from the crime lab would come back everything would be perfect.

"You know I think a power bigger than both of us had a hand in my not interrogating Gideon because I'd likely be in jail for beating the living hell out of the sonofabitch. Any man who would take advantage of a woman should have their conjones served to them for breakfast via their asshole."

"That was an interesting visual." She finished massaging his neck and shoulders, then suggested that they lie back down for a while and get a little rest.

"No. I'm going to my office. You rest. I can't sleep, so won't even try." He put his hands on hers and kissed one and then the other. "Thanks. Once my investigator calls and the results from the damn state crime lab come in, I'll sleep for a week."

Chapter Twenty-one

Deuce didn't know where the time had gone, but it had been three days since Gideon and Sylvie had been arrested. As anticipated, the DA's office had informed him that they'd cut a deal with Sylvie. In return for her testimony against Gideon, they would recommend probation. Of course, she'd lose her job with the government, but he'd given thought to asking Rainey if she'd consider giving Sylvie a job at the antiques store, since it was about to open and Sylvie would make a good employee.

Undoubtedly, one of the provisions of her probation would be to remain gainfully employed, plus she'd have monthly probation fees and a hefty fine to pay.

Gideon wasn't going to have to worry about Green-Mart putting him out of business because by the time the DA finished filing charges against him, the only work he'd be doing would be prison laundry.

Deuce watched Rainey as she prepared dinner. He'd really tried to be patient with her but wasn't sure how much more he could stand. If he could have one wish fulfilled it would be to pick her up, take her upstairs to his bed, and make love to her until the roosters crowed three mornings in a row. Hell, the living room sofa would do. Even the orange sleeping bag. He wanted her and wanted her badly.

"You know I made A's in French in high school, don't you?" Her comment brought him back to reality, but it seemed to come out of nowhere.

"No, I don't think I did but I'm not surprised." He tried to stop watching her fine heinie as she squatted down to get a pot out from under the cabinet.

"There are only three things I can do in French besides speak it. Make French fries, French toast . . . and French kiss."

"And you have to use frozen French fries and I know damn good and well you don't even know how to make French toast."

"But I do know how to French kiss." She came to him, sat on his lap, and kissed him in a way she'd never done before. Her tongue explored the recesses of his mouth, making the blood in his brain boil, not to mention what she did to him between his waist and knees.

"I think you've proven your point. I'll never eat another French fry or take a bite of French toast again without thinking about that kiss." He closed his eyes and thought that was probably the best kiss he'd ever had in his life. French or otherwise.

"Can you open this for me?" She interrupted his thoughts as she handed him a bottle of spaghetti sauce.

He opened the jar only to see her pour it in a pan on the stove.

Well, she might not know how to make spaghetti from scratch, but she sure knew how to French kiss.

Moving behind her, he stretched to reach for a bottle of wine in the cabinet above the stove. He deliberately pressed in enjoying— hell, loving—the feel of her rounded tush pressed against his groin. The way she twisted her bottom just a little, pressing her left cheek squarely into his manhood, was an indicator she knew what he was doing. He tried to hold off Mother Nature, who took exception to his efforts and fought back. She was winning, too!

Rainey walked over to the sideboard and picked up Deuce's sunglasses and put them on him. "Hey, wear these. They'll shade your eyes from your ego!"

Deuce should have been ashamed for deliberately riling her up, but he couldn't help himself. It was their way of handling each other. Habits were hard to break, and it made him feel eighteen again . . . just like he was in high school but with maturity.

His iPhone rang. One hell of a time for him to get a call, but then he was on call twenty-four hours a day, seven days a week.

Not being sure whether he would be receiving bad news or good from his investigator, Deuce walked out of the kitchen towards his study.

"Hey, man, I hope you have some good news for me."

"You're not going to like it, but nobody has been there to see Hunter in weeks, and before then it was only his attorney. The reason you've been getting the runaround from prison officials is because Hunter has been in a coma and on life support since he tried to commit suicide. They are trying to keep down the publicity."

"Damn it to hell. Did you find out if there was anything about Edgar Allan Poe in his cell?" Deuce asked.

"Yep. *The Complete Works of Edgar Allan Poe* and the portions of 'The Tell-Tale Heart' that were in the letters were highlighted. And there's something else. I noticed that the letters came from zip code 94964, which is the town of San Quentin so they were post-marked in the United State Post Office. The prison has their own post office and that zip code is 94974. One digit different, but if we could have discovered it, it would have answered a lot of questions."

"If he didn't have any visitors other than his appeals lawyer before he tried to end his life, how in the hell did he get the letters out of the prison?"

"This is going to make your balls turn inside out, but you'll never guess who his appeals lawyer was."

Deuce had a bad feeling about what he was about to learn, just by the way his investigator began the sentence. He really didn't want to ask but did. "Who?"

"Got your television on? You can find out for yourself. Don't wanna ruin your surprise."

"I can have it on in thirty seconds." Deuce rushed to the television remote and turned it on. "What station?"

"Any national news channel. And I'm bettin' that Miss Clarkson is going to want to be there when you watch the news report. Hurry, the Los Angeles County DA's office is about to have a presser."

Deuce called for Rainey to turn off the stove and come to the living room. Then he said to the investigator, "Send me your bill direct to my office."

"What's going on?" Rainey came in drying her hands on a tea towel. "And why do you have the TV on?"

"Sit down. Remember I told you that I hired a PI, since we were getting the runaround from the folks at San Quentin?"

"Yes, but what does this have to do with him?"

"Listen. I don't know either."

A portly woman with graying hair moved away from the camera and a reporter with a microphone stepped in front of the camera.

"That was the press secretary for the LA DA's office," Rainey said.

"I know."

They listened intently as the news correspondent began her report.

"As we learned from the Los Angeles County District Attorney's office, a grand jury has handed down indictments against former DA, Judith Mason, for domestic terrorism for her part in assisting mass murderer Alonzo F. Hunter in terrorizing the lead prosecutor on his case, R. Maressa Clarkson." She took a quick breath, and then continued. "In conjunction with the indictment of former LA County DA Mason, an arrest was made for a suspect who allegedly assisted Miss Mason in locating Miss Clarkson. Although they did not release the name of the individual, CNN has been told by reliable sources, but not independently confirmed, that it's an operator of a used car lot in East Los Angeles. We've been told also from a reliable source that the man was posing as a secret informant for the Los Angeles Police Department. It's also been reported, again not independently confirmed, that the motive behind the plot was revenge because Miss Mason blamed Miss Clarkson for the DA's losing in the primary to reelect her as the Los Angeles County District Attorney. In another unconfirmed report, Miss Clarkson's whereabouts are unknown. It has been reported that the indictments were sealed."

Deuce pressed the off button on the remote control and the screen went blank.

"Well, that explains the purse. She knew when I was planning to disappear so she followed me and took my purse out of the trash bin. When she couldn't get any more letters from Hunter to send me, she sent the purse as a last resort."

Pulling Rainey to his side, Deuce prayed that he had the words necessary to comfort the best thing that had happened to him in his life. "It's over," he whispered, as he caressed her cheeks with the back of his hand. "You don't have to live in fear any longer." He lifted her chin and stared into emerald-green eyes brimming with tears. "And I've been thinking. I'm tired of doing this one night you sleep in my bedroom and the next in the guest room, so I made a decision." He kissed her on her forehead and reached into his pocket.

Sliding on one knee in front of her, he took her hands in his. "Brainy Rainey, I want you in my life and in my bed forever." He looked up and saw that her beautiful green eyes were full of life and unquenchable warmth, but still a tinge of pain remained. "So Brainy Rainey, Maressa Clarkson, will you go steady with me?"

He pulled out his senior ring that he'd found at his mother's house and put it in Rainey's hand, folding her fingers over it.

"I'd be honored to go steady with you." She kissed him. "You're the only one who stood beside me and accepted me just like I am. You've never expected me to be perfect and weren't disappointed when I wasn't."

"I've got one more thing." He stood up and walked to the coat closet, where he retrieved a small bonsai plant and his football letter jacket from high school. He put the plant on the end table and slipped his jacket over her shoulders and said, "You should have had this in high school." He kissed her on the forehead. "There's one string attached. Other than always sharing my bed, my only other request is that you learn to cook. I'll send you to cooking classes or—"

"Shut up, you fool, before I change my mind and you have to ask Clara over at Pumpkin's to go steady."

Fifth-Generation Mrs. Grooms's Chocolate Cake

For my readers who want to enjoy a larruping good chocolate cake, whether you think it's the one baked by Winnie Mitchell or Clara at Pumpkin's Café, here's the history behind my Mrs. Grooms's Chocolate Cake.

My family grew up on Mrs. Grooms's Chocolate Cake made by my Grannie Johnson. A Godly woman, she swore that the recipe had been handed down generations and it'd originated with a neighbor named Mrs. Grooms.

The recipe had to be totally jinxed since neither my mother nor my aunt could make the cake as good as Grannie. I'm the oldest of four girls, and I ended up being the only one of my sisters who could prepare the cake where it'd come out like Grannie's. Only one of my two daughters can make it so it'll come out moist.

When my aunt by marriage, Aunt Martha, was nearing the end of her life, she finally gave up Grannie: The recipe may have been given to her by a neighbor but it actually appeared in a 1950s *Good Housekeeping*.

Maybe it didn't begin as a generations-old recipe, but it is now since it was handed down from Grannie to Mama and Aunt Bobbie, to me and my three sisters, to my daughters and now my granddaughters . . . so it truly is a fifth-generation cake.

Enjoy the Fifth-Generation Mrs. Grooms's Chocolate Cake.

2 cups sugar
2 cups flour
¼ teaspoon salt
2 teaspoons soda
1 cup oil
1 cup buttermilk

½ cup cocoa
2 eggs, beaten
1 cup boiling water
2 teaspoons vanilla

Preheat the oven to 350 degrees F.

Beat the eggs until fluffy, then add the buttermilk and oil, and beat together. Add all the remaining ingredients *except* the water. Stir everything until the mixture is smooth, then add water—make sure it's boiling! The mixture will be thin when poured in the pan. Bake in an oblong 13x9-inch pan for 35–40 minutes. Allow to cool before adding the icing.

Chocolate Icing

2¼ cup powdered sugar
4 tablespoons cocoa
1 stick softened butter (do not use tub butter—use stick butter
   or margarine only)
4 tablespoons water
1 teaspoon vanilla

Mix all ingredients and beat until smooth.

Tip: If you want glossy icing, melt your butter; but if you want an opaque icing, just use softened butter.

Now it's time to expose my secret. To add extra moisture and richness, I slip in about a ¼ cup of Hershey's Genuine Chocolate Syrup to the cake batter.

ABOUT THE AUTHOR

A native Texan, *New York Times* and *USA Today* bestselling author PHYLISS MIRANDA still believes in the Code of the Old West and loves to share her love for antiques, the lost art of quilting, and the Wild West.

Visit her at phylissmiranda.com.

Don't miss Phyliss Miranda's *The Tycoon and the Texan*, available now wherever Kensington e-books are sold!

He's got everything
in the world
— except her…

THE
TYCOON
AND
THE
TEXAN

PHYLISS MIRANDA